Ryder's Storm is a work of fiction. Names, characters, places, and incidents are the products of the author's imagination and are used fictitiously. Any resemblance to actual events, locales, or persons, living or dead, is entirely coincidental.

Copyright © 2022 by Tina Folsom

Published in the United States

Cover design: Leah Kaye Suttle
Cover photo: Shutterstock
Author Photo: © Marti Corn Photography

Printed in the United States of America

Books by Tina Folsom

Samson's Lovely Mortal (Scanguards Vampires, Book 1)
Amaury's Hellion (Scanguards Vampires, Book 2)
Gabriel's Mate (Scanguards Vampires, Book 3)
Yvette's Haven (Scanguards Vampires, Book 4)
Zane's Redemption (Scanguards Vampires, Book 5)
Quinn's Undying Rose (Scanguards Vampires, Book 6)
Oliver's Hunger (Scanguards Vampires, Book 7)
Thomas's Choice (Scanguards Vampires, Book 8)
Silent Bite (Scanguards Vampires, Book 8 1/2)
Cain's Identity (Scanguards Vampires, Book 9)
Luther's Return (Scanguards Vampires, Book 10)
Blake's Pursuit (Scanguards Vampires, Book 11)
Fateful Reunion (Scanguards Vampires, Book 11 1/2)
John's Yearning (Scanguards Vampires, Book 12)
Ryder's Storm (Scanguards Vampires, Book 13)

Lover Uncloaked (Stealth Guardians, Book 1)
Master Unchained (Stealth Guardians, Book 2)
Warrior Unraveled (Stealth Guardians, Book 3)
Guardian Undone (Stealth Guardians, Book 4)
Immortal Unveiled (Stealth Guardians, Book 5)
Protector Unmatched (Stealth Guardians, Book 6)
Demon Unleashed (Stealth Guardians, Book 7)

Ace on the Run (Code Name Stargate, Book 1)
Fox in plain Sight (Code Name Stargate, Book 2)
Yankee in the Wind (Code Name Stargate, Book 3)

A Touch of Greek (Out of Olympus, Book 1)
A Scent of Greek (Out of Olympus, Book 2)
A Taste of Greek (Out of Olympus, Book 3)
A Hush of Greek (Out of Olympus, Book 4)

Venice Vampyr (Novellas 1 – 4)

Teasing (The Hamptons Bachelor Club, Book 1)
Enticing (The Hamptons Bachelor Club, Book 2)
Beguiling (The Hamptons Bachelor Club, Book 3)
Scorching (The Hamptons Bachelor Club, Book 4)
Alluring (The Hamptons Bachelor Club, Book 5)
Sizzling (The Hamptons Bachelor Club, Book 6)

RYDER'S STORM

SCANGUARDS VAMPIRES #13

SCANGUARDS HYBRIDS #1

TINA FOLSOM

1

Ryder stepped out of the shower and dried off. He'd slept well and had woken two hours before sunset. His parents, Gabriel and Maya Giles, were still sleeping. As vampires they had to avoid daylight, but Ryder and his younger siblings, twenty-nine-year-old Ethan and twenty-seven-year-old Vanessa, were hybrids and had a crucial advantage: the rays of the sun couldn't hurt them.

In most other things they were like their parents. Silver could burn them; drinking human blood made them strong, though they also ate human food; they stayed young forever; and only a few things could kill them: silver bullets, and a wooden stake through the heart.

Ryder stood in front of the full-length mirror in his room. While a full-blooded vampire didn't have a reflection, a hybrid did. Ryder averted his eyes. He knew what he would see. Yes, he had a muscular body and a handsome face—his mother kept telling him so, and he knew many a woman turned her head to give him a second look—but there was a part of his body he didn't like to show to anybody.

He'd grown up with it, as had Ethan. Their father had told them early in their childhood not to be ashamed of the trait they had inherited from him. Ryder knew that the mass of flesh and skin that sat a little over an inch above his cock would change one day. It would become a fully functioning second cock. When he and Ethan had asked how long it would take until it happened, their father had cast a loving smile at their mother.

"When you meet your mate, your body will change, and the satyr in you will surface and make you whole."

"You always said that there aren't a lot of satyrs in this world. What if my mate doesn't even live here? What if she lives in Europe or Australia or Africa, and I never cross her path?" Ryder had wondered.

"Your mate doesn't have to be satyr. She can be human, or a witch, or even a vampire. It doesn't matter."

"And how and when will I get my second cock?" Ethan had blurted.

"Shortly after you make love to her for the first time."

Ryder had immediately realized what this meant. His future mate would have to see the deformity and agree to sleep with him despite the ugliness of it. It reminded him of the Grimm fairy tale *The Frog Prince*, where the princess had to kiss an ugly frog who would then transform into a handsome young prince.

While Ryder was still thinking about the fairy tale, wondering what would make a girl kiss a frog, his father had added reassuringly, "Your mother accepted me, and I'm only half as good looking as the two of you. You're both handsome, and you can thank your mother for that. You'll never have to jump over the hurdles I had to."

His father had turned the left side of his face to them, emphasizing his point. An angry-looking scar ran from the corner of his left eye down to his chin. His first wife had cut him on their wedding night believing him to be the devil incarnate. The scar had formed long before he was turned into a vampire, and thus was permanent. Gabriel Giles had thought himself ugly and unlovable for over a hundred-and-fifty years. Until he'd met Maya and won her love.

Ryder shook his head. His father was an attractive man despite the scar, or maybe because of it. And there was no doubt that Ryder's mother loved him deeply and unconditionally. But his mother was an extraordinary woman who'd overcome insurmountable obstacles herself. What if Ryder's future mate wasn't as strong and as tolerant as his mother? What if she took one look at him and ran? What then?

Ryder shook off the thought and zipped up his low-riding pants. Feeling a pang of hunger, he went to the tiny fridge next to the comfortable couch in his over-sized bedroom, which was more like a suite than just a bedroom. Inside the refrigerator were several small bottles of fresh blood, all marked with AB+, his favorite blood type. He took one bottle, unscrewed the lid, and gulped down the viscous liquid. It coated his throat. As a response, his fangs descended, and his fingernails turned into sharp barbs. He enjoyed this moment where his vampire side gained the upper hand and reminded him that he wasn't human. Ryder felt his cells infuse with strength, his senses sharpen, and his mind become more focused.

He was a powerful preternatural creature. But with this power came responsibility. He'd sworn an oath to his father, and to everybody at Scanguards, the security company his entire family worked for, that he would never use this power to harm an innocent. All of the vampires and other preternatural creatures who worked for Samson Woodford, the powerful vampire at the helm of Scanguards, had sworn the same oath. And they were all determined to keep it.

It happened more often lately that Ryder thirsted for blood shortly after rising the same way a full-blooded vampire did. Not all hybrids like him and his siblings, or the sons and daughters of Samson and the other vampires in his employ, experienced the same kind of thirst for blood at the same times in their lives. The thirst was as individual as their personalities. Ryder had always thought himself above such a base need, but it appeared that at his core he was just as much a vampire as he was a satyr. Two strong needs, one for blood, the other for sex, would one day collide. When they did, he had to exercise all his restraint in order not to hurt anybody around him, because once he met his mate, he had to hold back the urgent need to mate with her, until she was ready to accept him. But he had no way of knowing when this would happen, whether it was tomorrow or in a hundred years.

Ryder went back to his closet and pulled a casual shirt from it. He put it on, when the door opened.

"Hey Ryder, can I borrow your brown leather jacket?"

His younger brother waltzed into the room without as much as a knock or a perfunctory apology for barging in. Ethan had no boundaries, no sense of personal space. Still, they were brothers and would kill for each other if it came to it. It didn't mean that Ryder didn't occasionally get annoyed with him.

"Given that you'll take it anyway the moment I leave the house, why even ask?"

"You're the best," Ethan said and opened the closet. He reached for the jacket in question. "Wanna come out with me tonight? It's your night off, right?"

"Yep. And no, I don't wanna go out."

"You don't even know where I'm going." Ethan put on the leather jacket and admired himself in the mirror.

"Let me guess: a nightclub."

"Not just any nightclub. It's ladies' night at the Mezzanine. It's gonna be a crush!" Ethan grinned from one ear to the other.

Not only was he handsome in a boy-next-door kind of way, he had the charm to go with it. People who didn't know him would never guess that he was a predator, a hybrid vampire with an insatiable appetite for sex and blood. When Ethan had hit puberty, he'd become restless and made one conquest after the other, sleeping with any girl who'd have him. Ryder, on the other hand, had never gone through that rebellious teenage stage, nor was his appetite for sex as pronounced as his brother's. He was in control of himself at all times.

Ryder rolled his eyes and calmly buttoned his shirt. "I'm planning on getting a bite to eat at Carlito's in North Beach and then read. Baldacci's latest thriller just released—"

"Oh my God," Ethan said with disgust in his voice. "Could you sound any more like an old college professor? Nobody would ever guess that you're one of the best bodyguards at Scanguards." He shook his head. "You want to read on your night off? Are you for real? You sound like you're decades older than me, not just a year."

"It has nothing to do with age," Ryder said.

"Come on, don't be so boring. Don't you wanna get laid?"

"I'm not like you."

It was true. Where Ethan was impulsive and carefree, Ryder was thoughtful and responsible, just like an older brother should be.

"You can't tell me that your sex drive isn't just as high as mine. You're thirty, look decent enough"—Ryder scoffed at that—"and are free to fuck whomever you want. So why aren't you bedding a different girl every night?"

Ryder snatched his brother by the lapels of his jacket and pushed him against the wall. "Because I..." He sucked in a breath and tamped down the anger that was churning up inside him. "... because I don't want to subject every girl in San Francisco to... to... you know what I mean."

He let go of his brother and took a step back, regretting his sudden outburst already. It wasn't like him to get physically violent.

"So you'd rather pay for the pleasure?" Ethan spat.

Ryder's eyes widened.

"Oh please! As if you could fool anybody. I know you've been going to Vera's for years."

Stunned that his brother knew that he'd been frequenting Vera's club, an upscale brothel run by a vampire whose girls were kind and looked past the fact that Ryder sported an ugly deformity. He felt comfortable there, because none of the women had ever looked at him with disgust. They'd helped him slake his lust. But if he was honest, he'd never felt a true high with any of them, even though all of Vera's girls were beautiful and well-versed in all kinds of carnal pleasure. His orgasms had stilled his need temporarily, but he'd never felt the kind of satisfaction after sex that he'd heard his friends talk about.

"It's none of your business," Ryder said and turned away.

"Come on, bro, don't be like that. Honestly, most of the girls I sleep with really don't care what I look like as long as they get what they want. Hey, some of them even find it cool. And if a girl really rejects me because of it, then I just glamor her so she won't remember what she's seen. Besides, most of the girls at the club will be half-drunk anyway."

Ryder scoffed. "You think sleeping with girls that are too drunk to care makes it any better than sleeping with prostitutes?"

"Trust me, I make sure they have their fun. I'm not a selfish lover," Ethan claimed. "Plus, the more girls I sleep with, the better my chances of finding my mate, right?"

He had to admire his brother's optimism despite the questionable methods he employed. His own ethics prohibited him from taking advantage of a girl, whether she was half-drunk or not. "Guess that means you can't wait until you finally have two cocks. Good for you."

A chuckle from the door made Ryder snap his head to it. Vanessa stood there, giggling. She was as beautiful as their mother, with long dark hair and expressive eyes. And even though she was the youngest of the siblings, she seemed more mature than her brothers. It was true that girls grew up faster.

"Men! At least you get something out of it once you find your mate, while I'm in heat at least four times a year. Do you hear me bitching constantly?"

She walked into the room and looked at Ryder. Then she shook her head. "That button is loose. And that shirt doesn't look good on you anyway. Why don't you wear the linen shirt?"

Ryder let out a breath. "I'm not going anywhere special, so it doesn't matter."

"Take it off," she insisted and pulled out a different shirt from his closet.

Ryder hesitated. "Fine. I'll get changed. If you both leave my room."

Ethan and Vanessa exchanged a look.

"Now," he added.

"You're a hopeless case," she said.

Ryder took the shirt from her hands, then ruffled her hair. "Thanks, Nessie. Now get lost, before I lose my patience."

"Yeah, I wanna see that," Vanessa joked.

"No, you don't."

Vanessa looked at Ethan. "I bet he doesn't even wrinkle the sheets when he has sex with a girl."

"Good one, Nessie," Ethan said, laughing.

"You do know that I'm right here, and there's nothing wrong with my hearing, right?" Ryder said.

"Then you should take some well-meant advice," Ethan said. "Let loose once in a while, or that stick that's up your butt will become permanent."

2

Scarlet was in the kitchen, when she heard the chiming of her cell phone. Her father, Brandon King, was calling her on FaceTime. She clicked accept.

"Hey, Dad!"

His handsome face was pixilated for a moment, before it became sharper. "Hey, honey, what are you up to?" His voice was a deep baritone, and he smiled warmly at her. There was something youthful to him, even though he was fifty-five years old, and he had streaks of gray in his dark hair.

"I was working on my thesis all day. Now I'm beat."

"And your health? Any episodes?"

"I'm fine, Dad. How's your ankle?"

"It's healing, no worries."

"I can't believe you slipped in the bathroom. How did that even happen?" After all, her father wasn't an old man or an invalid. In fact, he played tennis regularly, and was in shape.

"I just slipped on something wet. Some shampoo must have dripped from the bottle to the floor. You know how many shampoos and lotions Claudia has. I'll be more careful next time. So, how are your studies?"

"I'm making good progress. It's just really busy."

Scarlet had transferred to San Francisco University the previous fall, and moved into her father's Victorian in Pacific Heights rather than staying in their mansion in Palo Alto where she'd lived while she'd gotten her degree at Stanford University. Not only did she want to get her PhD at the somewhat smaller private university in San Francisco, she also wanted independence, as well as grant her father and her stepmother, Claudia, some privacy.

Claudia, whom her father had married six years earlier, long after Scarlet's mother had died of an unexpected heart attack at age forty, was a wonderful woman, even though Scarlet had at first thought that she was far too young for her father. Despite the eighteen-year age gap between them—Claudia was thirty-seven—they seemed to be happy together. Scarlet had expected that they would be overjoyed when she'd announced that she would move to San Francisco. Far from it. Both of them had protested, wanting her to live with them on the Peninsula.

But she'd put her foot down. After all, she was twenty-four and an adult. Still, her father had agreed only grudgingly. And under one condition.

"How's the new bodyguard working out? Do you like him better than the last?"

Scarlet didn't even bother to hide her eyeroll. "He's annoying and clings to me like a bad outfit."

Her father chuckled softly. "That's his job. He has to protect you."

"Really, Dad? Haven't I proven to you that I can look after myself and don't need a babysitter? You're not applying the same rules to Claudia!"

"Because Claudia agreed to have a gun in the house so she can defend herself when I'm away on business," he countered.

"And I took the self-defense class, just like you asked me to, and I'm even learning karate, so that I can defend myself if I'm attacked. But I don't want a gun in the house. Statistics say that people are more likely to be killed by their own guns than not."

"I don't care about statistics. I care about your safety."

"I really don't need a constant shadow. Frankly, it's humiliating showing up everywhere with a bodyguard in tow. People look at me strangely."

And it made it hard to really get to know the other students on campus. They all assumed that she was aloof, or something better, and didn't want to mingle with her peers.

"Honey, you know we had an agreement. Besides, Scanguards is the best security company in the entire country. They have the best people."

Scarlet huffed. "I'm not saying that the bodyguards Scanguards provides are bad. They're just not for me. I don't—"

"Scarlet, please! You've already churned through four of their bodyguards. And now the owner's son has been assigned to you. Trust me, after you alienated each of your previous bodyguards, it's a wonder they haven't terminated the contract."

"I haven't alienated anyone," she managed to interject.

Her father grimaced, showing her that he didn't believe her. "Last month, Samson Woodford called me personally to assure me that you'll get the very best they have. That's all I want for you: to be safe. I can't lose you too. It would break my heart."

She hated it when her father tugged at her heartstrings by reminding her of their recent loss. She was still grieving too. She'd loved her half-brother, and his death had been a shock for all of them. Scarlet looked at her father, silent for a moment. He wasn't doing this to control her, he was doing this to protect her, because if he lost her too, it would destroy him. He would never recover from that, not even with Claudia by his side.

"I'm sorry, Dad. I understand." She forced a smile, despite having lost another argument with him. No wonder her father was a successful businessman. He always got what he wanted. "When are you coming to the city?"

"Not for a few days. I have to fly to Phoenix tomorrow on business. But Claudia might come up tomorrow. She has some things to do in San Francisco."

"Oh, she's not flying to Phoenix with you?"

"No, you know she hates the desert heat. But I won't be gone for long. Promise."

"I miss you," she said. It was the truth. She and her father had always been close.

"Miss you too, honey. Chin up! I'm told that Grayson Woodford is a handsome young man."

Her father wasn't wrong. "Trust me he has the arrogance to go with his looks."

"Just don't make his life hell, okay?"

"Okay, Dad. Have a good flight."

"Bye, honey."

Scarlet disconnected the call, when she heard a sound from the door. It startled her. She spun around and saw Grayson standing in the door, a frown on his face.

He was handsome, she had to give him that. Tall, dark hair, fit body. He probably had a swarm of women drool over him wherever he went. But Scarlet didn't like him. After all, he was her jailor, and he was full of himself. Clearly, the heir to the Scanguards empire was spoiled rotten. She'd looked into Scanguards before her father had hired them. Unfortunately, she hadn't found anything that would disqualify them in her father's eyes, or in her own. They were a very well-run operation with glowing reviews from previous and current clients.

Nevertheless, Scarlet didn't like the idea of having a bodyguard in general, nor Grayson in particular. He couldn't be much older than her. How much experience could he really have at this age? He didn't strike her as somebody who spent his days and nights training to be the best in his field. Clearly, he'd gotten the plum assignment because he was the owner's son.

"So you think I'm arrogant," Grayson said while he ran his eyes over her.

His look said that he didn't like what he saw. It didn't bother her. She liked wearing her long hair in an efficient ponytail, liked the casual clothes, the worn-out jeans and the oversized sweater that hid her curves. Her clothes made her feel safe, because she could hide behind them, just like she hid behind metal-rimmed glasses that made her look older than she was, even though she didn't need them. She had perfect vision. Just like her clothes, her glasses were part of her image: the bookworm and PhD candidate who was focused only on her studies and was not interested in men.

Unfortunately, over the last few years, a sexual need had arisen in her that she couldn't deny anymore. Every so often, she had to leave the façade of the demure bookworm behind, and take what she needed to feel better. She couldn't deny herself the carnal pleasures that her body demanded from time to time. She could only suppress them for so long, before she lost control over her actions and did what she needed to do to find peace, if only for a little while.

"Was that a question?" Scarlet asked.

He raised an eyebrow. "I don't have to make conversation."

"Then don't." She looked at the clock on the kitchen wall. "My takeout from Tomaso's should be ready. Let's go." She grabbed her handbag. It was her largest one, large enough to hide the things she needed for tonight.

"You're eating that late? I thought you had dinner already."

"Well, working on my thesis burns a lot of calories. I need food. And since I don't want to cook, I need takeout. And before you ask, no, they don't deliver. They're short on drivers. If you don't want to drive me, then I'll go by myself." She knew his answer before he gave it.

Grayson glared at her. "Nice try. Not a chance. I'll drive you."

"Thank you," she said, giving him an overly sweet smile, because she knew it pissed him off. There was something rather satisfying about pushing Grayson's buttons.

Grayson's Audi TT was parked in the driveway. They jumped in, and without a word, Grayson drove off. Scarlet settled into the leather seat. She felt hot beneath her bulky sweater and reached for the button to switch on the air conditioning.

Before she could touch it and turn it cooler, Grayson barked, "Don't touch the controls. I'll do it."

"Then turn the heat off already."

"The heat isn't on. It's a comfortable 68 degrees in here."

"Comfortable for you. But I'm hot, so put the air conditioning on."

"You can't be hot."

She shot him an annoyed look. "Says who?"

"Fine, the air conditioning it is," Grayson said, a growl in his voice. He turned the temperature dial.

She couldn't help but add, "Well, was that so hard?"

Grayson had the good sense not to reply. She wasn't mad at him, not really. Rather, she was mad at the hand she'd been dealt. She was close to exploding. It was like PMS times a hundred. She knew that some of her girlfriends from college had the occasional PMS symptoms, but Scarlet always got a full blast of it. And when it happened, she had to get out of the house or she would climb up the walls. Cabin fever, she called it. Episodes was what her father called it.

When they reached Tomaso's restaurant in the Mission, there was no parking anywhere close to it. Traffic was heavy in the neighborhood famed for its great restaurants and bars. It was hopping even on a weekday night. Scarlet had counted on it.

Grayson circled twice around the same block, but there was nowhere he could park.

"Come on, Grayson, just double park and let me jump out, or my food will get cold," she said.

"No way. I'm not that stupid to let you go inside so you can run out the back exit and ditch me."

Scarlet tossed him a glare. "Then you go in and get the food, and I'll stay with the car."

Grayson grimaced, before he finally stopped the car in front of the restaurant's entrance, double-parking it. "Fine, but I'm taking the car key with me."

Scarlet rolled her eyes. "Like I want to drive your precious car."

Fuming, Grayson switched off the engine and got out. She watched him as he ran around the car's front and rushed into the restaurant. She could see from where she was that the hostess was dealing with several customers, and Grayson would have to wait a minute or two. It was enough time for her to do what she needed to do.

The moment Grayson was inside the restaurant, Scarlet jumped out of the car and hurried toward the intersection, where a crowd of partygoers waited for the pedestrian light to give the walk signal. She quickly pushed through them, so that she ended up in the middle surrounded on all sides by people.

When the signal turned, she crossed the street with the other young people around her, and hurried to the entrance of the MUNI station. She ran down the stairs, already pulling out her monthly pass, so she could pass through the turnstiles. She heard a subway train coming, and hoped it was heading in the right direction. Moments later, she reached the platform, and looked at the display.

She was in luck. The train was an inbound train. It was busy, but she managed to get on it. She cast a look over her shoulder, her heart beating frantically, worried that Grayson had seen through her ruse and was on her heels. But she didn't see him. She'd successfully shaken him off like a bad cold.

Scarlet let out a sigh of relief. She didn't care if Grayson got in trouble for this, or even if he told her father. By now, her body had such an amount of pent-up energy that she had to do something about it. She could barely wait until the train finally stopped at the station closest to her destination. Once above ground again, she walked two blocks to a bar she'd been to before. There was no hostess or bouncer at the door, making it the ideal place for her to slip in and get changed.

Scarlet headed for the bathroom and went inside. Two girls were washing their hands, but the three stalls were empty. Scarlet chose the largest one, entered and locked the door behind her. Quickly, she rid herself of her sweater. Underneath it she wore a black bustier that hugged her breasts tightly. She took off her long black boots, an essential item for San Francisco's notoriously cool weather throughout the year, and wriggled out of her jeans. Earlier, she'd stuffed a short skirt into her handbag, and she now pulled it out and slipped it on, then donned her boots again. She folded her jeans and sweater and squeezed them both into a plastic bag she'd brought. By the time she left the stall, the two women were gone. Scarlet stuffed the plastic bag containing her clothes into a cabinet that held extra toilet paper. With some luck, the bag would still be here when she came back later. If not, she didn't care. She'd never much liked that sweater anyway, and she had plenty of jeans.

Scarlet stopped in front of the mirror and undid her ponytail. She shook out her black curls, then took off her glasses and slipped them into her handbag. She applied only a little bit of make-up, just enough to accentuate her blue eyes and her long black lashes. Her lips were a deep red even without lipstick.

When she looked into the full-length mirror, she didn't see the unassuming PhD candidate looking back at her. No, the reflection was that of a temptress flaunting her curves, a woman with an unquenchable carnal need visible to anybody who cared to look. Now all she needed was the right man to quench that hunger for physical touch that was becoming more unbearable by the minute.

It was time to hit the nightclubs and let off steam.

3

Ryder had dinner at Carlito's restaurant in North Beach. Even though he'd gorged himself on blood earlier, he enjoyed the human food Carlito's served. Food choices in San Francisco were endless, and over the last few years he'd been to almost every place that offered good cuisine. When it came to blood, however, he had an absolute favorite: AB positive. Every blood type tasted slightly different. He found that AB positive gave him the right mix of sweet and tangy to satisfy his thirst. Most of the time, he drank bottled blood, which Scanguards procured via a medical company, and distributed to their staff for free. Many of the vampires Scanguards employed appreciated this service. But Samson, the founder and CEO of Scanguards, didn't judge. If a vampire preferred drinking from a human directly, he didn't stop them. He had only one rule: no human would be harmed in the process.

Ryder, on occasion, drank from the girls in Vera's employ. Some of them were human, some vampires, but all of them were discreet and loyal to Vera. The human women knew about the vampires in their midst but kept their secret. Just as they kept Ryder's secret.

After his dinner at Carlito's, Ryder took a stroll through North Beach and made his way up the hill to Nob Hill, where Vera's exclusive club was located. At the unassuming door of the stately corner building, he rang the bell and announced himself. Somebody buzzed him into the building. Inside, it looked like an elegant hotel lobby. Soft music came from loudspeakers in the ceiling, and the lush carpet under his feet swallowed his footsteps.

Vera, the vampire who ran the establishment, walked toward him with a smile. She was a petite Asian woman with stunning looks, who'd assisted Scanguards in several cases in the past few years. "Ryder, it's been a while." She hugged him.

"It's been busy at work," he said apologetically, though it wasn't the reason why he hadn't visited in almost a month. He'd wanted to see how long he could suppress his sexual needs. Apparently a month was his limit.

Vera released him and sighed. "I'm so sorry, Ryder, but none of the girls are available. There's a big congress in town, and all the girls are triple-booked tonight. And you know I don't like to make them take more than three bookings a night."

"Oh, I understand," Ryder said quickly, even though he was disappointed. But he knew Vera well enough to know that her first concern were the women who worked for her. They were treated well and paid even better. None of them was forced to do anything she wasn't comfortable with.

"I should have called ahead. My fault."

Vera squeezed his hand. "The clients will be gone in two days. Why don't you come back then? And you can choose whom you want."

"Perfect," Ryder said and forced a smile to hide his disappointment. "Enjoy your evening, Vera."

When he closed the door behind him and stood outside in the cool night, he looked down the hill. The lights sparkled. He loved the view from up here, where he could see all of San Francisco. He wasn't in the mood to go home and use his own hand to find the satisfaction he needed. Tonight, he had to find a woman who was willing to slake his lust.

"Guess I'm going clubbing after all," he murmured to himself and hailed a cab to take him to a club that would be teeming with women tonight.

"The Mezzanine in SOMA please," he told the cab driver and settled in for the short ride.

The Mezzanine was a nightclub that had been around for several decades. Amaury, one of Scanguards' directors had been a part-owner of the club for a long time. When one of his twin sons, Damian, had shown interest in the club, he'd handed the management over to him and arranged for Samson to buy the other half of the club for his son Patrick. Now, Damian and Patrick, both hybrid vampires, ran the club on the side, while still working as bodyguards for Scanguards.

They had remodeled the club extensively, and it had become a hotspot in San Francisco's nightlife. The bouncers were vampires and assured that the clientele remained classy. Anybody who exhibited any kind of violence on the premises was promptly removed and barred for life.

Ryder flashed his Scanguards ID at the bouncer, who waved him through, past the waiting line that stretched nearly half a block. Inside, music droned, and lights flashed in the rhythm of the music. The dance floor was packed, and the crowd seemed to move in synch like a flock of birds. Ryder let his eyes roam. He couldn't see his brother, nor anybody else he knew. He took that as a good sign. He didn't like the idea of Ethan watching him as he tried to pick up a girl. He was a little rusty in that department.

Ryder strode down the stairs that led to the dance floor and paved his way through the throng of dancing women and men to get to the bar. It wasn't as easy as it sounded. There was definitely an abundance of women and a shortage of men. Every other woman he passed put her hands on him, trying to pull him toward her, her intentions clear. If he wanted to, he could pick anyone. But for some reason, none appealed to him.

Despite their skimpy outfits, their perfect make-up, and their unmistakable offers, he wasn't even close to getting hard, when just entering Vera's club he'd been ready and raring to go. But in a nightclub with a whole army of sex-hungry women, he didn't see a single woman whom he wanted to touch.

Maybe a drink was in order, though alcohol did very little for a vampire. It would take gallons of hard liquor to get a vampire even slightly inebriated. But perhaps a drink would make him feel more comfortable in this environment. It took a while until he reached the bar, where the three bartenders were inundated with orders. Ryder let his gaze roam while he waited for his turn.

When somebody elbowed him in the side, Ryder spun around, ready to punch the person. Instead, a woman with long black curls, her back to him, bumped into him, and only Ryder's vampire-speed reaction saved them both from crashing to the floor. He caught the woman beneath her armpits to put her back on her feet, and now saw the reason why she'd lost her balance. A rather drunk guy who looked like a surfer, was trying to grab her and force her to dance with him. Ryder let go of the girl and stepped past her to confront the surfer dude.

"She doesn't wanna dance with you. So piss off!" Ryder growled and felt his fangs lengthen. His eyes were probably already flashing red, but inside the club, he wasn't concerned about his vampire side emerging. An abundance of colored lights in the club could easily explain his red eyes away as a reflection.

The surfer dude withdrew with a stunned look on his face. Ryder watched him retreat and turned back to the girl to see if she was all right.

The question was already on his lips, but Ryder froze, unable to say a single word. The girl just stood there, looking straight at him. Long black hair framed her heart-shaped face. Her eyes were of a stunning blue, and her lashes thick and rich. Her cheeks were flushed, and her lips red and plump. She wore a short black skirt and a bustier that revealed more than it concealed, keeping her midriff bare. Her breasts were petite, and her skin creamy and unblemished. Instinctively his gaze swept to her neck where her carotid artery pulsed as if it was sending him a secret message in Morse code.

Ryder's cock turned hard in a second. He couldn't tell how old the girl was, but he knew she had to be over twenty-one, or she would have been turned away at the door. That was reassuring, because what he wanted from her was definitely… yeah, most definitely nothing for an underage virgin.

"Hi," he said, his throat as dry as sandpaper. "I'm Ryder."

She licked her lips and took a step closer. Only an inch or two separated their bodies now. She lifted her face to him and sucked in a long breath, drawing his eyes to her cleavage as it rose with her breath.

Fuck! He couldn't look away. Couldn't step back. Without any conscious thought, he put his arm around her waist and pulled her to him, bringing her body flush with his.

Her lips parted, and a breath rushed from her lungs, but she didn't free herself from him. Instead, she pressed her pelvis to his. He felt her stomach rub against his hard-on, while she locked eyes with him.

"What's your name?"

"Sara," she said. "Dance with me."

Sara put her arms around him, and slid one hand on his ass, as they started moving to the rhythm of the music. What they did could hardly be called dancing, because they didn't move from their spot close to the bar, their feet remaining firmly planted on the ground, only their bodies writhing. With every second of feeling Sara rub herself against him, clearly fully aware of his arousal, Ryder's heart beat faster. He dipped his head to her neck and inhaled the aroma of her skin.

"Let me feel you," she murmured in his ear.

He slid one hand on her backside and squeezed one cheek, drawing her harder against his rampant cock. "Is that what you want?" he replied. "My cock?"

At the word, she moaned, and Ryder couldn't help himself and inserted one leg between her thighs.

"That's it," she said, clinging to him as she began riding his thigh.

Fuck! What was happening here? He hadn't given her more than his name, and already they were practically fucking. Yet, he couldn't stop himself, couldn't find the decency to pull back. He was instinctively drawn to her. She was probably drunk, or why else would she allow him to touch her like this? His good upbringing and manners dictated that he stop this madness, but apparently he'd left his upbringing and manners at the door.

Ryder felt Sara's breasts crushed against his chest, loving the feel of them hugging his hard muscles. He lifted his head from her tempting neck and met her gaze. Her eyes were dilated, her breath choppy, and her lips inviting.

He captured her mouth and drank her in. She kissed him back without hesitation, allowing him to explore her with his tongue, while he used his hands to guide her hips and make her ride his thigh with an increased tempo.

All of a sudden, he felt her shudder in his arms and realized that she'd climaxed. He ripped his lips from hers and stared at her, stunned. Her blue eyes were even more beautiful now, and in them he saw raw desire and unbridled lust.

"I need you to take me…" She slid her palm over his erection.

He clenched his jaw so he wouldn't come right here in public.

"Please," she begged.

Her plea sent a spear of fire into his balls. If he didn't take her somewhere else right away, he would have to press her against the bar and fuck her right here. And he couldn't allow that to happen. Not in public. It would have devastating consequences, for both of them.

"I know a place where we can be alone."

4

Scarlet followed Ryder, her hand in his, as he paved a way through the crowd to a different part of the club. She'd given him a fake name, which was something she always did when she sought anonymous sex. In a way it helped her distance herself from the person she became when her sexual urges overpowered her.

Ryder headed for the corridor that led to the restrooms, but he passed them and pushed another door labeled *Staff only* open and walked through. There he took an immediate right and opened another door, peered into the room, and then ushered her inside. He closed the door behind them and flipped the lock shut.

The light was dim, and from what Scarlet could see, this was a storage room of some sort. There were extra tables and chairs, a few armchairs, as well as partitions and other furniture. She didn't care where she was. She'd climaxed while rubbing herself on Ryder's leg. That had never happened before. But then, everything was different tonight. Several men had approached her in the club, but despite her hunger for sex, she'd rejected them all. None had measured up.

But the moment Ryder had prevented her from falling, the moment he'd put his hands on her to steady her, she'd felt it. Her body instantly responded to him, even before he'd turned back to her so she could see his face. And when she laid eyes on him, every cell of her body, everything female awakened and drew her to him. He was perfect. He would be able to give her what she needed.

Ryder was tall and handsome. His hair was a light brown, his eyes a deep chocolate brown, his skin a light olive shade. He looked slender, though his muscles seemed to bulge under his shirt. There was a magnetism to his gaze, one she couldn't tear herself away from. As if he were a magnet, and she a mere metal nail.

"Sara," he murmured at her lips. "Tell me what you want."

She let out a breath. "Your cock inside me."

"Good, cause that's what I want too." He pressed her back against the wall and drew her bustier down until her breasts popped out on top. "I've never met anybody like you."

His hungry mouth met her skin, kissing her sensitive nipples, and her clit began to tingle again, still sensitive from her orgasm. She snatched Ryder's shirt and pulled it from his pants, so she could put her hands on his naked skin. It felt as hot as her own.

"You made me come so hard," she whispered, enjoying the feel of his tongue licking her breasts, while his hand swept under her skirt and slid between her thighs, where her panties were drenched in her own juices.

"You wanna come again?" he asked and already pushed her panties aside to rub his fingers along her cleft, his action bold, yet more than welcome.

His touch was electrifying, and she closed her eyes and let herself go in the arms of this stranger who seemed to know what she needed.

"You're weeping for me. I like that," Ryder rasped. "This time when you come, do me a favor, and say my name."

"Yes."

The word hadn't left her lips yet, when he thrust his finger into her, making her gasp at the unexpected invasion. She loved his finger exploring her, but it wasn't enough.

"Ryder, I want your cock."

He chuckled unexpectantly. "You'll get my cock, don't worry, baby. But first I want you to come again. Can you do that for me?" He pumped his finger into her slowly, then added a second one.

"Oh, oh, that's better… yes…" She leaned her head back against the wall, enjoying the fullness in her intimate channel.

Ryder thrust again and again, and every time his fingers descended as far as they could, he brushed his thumb over her clitoris, eliciting moans from her. Her knees felt weak, and if he kept this up, she would surely collapse.

He lifted his head from her breasts and met her eyes. "You like that, don't you?"

"Yes." More than he could know.

"Say my name."

"Ryder, you feel good. I can't wait to feel your cock where your fingers are now." If he could bring her to such ecstasy with his fingers alone, what would she feel with his cock inside her? Finally, she would get what she needed. Ryder would quench her thirst for no-holds-barred sex.

"Fuck me harder," she demanded. "Ryder."

He did as she commanded, thrusting his fingers deeper and harder into her, while his thumb worked her clit with such skill that she was only seconds away from another climax.

"Yes, yes, Ryder, yes!"

She shuddered. Her muscles spasmed around his fingers as she came, the waves rocking her body as if an explosion had knocked her off her feet. Ryder didn't withdraw his fingers. He kept his thumb on her clit, and just as she thought her orgasm was subsiding, he strummed her clit once more like a talented musician, igniting her again.

She met his gaze and saw male satisfaction in his deep brown eyes that looked almost like molten lava now, a red hue around his irises as if a fire was burning in them.

"You still want my cock?" he asked, his voice reaching every cell of her body and resonating there.

"Yes, I need your cock. Please." It was true. Despite the earth-shattering orgasms he'd given her, she needed more. Almost as if every orgasm fueled her hunger even more.

"Good, cause now you're ripe," he said and removed his fingers from her.

~ ~ ~

Not able to wait a second longer, Ryder pushed Sara's skirt up to her hips and pulled her panties to her knees, before turning her around and bending her over one of the armchairs, her pretty ass pointed at him. Impatiently, he opened his pants, pushed them down, and made his boxer briefs follow. His cock was harder than it had ever been, and the mass above it seemed to pulse. But in this position Sara would never see it. He didn't bother using a condom. Vampires didn't carry disease and could neither contract a venereal disease nor infect somebody else. An unwanted pregnancy was also impossible. Only blood-bonded vampires could impregnate their mates.

Gripping her hips with both hands, Ryder positioned himself behind her and sank his cock into her drenched pussy until he was seated to the hilt. The sensation of being gripped by her still pulsing muscles almost robbed him of his self-control. He'd never felt anything so perfect.

"Fuck, you're tight."

Sara turned her head to look over her shoulder. Just as well that he'd kept his shirt on, which hid his deformity.

"Fuck me hard. Can you do that for me, Ryder?" Her eyes glistened as if she was delirious, but her demand was clear.

"Nothing will please me more than to fuck you until you can't move another muscle."

Ryder took her hard, impaling her on his cock with such force that he was worried he'd hurt her, but she didn't bail on him. Instead, she demanded more, as if she couldn't get enough of his cock pounding into her. He'd never dared to do this to another human woman. Not even the vampire females he'd been with at Vera's had gotten him so randy that he couldn't restrain his primal need to fuck her as if she belonged to him, as if she was his.

And every move Sara made, every moan that rolled over her lips, and every thrust she met, drove him closer to the point of no return. Even if she begged him to stop now, he didn't have the self-control to follow such a demand. He was no longer master of his own body. The vampire and the satyr inside him were ruling him now, demanding their due. He'd suppressed the inner beasts in him for too long. Now they were free, unleashed from their cages.

His satyr side reared up, pushing the vampire's need for blood aside. Ryder knew what the satyr wanted. He was no fool. He knew why a satyr had two cocks. Nobody had to explain it to him. He felt it now, felt the need to fuck Sara the way a satyr fucked his woman. But his yet unformed second cock was incapable of such an act. Still, the satyr wanted to feel her. All of her.

Ryder released Sara's right hip and stroked his index finger along the crack of her ass. His finger was still wet from her juices, and he couldn't resist the temptation any longer. With the tip of his finger, he rubbed over her puckered hole and felt her shiver in response. His cock thrusting without pause, Ryder pressed against the tight ring.

"I'm sorry, Sara, I have to..."

He drove his finger into her forbidden hole and braced for resistance. But Sara didn't push back, didn't protest, didn't ask him to withdraw. Instead, a long moan rolled over her lips.

"Ryder..."

Whatever she wanted to say didn't come over her lips. Her muscles convulsed around him, her orgasm slamming into him like a gigantic ocean wave, ripping him with her, making him spill inside her until she'd wrung every last drop from him. All the while, he continued pumping his finger in the same rhythm as his cock.

Sex with Sara was the best he'd ever had.

5

Scarlet felt awash with all kinds of sensations when Ryder withdrew from her. For a moment, she couldn't even move, her last orgasm so powerful that she'd seen stars before her eyes. She'd never felt so... so sated.

"Let me get cleaned up in the bathroom. I'll be right back," Ryder said. "I'll bring you a towel."

She looked over her shoulder, but he'd already turned around and headed for the door. She appreciated that he opened it only a fraction to make sure nobody was outside in the hallway, before he slipped out and closed the door behind him.

Scarlet straightened. Her legs felt like jelly, and she steadied herself with the help of the armchair. She'd enjoyed every single second of her encounter with Ryder, but something was different now. Her episode, the almost feverish need for sexual gratification, had passed. Looking around her in the storage room now brought her to her senses again. It was as if somebody had doused her with a bucket of ice. She'd behaved like a common slut, begged a stranger to fuck her, and... do other things. She didn't even want to think about... *that*. What must he think of her? She'd never behaved like that before.

At least when she'd had her previous sexual exploits, she'd had sex with guys in their cars, or even in their flats, never in a storage room, and never like this. Sex with strangers had never been that primal, that raw, that taboo. She knew it was all her own doing. She'd practically fucked Ryder at the bar. Hell, she'd begged him to take her. She'd asked for his cock. Sure, he'd agreed to fuck her. What young single guy wouldn't? But the moment he was done, he'd hightailed it out of here. He hadn't even looked back.

Damn! She had to get out of here and forget what happened.

Scarlet made sure her clothes covered her body before she rushed out of the door. A breeze blew through the corridor, and she realized that a back door was open at the end of the corridor. She turned toward it. She was relieved that she didn't have to go back through the club. Who knew how many people had seen how she'd practically rubbed herself on Ryder's cock in public for the entire world to see?

Scarlet rushed outside into the dark. As if in a trance, she made her way back to the bar where she'd stashed her clothes. She was lucky. Nobody had taken them. After she dressed and left the place, she called an Uber and headed home.

In the back of the car, she closed her eyes. But she couldn't push the events of the last hour out of her mind. There was no denying it: she'd enjoyed sex with Ryder. Hell, she'd enjoyed every single second of it, and every single thing he'd done. Even when he'd penetrated her in a place where nobody had before. The sensation of his finger inside her had aroused her more than anything else. Christ, she was depraved. How could she, an educated woman, like such a debauched act? Not just liked, no, loved.

Scarlet felt the shame of it now. She was glad that she hadn't given Ryder her real name, just in case he went back to the club on another night and asked about her. Not that she thought he would. To him she was probably just a quick fuck, a slut with whom he could do things no decent girl would allow.

By the time the Uber dropped her off outside her home in Pacific Heights, she'd made a promise to herself: next time she felt the urge to go on a sexual bender, she would lock herself in her room and toss the key out of the window.

Scarlet unlocked the front door and entered the house, letting the door close behind her. She headed straight for the stairs, in need of a shower to wash the shame from her body. But she didn't reach the stairs.

"Well, look what the cat dragged in."

Scarlet spun to the left and saw a dark shadow. Grayson. Figured that he was here waiting for her. He flipped on the light switch. She would have preferred to stay in the dark. Did she show signs that she'd been thoroughly fucked less than an hour ago? Was it written on her face how wild she'd gotten, and what liberties she'd allowed her sexual partner?

"What do you want?" she asked.

"You tricked me. You never ordered takeout. You made me go in there so you could ditch me while I was busy arguing with the hostess about them not preparing your order." Grayson looked as if smoke would come out of his ears at any moment.

"Well, at least you had fun." Because for certain he enjoyed arguing.

"Where the fuck were you?"

"None of your business. You work for me, not the other way around."

"Correction: I work for your father." He stared at her, his jaw clenched. "And when I tell him where you were, I'm sure he won't be pleased."

Scarlet took a step toward him and braced her hands at her hips, not at all intimidated by him. "First: you have no idea where I was, or you would have gone there to fetch me. But you didn't. Ergo you had no clue where I was. And I'm not gonna tell you. And second: go ahead, and tell my father. And while you're at it, explain to him how you, the supposedly best bodyguard Scanguards has, managed to lose sight of me, a quiet, introvert twenty-four-year-old PhD candidate half your size. I'm sure he'd like to hear your excuse."

"You... you..."

With satisfaction she saw that for the first time since Grayson had become her bodyguard he was speechless. Unfortunately it didn't last long.

Grayson had a comeback after all. "Then I think I'll speak to my father. I'm sure he'll terminate his contract with your dad. And you won't be able to hire anybody else in this city."

"Well, go ahead. I'm not the one who wants a bodyguard! And while you're chatting with your father, you might as well tell him that the moment I turn twenty-five, I'll be able to access my trust fund, and then nobody can tell me any longer how to live my life. So tell him, in three months, I'll be firing you anyway!"

"That day can't come soon enough," Grayson replied. "But I'm afraid I'm not gonna waste my energy on you any longer. You're a spoiled, rotten little bitch!"

"It takes one to know one," she shot back.

His face flushed, and the chords in his neck seemed to bulge. He reached for his cell phone and punched in a number.

"Calling daddy 'cause somebody was unfair to you?" she asked. "Booohooo!"

He glared at her, and a red glint shone from his eyes as if he was about to pop a blood vessel. But he didn't reply. Instead, he turned his back to her.

"Benjamin, you're up. I need you to relieve me at the King's. Yep, make it quick. I'll wait outside for you."

Without a look back, he opened the front door and walked outside. The door fell shut behind him.

"Good riddance!" she murmured to herself and walked upstairs.

In her room, she undressed and looked at herself in the mirror. She felt different, though she looked the same. For the first time since puberty, she felt—for lack of a better word—complete. Her body still hummed with pleasure. Not even the shame about her actions could wash that feeling away.

All her life, ever since her mother had died, she'd felt like she didn't belong anywhere. That she was different from her peers. She had no idea where that feeling came from, only that tonight, Ryder had made her feel understood, if only for a short time. It gave her hope that maybe one day in the future, she would find the happiness she was yearning for and be as normal as everybody else.

6

Grayson parked his Audi in his assigned spot in the parking garage below Scanguards HQ in the Mission and killed the engine. He was fuming. He was done looking after Scarlet King. She was a manipulative spoiled little rich girl.

The elevator dinged, and Grayson got in, swiped his access card and punched the button for the top floor where the executive offices were located. He waited impatiently for the doors to close.

"Hold the door!"

He recognized his older sister's voice, and pressed the button for the door to close immediately, not in the mood to speak to her, but Isabelle was faster.

"Hey, Grayson," Isabelle said as she jumped into the elevator just before the doors closed.

Isabelle was only a year older, and the spitting image of their mother, Delilah. At thirty-two, she was still single, though she'd had her share of boyfriends. But whenever things got serious, she bowed out. In that respect they were very similar. Grayson too, wanted to play the field for as long as he could before committing to one woman for the rest of his life. Frankly, he found the idea unappealing. To have sex with the same woman for centuries? Where was the fun in that? He liked variety. It added spice to his life. It would take a very special woman for him to give up his bachelor life.

"Back already? I thought you were on an assignment," Isabelle said.

He forced himself to be civil when he felt anything but. "I finished it."

"Oh, great, then you've got time."

Figuring that she was about to recruit him for one of her many projects of improving the lives of vampires in general, and members of the extended Scanguards family in particular, he replied, "I don't. I've got a meeting."

Sometimes he couldn't take Isabelle's constant positivity. How could somebody be so happy and cheerful all the time? What the fuck was she on?

"Well, maybe after your meeting I could run something by you."

He took a breath. "You know what, Isa? Whatever it is, I'm not interested. I've got enough on my plate."

She lifted her eyebrows and gave him a once over. "Somebody's in a bad mood tonight."

He glared at her, ready to tear into her, but then he stopped himself. "Forget it."

The elevator stopped and the doors opened. He charged out, glad to not have to continue a conversation that would inevitably lead to an argument. Isabelle fought with him constantly, whereas their younger brother, Patrick, could get away with murder without as much as a reprimand from Isabelle. Fighting with her was never very satisfying, because she was rational and won far too often. It pissed him off.

Grayson headed for his father's office, and opened the door after a cursory knock. Samson Woodford stood near the window looking out over the lights of the city, his second-in-command, Gabriel Giles next to him.

Both looked over their shoulders. His father looked less than two decades older than Grayson, even though he was over two-hundred-and-sixty years old. He made a striking figure. Tall, slim, with dark hair and hazel eyes, he drew everybody's attention to him without uttering a single word. They'd had their differences, but when it came down to it, Grayson admired his father and wanted to emulate him. But it was harder than he thought.

"Can it wait?" Samson asked. "Gabriel and I are in the middle of something."

Gabriel was one of his father's closest and oldest friends. On the surface, Gabriel looked like a thug. He had the hideous scar that ran from his eye to his chin to thank for it. But everybody who knew Gabriel, knew that he was fiercely loyal to Scanguards, and protective toward his family, an honest man with strong morals. He would take a silver bullet for his mate and children. Come to think of it, so would all the mated vampires in Scanguards' employ.

"No, it's urgent," Grayson said. Patience had never been his strong suit. He wasn't going to start with it now.

"I'll leave you two to talk," Gabriel said and made a motion to walk toward the door.

"No, stay," Grayson said. "You might as well hear this. It concerns our contract with Brandon King."

Samson and Gabriel exchanged a look.

"Please tell me you didn't piss off his daughter," Samson said on a sigh.

"I didn't piss her off. She pissed *me* off," Grayson started. "You know what she did?"

"I'm sure you'll tell us any moment now," Samson said.

"She manipulated me into taking her with me to pick up a takeout from Tomaso's. Of course, there was no parking outside, so I had to double-park and hop inside. And while I'm arguing with the hostess because she couldn't find Scarlet's order, she just ditches me and disappears. Turns out she never ordered takeout from Tomaso's. She sent me in there knowing that it would give her plenty of time to escape."

"You do know that she's not your prisoner, right?" Samson said with a hint of a smirk on his face.

"Yeah, but that doesn't mean she can just take off. She was gone for hours. I looked everywhere for her. And then she just waltzes in after midnight and tries to sneak past me. That devious little b—"

"Don't say it," Samson warned.

Gabriel glanced at Samson. "Do you wanna tell him what went wrong there, or should I?"

"I'll do it."

What the fuck where they talking about? "I know what went wrong: Scarlet is a headstrong, manipulative, spoiled—"

"Enough!" Samson said with a raised voice. "You let yourself be outmaneuvered by a twenty-four-year-old introvert and quiet PhD student? Have you learned nothing? Why didn't you track her phone to find her? Or did she switch it off?"

Shit! He hadn't even checked, too annoyed that she'd left the car and disappeared. "Uhm…"

"You didn't?" Samson shook his head. "Where was your head?"

"Not my fault!" Grayson protested. "Every single day, Scarlet pulls another stunt to piss me off."

"And clearly it worked," Gabriel said with a sideways look at Samson. "She pushed all your buttons."

Grayson ignored Gabriel's comment. "And she's neither an introvert, nor quiet! She came back reeking of sex. She doesn't want a bodyguard. When she turns twenty-five in three months, she'll fire Scanguards anyway. She told me so herself. So I say, cut her loose now. She's not worth the trouble."

Samson let out a breath. "I didn't know you were the boss here." He paused for effect. "Oh, wait, you're not. I'm still the boss. And as much as you'd like to take over so you can run Scanguards the way you want to, you've still got a lot to learn."

The reprimand stung. He wouldn't let his father dress him down, particularly not in front of Gabriel. "I—"

"I'm talking," Samson thundered. "If you had bothered reading Scarlet King's file, you would know that we can't cancel her protective detail."

"What's that supposed to mean? Since when don't we have an out clause?" Grayson growled.

"I gave her father my word," Samson replied. "Scarlet is delicate—"

Grayson huffed.

"—She's sick. Her father suspects that she suffers from the same ailment as her late mother. He worries about her, even more so after the death of his son. I promised to do everything in my power to protect his daughter so nothing bad happens to her."

Stunned, Grayson digested the news. "What does she have?"

"That's confidential. Besides, you're not on her detail anymore."

Grayson felt relief flood him. "Thanks, Dad."

"I'm not doing this for you," Samson snapped. "I'm doing it for Scarlet's sake. She needs somebody she can't easily manipulate. You're like a bull. She waves a red cloth, and you charge without thinking. We need to find somebody who can keep a cool head."

"The twins can do it. Benjamin is already the backup on her security detail," Grayson said. "Just make him the primary, and have Damian take over backup."

"Damian is moonlighting at the Mezzanine with Patrick. He's already spread too thin," Samson said with a shake of his head. "And Benjamin has already expressed that he prefers to be the backup."

"Oh, *he* gets a choice?" Grayson spat. "But when *I* complain about my assignment, *I* get dressed down?"

In the blink of an eye, Samson was on Grayson, and pinned him against the wall. "You still haven't learned when to quit. Another word out of you, and I'll assign you to babysitting duty for the next twelve months. Nod if you understand me."

Grayson swallowed hard. What everybody at Scanguards called *babysitting duty* was the most boring assignment for any bodyguard. Nobody volunteered for it. Everybody dreaded it. It meant spending his days at an exclusive daycare center to watch over the kids and teachers. Nothing ever happened there. Boredom and the constant chatter of four- and five-year-olds would drive him insane.

Grayson nodded. Finally, Samson released him.

"You may leave," Samson said.

Grayson pivoted and opened the door.

On his way out, he heard Gabriel say, "I think I know who'd be perfect for taking over Scarlet King's protection."

Grayson left, not even curious who would have to deal with her from now on. As long as it wasn't him, he didn't care.

7

Scarlet stirred. It took her a few seconds to focus her eyes so she could see the clock on her bedside table.

Twelve fifteen.

She shot up to sit. It was past noon? She never slept longer than seven o'clock, maybe eight o'clock on the weekend. She was fully aware of the reason why her body had needed the extra rest. Not only had she had cabin fever last night, she'd also had mind-blowing sex with a handsome stranger who'd made her come three times in the span of less than an hour.

Every moment of the previous night replayed in her mind. In fact, she'd dreamed about it. About him. About Ryder. But the ending had always been different. In one version, Ryder had taken her again, this time facing her, and they'd both been naked. In another, he'd lain on the floor, and she was riding him until he begged her to let him come. In none of these versions had she felt any shame about allowing him to do things that were considered taboo. Nor had he looked at her as if he thought her a slut. On the contrary, in her dreams, Ryder had looked into her eyes and professed that he was looking for somebody like her, a woman who had no inhibitions, no matter what he wanted to do.

But those were only dreams, not reality. However, this morning, in the light of day, she didn't feel as embarrassed as she had the night before. After all, Ryder had been a willing participant, eager to explore her. And he'd been a rather considerate lover. Most guys she had one-night stands with didn't care much whether she orgasmed or not. Ryder had made sure she found her pleasure before he took his own. What stranger did that?

Had it been a mistake to leave? Perhaps he had come back to the storage room after all. She would never know now. Crap, she was a hot mess! One minute she was satisfied, the next ashamed, and the next after that full of doubt about everything. And she'd thought her adolescence had been difficult. Her problems had only magnified ever since she'd become an adult. At least in her teenage years she'd found solace with her girlfriends, who'd all gone through the same issues, always doubting themselves, always worried about what others thought of them. Now she was an adult, and very soon, truly independent, yet she wasn't confident that independence would change anything for her. Inside, she was still an insecure little girl who wasn't sure where she belonged.

"Scarlet, are you home?"

Scarlet jumped up. "Claudia?"

The door opened, and her stepmother entered. As always, she was dressed to the nines. She was almost twenty years younger than her father, and at age thirty-seven she looked stunning. Her blond hair reached to her shoulders, and her gray eyes were framed by long lashes. She always wore a warm smile and spoke with a soft voice. Whenever Scarlet saw Claudia with her father, she saw how happy her father was. She herself had accepted Claudia wholeheartedly and welcomed her into their family. After having lost her own mother at a young age, it was good to have another woman to confide in, even though Claudia was hardly a conventional stepmother. In fact, they weren't that far apart in age at all. Only thirteen years separated them.

"You're still in bed? Are you all right? Did you come down with that cold that's been going around?" Claudia walked closer, a concerned look on her face now.

"No, no, I'm fine, honestly." She gave her a disarming smile. "I got to bed really late. I was working on my thesis last night, and when I looked up, it was four o'clock."

Liar.

"Scarlet, you're working too hard. There's no need to rush your thesis. You don't have to do everything in record time. You should enjoy your studies, breathe a little."

"I do," she insisted. "It's fun working on my thesis." Then she changed the subject. "You look nice. I like that outfit on you. Well, anything looks great on you." It was true. Claudia had the body of a model.

Claudia beamed. "Thank you. I bought it when your father and I went to Santa Barbara last month."

"He said last night that you'd be coming to the city today to run some errands."

Claudia winked conspiratorially. "Don't tell your dad, but I'm shopping for a birthday present for him. He thinks I'm meeting with my old law firm. Though I went to see the trust lawyers and brought a document for you to sign."

"For me?"

"Yes, it's time to get ready for the trust to be transferred so you can access it when you turn twenty-five."

"I thought that was automatic."

"Nothing is automatic," Claudia said with a chuckle. "Or the lawyers wouldn't be able to charge their exorbitant fees for anything. There are always more documents to draw up so they can justify their fees."

"Well, I guess more paperwork it is. Not that I'm looking forward to reading another stack of legal mumbo-jumbo."

"Don't worry about that. I've already started reviewing it for you to make sure it's all in order, so there won't be any delay. Consider it a birthday present from me."

"You're the best, Claudia."

"It's nothing."

"Do you miss working as a lawyer?"

She shrugged. "Yes and no."

"It can't be easy to change your life completely for a man."

"It's easy when you love that person. I'm sure, one day you'll figure that out for yourself."

Scarlet nodded. For some inexplicable reason, her mind instantly went back to Ryder. If she'd met him under different circumstances, and not during one of her episodes, when the only thing on her mind was sex, perhaps they could have gotten to know each other and perhaps had a real relationship.

"I should get dressed. Can't laze about all day. I have to go over some of my work so I'm ready for when I have to see my professor this week."

"I hope that won't take too long, will it?"

"No, just an hour or two. Why?"

"Well, my nephew is visiting this week."

"Your nephew?" Scarlet furrowed her forehead. This was the first time she'd heard about a nephew. "I didn't realize you had a nephew."

"Well," she said sighing. "He's my older sister's kid."

"You have a sister?"

"Yes. But we've been estranged for a long time. It's a long story. It was my fault as much as hers. But her son and I remained in contact all these years, and I've asked him to visit. Derek's a charming young man"—she leaned in—"and unattached. So, I hope you'll make time to show him the sights."

Scarlet walked to the closet, turning her back to Claudia to hide the dread on her face. "Yes, sure, but I don't know how much time I'll have this week."

She hated being set up. Normally, she found it easy to rebuff any unwanted male attention, but knowing that Derek was related to Claudia, and she didn't want to hurt the woman who'd been so good to her, she knew she had to go easy on the guy.

"I think you'll enjoy his company," Claudia said softly. "No pressure."

Scarlet took a pair of tight jeans out of the closet, then looked at the sweaters. "Is it cold outside today?"

"The fog already burned off," Claudia said. "It's actually quite nice weather for San Francisco."

"Well, a T-shirt it is," Scarlet said with forced cheerfulness and snatched one from the stack. Then she turned back to her stepmother and smiled. "I'd better take a shower."

Despite the fact that she'd taken one the moment she'd returned home.

"Don't take too long," Claudia said as she walked to the door. "Your new bodyguard is supposed to show up pretty soon."

Scarlet pivoted, her heart pounding. "My new bodyguard?"

"Yes, Scanguards assigned somebody else to you."

"They called you?"

She shook her head. "No, they called your dad just before he left for the airport. He asked me to meet him since he didn't have time."

Had Grayson made good on his threat to tell her father that she'd slipped out and not come back until the early hours of the morning?

"Did he say why I'm getting a new bodyguard?" Scarlet asked casually as if she didn't really care.

"Apparently there was some scheduling conflict. Some other client that Grayson has been working for needs him on short notice, so they assigned somebody else to you. Don't look so worried. They assured your father that the new guy is just as qualified and capable as your previous bodyguards."

And just as annoying.

But she didn't say that. "Oh, good."

Three more months, and she would finally be able to make decisions about how to live her life. And one thing was certain: she would no longer have a bodyguard following her like a puppy.

8

Ryder had gotten very little sleep after returning home from the nightclub, his entire body still humming from the amazing sex he'd had with Sara. He'd thought that she'd enjoyed it as much as he had, but it appeared that he'd misjudged her and taken her apparent compliance for approval when she'd probably been unable to stop him. No wonder she'd disappeared the moment she had the chance. He'd gone too far. What was he thinking engaging in anal sex with a woman who didn't know him from Adam? Fuck! How had he screwed this up so quickly so badly?

He'd gone back to the bar and the dance floor to look for her and even stopped at the ladies' room where he'd asked a girl to check if Sara was inside. She wasn't. She'd vanished into thin air. Disappointed and angry at himself, he'd walked all the way from SOMA to his home on Nob Hill. He was glad that nobody was home when he returned.

His parents were at Scanguards: Gabriel was one of the directors of the company, and Maya operated a small medical center for vampires and other preternatural creatures on a lower level of Scanguards' headquarters located in the Mission. Ethan was probably still at the club, and Ryder was grateful that he hadn't run into him there, or his perceptive younger brother would have had no trouble picking up the scent of sex on him. Ethan would have grilled him about who the girl was, and Ryder had no answers.

Where Vanessa was at this time of night, was anybody's guess. She handled a variety of things at Scanguards. Most of her time was spent doing outreach, patrolling the city streets to find at-risk youth, victims of crimes, and check up on the city's sex workers to see how Scanguards could help them. This service was part of the agreement Scanguards had struck with the Chief of Police many years earlier. In exchange for keeping the city's residents safe, the police didn't investigate crimes committed by vampires, and instead allowed Scanguards to punish vampires who'd broken the law—and if necessary send them to the vampire prison in the foothills of the Sierra Nevada.

When his parents returned shortly before sunrise, his father had informed Ryder of a new assignment.

"Grayson was pulled off the Scarlet King detail."

Ryder smirked. "So he threw in the towel. No surprise here." Everybody had been taking bets as to how long Grayson would stick it out, before he gave up. "That girl can't possibly be all that difficult."

"She's not," Gabriel agreed. "But I think their personalities clashed big time. That's where you come in."

"Let me guess: I'll be the one to calm her down, and give her some space, while still keeping a close eye on her?"

"You know the drill. I know I can rely on you. You always keep a cool head."

Normally that statement was true, but his father didn't know that he wasn't always this cool. He'd felt anything but cool when he'd been with Sara, and the result had been disastrous. He'd scared her off. Maybe it was good to get this assignment. It would help him find his inner peace again. How hard could it be to watch a young woman who kept to herself and had her head in a book all day? Piece of cake.

"Grab a couple of hours of sleep. You'll need to relieve Benjamin at one o'clock. He'll text you the address. Thanks, son, I know I can count on you."

He squeezed Ryder's shoulder, before he walked up to the third floor where the secluded suite that Ryder and his siblings considered their parents' love nest was located. It was off-limits, not because his parents had said so, but because no-one—human, witch, or vampire—wanted to walk in on their parents having sex. And their parents had a lot of sex.

Around a quarter to one in the afternoon, Ryder jumped in his car, an SUV with windows tinted with a special coating that blocked all types of UV light that could burn a vampire. He'd opted for this practical vehicle rather than the flashy sports cars Amaury's twins, Benjamin and Damian, drove because he was the one person most full-blooded vampires called when in trouble, trouble being the rising sun. He didn't mind. It was part of his job to help out where his full-blooded vampire colleagues had obvious limitations.

Benjamin was leaning against the hood of his black Porsche, when Ryder pulled up in front of the Victorian mansion belonging to Brandon King, the father of his new charge. Ryder parked behind him, and got out.

Benjamin grinned and jerked his thumb toward the house. "Looks like you pulled the short straw this time."

"And you owe me twenty bucks," Ryder retorted good-naturedly. "I told you Grayson couldn't hack it for a full month."

Benjamin pulled out his cell phone and tapped on it. "Just sent it." He grimaced. "Spoiled brat."

Ryder's phone pinged, announcing the receipt of the money. "Who? The girl? Or Grayson?"

"Grayson, of course. The girl is fine. Nice, quiet, you know, a bookworm. You might like her. You probably read the same books."

Ryder ignored the obvious dig at his pastime, which most of his fellow hybrids found boring. "Anything else I should know?"

"Stepmother arrived this morning. Hot babe."

Rider shook his head. "You serious? Since when do you go for MILFs? Aren't they a little too old for you?"

"She's barely a day over thirty-five. Claudia could be my own personal Mrs. Robinson." Benjamin waggled his eyebrows in Groucho Marx fashion.

"Claudia? You're on a first-name basis with the wife of our client?"

Benjamin grinned and leaned in. "In my mind we're on a way more intimate basis. The things I'm already—"

Ryder put his hand on Benjamin's chest. "No need to elaborate. I've seen *The Graduate*."

"Well, then you know what I'm talking about, but I've got dibs on her," Benjamin said before he jumped in his Porsche. "No poaching, bro."

"I wouldn't dream of it." He wasn't into over-sexed bored housewives.

"Almost forgot." Benjamin reached into his jacket pocket and pulled out a key. "That's your key to the house. I've got my own."

"Thanks, call you when I need to be relieved."

"Sure thing." Benjamin closed the driver's door, and sped away.

Ryder crossed the street and looked up at the impressive house. By the looks of it, this Victorian had been renovated from top to bottom, no expenses spared, while retaining all the historic details that made San Francisco's architecture so rich.

Since this was his first day of this assignment, Ryder decided to ring the doorbell instead of using his key. It was best to start off on the right foot.

Ryder heard the sound of footsteps approaching. His schooled ear recognized the click-clack of high heels. The door was opened by an elegantly dressed blond woman. This had to be the stepmother. Benjamin was right. She was stunning, and definitely not older than her mid to late thirties. But nothing stirred in Ryder. She wasn't his type. Not even close.

"Mrs. King? I'm Ryder Giles from Scanguards. I was assigned—"

"—to protect my lovely stepdaughter, yes, my husband told me. Please, do come in," she said with a warm smile. "The living room is the first door on the left."

"Thank you, Mrs. King."

"It's Claudia, please. Mrs. King makes me sound so old." She laughed. "Scarlet should be down any moment. She's got a bit of a late start today. She studied all night again. I wish she'd get that head of hers out of her books occasionally. She's so ambitious."

In the living room, Ryder glanced around, making himself familiar with the windows and any doors, without being too obvious. "Nothing wrong with a good book, Mrs.... uhm, Claudia."

"I'm glad I could arrange to meet you in person today. Transitioning to new security personnel is always hard for Scarlet. So I drove up from Palo Alto this morning."

"You and your husband don't live in the city on a permanent basis?" Ryder asked politely.

She shook her head. "Brandon—uh, my husband—prefers the peninsula. He hates the fog. But this house has been in his family for decades. We come here occasionally, but he travels a lot for his business, and whenever I can, I accompany him on his trips."

Ryder heard the creaking of the stairs before Claudia turned her head to the sound.

"Scarlet," she called out toward the hallway. "We're in the living room." Then Claudia whispered to him, "She's a little shy at first when she meets new people. Don't worry, she'll warm up to you eventually."

Ryder turned to look at the girl entering the living room. The moment their eyes met, Ryder froze.

As if paralyzed, she stood there, still a good eight feet away from him, dressed in a pair of jeans and a casual white T-shirt, wearing sneakers. Her long black hair was tied back in a low ponytail, and on her nose sat a pair of metal-rimmed glasses. She looked like an unassuming studious girl. But he knew better.

This was Scarlet's disguise. Because he'd seen the real Scarlet last night. Or should he call her Sara? Because the woman who stared at him as if he were a ghost was the same woman he'd fucked senseless at the nightclub.

9

Scarlet stood frozen in shock at seeing Ryder standing in her living room. How the hell had he found her? And what had he told Claudia? And why had he even bothered to look for her? Did he want a repeat of what had happened the previous night? But then why did he look at her with an expression of utter surprise on his handsome face?

"Come in, Scarlet," Claudia coaxed. "Meet your new bodyguard. He's replacing Grayson as of today."

Her new bodyguard? No, no, that couldn't be! How had this happened? This wasn't fair! No wonder he was looking so shocked. He hadn't been searching for her after all. He was here because he worked for Scanguards. And there was nothing she could say to him to make him leave her home immediately. Not in front of Claudia in any case. Neither Claudia nor her father could ever find out that she'd had mind-blowingly fantastic sex with Ryder.

When Scarlet didn't move, and Ryder remained just as frozen, Claudia added, "Is something wrong?"

"Not at all, Mrs. King, uhm, Claudia…" Ryder said with an innocent smile. "I'm sorry for my momentary silence. It's just, whenever I take on a new assignment, I'm somewhat anxious whether I'll measure up to my clients' expectations and vice versa. But I think all my worries were entirely unfounded."

What an actor he was! Christ, even Scarlet believed his statement even though she knew he was flat out lying.

"Your openness is so refreshing," Claudia said with a broad smile, eating up Ryder's boy-next-door charm like a cat a bowl of cream.

Ryder took a step toward Scarlet and stretched out his hand in greeting. "It's very nice to meet you, Scarlet."

She was forced to shake his hand. The warmth of his touch sent the same tingling feeling through her body that she'd felt when he'd touched her clit and made her come. Judging by the way he locked eyes with her, he probably knew what she was thinking. She felt her cheeks flush with heat, embarrassment making her tongue-tied.

"Nice to meet you too," Scarlet said, knowing if she continued her silence any longer, Claudia would suspect that something was wrong. At least Ryder had the decency to pretend that this was their first meeting. She was grateful for that.

As quickly as she could, Scarlet let go of his hand.

Claudia looked at her wristwatch. "It's getting late. I'd better get my errands done. Scarlet, why don't you show Ryder around so he knows his way around the house. I'm assuming you already have a house key, Ryder?"

"Yes, thank you. I was given Grayson's key."

"Perfect," Claudia said. "Scarlet, make sure you give Ryder a schedule of all your appointments, and don't forget that my nephew will visit in a couple of days. Keep some time available. Don't over-schedule yourself, okay?"

"Okay," Scarlet said.

Claudia's cell phone chimed and she looked at the message. "I have to run."

"When will you be back?" Scarlet asked.

"Oh, I won't be staying the night. I'll drive back to Palo Alto after I'm done with my last appointment. The contractor who's designing my new walk-in is coming bright and early tomorrow morning, and I don't wanna be caught in morning rush-hour traffic."

"Oh." She didn't know whether to welcome the fact that Claudia wasn't staying. It meant that she wouldn't interrupt the talk she needed to have with Ryder just as soon as she left the house. But it also meant Claudia wouldn't be here to stop her from doing something stupid.

"Again, nice meeting you, Ryder. Bye, Scarlet," Claudia said before she hurried out of the living room and left the house.

Scarlet listened for the garage door to open, the sound of the car's engine reverberating from the garage below the house a moment later, and for the car to exit. It appeared Ryder was doing the same, because he too remained silent until it was certain that Claudia had left.

"So your name isn't Sara but Scarlet," Ryder finally said. She detected no malice in his voice. "Scarlet suits you better."

She tipped her chin up. "Did you know last night that you would become my bodyguard?"

"Trust me, had I known, I would have never touched you. I don't need that kind of trouble in my life."

That annoyed her. He called her trouble? How dare he? After what had happened last night, he insulted her? "Clearly, last night was a mistake." She pressed the words out with as much conviction as she could muster.

"I see."

Well, it sounded like it pissed him off that she'd said it first. "Well, then we're in agreement. You'll tell your boss that you can't be my bodyguard because you've taken an instant dislike to me, and the feeling is mutual and—"

"That would be a lie," he interrupted.

"Which part?"

"Everything. I haven't taken a dislike to you."

"Of course you have. You just said so yourself."

"I said nothing of the kind."

There was nothing wrong with her short-term memory. "You said, and I quote: had I known, I would have never touched you. I don't need that kind of trouble in my life."

"And from that you conclude that I dislike you?" Ryder shook his head.

"It's pretty evident from where I stand." She crossed her arms over her chest.

"How about your claim that the dislike is mutual? It's pretty evident to me that that's not the case."

It was clear that he was talking about their sexual encounter.

"Are you saying I'm lying?"

"If I remember correctly, last night you liked me just fine. Or do you fuck any guy, whether you like him or not?"

Scarlet glared at him. "That's none of your business."

"Fine. Don't tell me. I don't care. For all intents and purposes, last night never happened."

His voice had an edge to it that sounded like retaliation for hurting his pride. Well, she could play the same game.

"Fine. Let's pretend it never happened. It's better that way." Though it didn't mean that she could forget about it. Her mind kept going back to the way Ryder had made her feel. What if no other man could ever make her feel that way again? "If you ever tell anybody what happened, I will go to your boss, and I will have you fired."

"Well, then we're in agreement," he said icily. "You'll see as little as possible of me. All I need is your schedule of all your appointments that require you to leave this house. While you're home, I'll stay out of your way. Just pretend I'm not here."

As if that was possible!

Ryder's words were matter-of-fact. It further proved to Scarlet that the previous night had meant nothing to him. But she couldn't pretend that his presence didn't affect her. Even now, her body betrayed her. She felt her nipples transform into hard peaks and her pussy turn wet at the mere memory of the things Ryder had done, the way he'd touched her, how he'd made her feel. How hard he'd come inside her. She'd felt his cock spasming inside her, had enjoyed how his hot semen had filled her.

Her memories screeched to a halt. It had never even occurred to her until now, but all of a sudden, she remembered it very clearly. Ryder hadn't used a condom. And she'd been so delirious with lust that she hadn't insisted on it. That was the first time it had ever happened to her. She'd always been so careful.

Fuck! How could she have been so stupid? Not only had she slept with a stranger who turned out to be her new bodyguard, she'd put herself at risk for an STD, and even worse, a pregnancy.

"I need to go to a pharmacy." She prayed that it wasn't too late for the morning-after pill.

"Are you feeling sick?" he asked. "What do you need?"

"Not that you care, but I need the morning-after pill. And probably some antibiotics. She turned to the door. "Let's go. Now."

Ryder snatched her arm and made her turn back to him. "You won't need any of that."

She ripped her arm free and glared at him. "I wouldn't if you had worn a condom, damn it!"

"You won't get pregnant," he said.

"What are you, a doctor now?"

"No, but I'm sterile. You won't need the morning-after pill."

"Oh." That surprised her—if he spoke the truth. "Are you making this up?"

He simply shook his head. "I was born sterile. As for antibiotics, I assume you're worried about STDs?"

She looked at him, trying to read his expression, but she couldn't.

"I don't have any STDs. We get tested regularly at Scanguards. I'm clean. And I don't sleep around."

She raised a doubting eyebrow.

"Last night was an exception," he claimed. "Doesn't matter if you believe it or not. I guess the evidence speaks against me on that." He paused. "But I would never lie to anybody where their health or safety is concerned. I took an oath when I became a bodyguard. I've never broken it, and I'm not gonna start now."

Scarlet surprised herself when she realized that she believed him, even though she had no reason to know whether he spoke the truth. But she saw something in his eyes, something that made her hear the truth in his words.

10

Ryder arrived at home shortly after sundown. He'd spent the entire afternoon in Scarlet's home. Scarlet had studied in her room, working on her computer, while Ryder had tried to read in the living room, staying out of her way. But despite the suspenseful thriller he was reading, he couldn't concentrate on it, and kept re-reading the same few pages.

He was fuming that Scarlet had dismissed their sexual encounter so easily. She'd called their perfect coupling a mistake. It had enraged him so much that he'd let himself be baited into saying that it was best to pretend it never happened. As if he could forget what had passed between them. For the first time in his life he'd felt true passion, true desire.

Knowing he needed to clear his head, he called Benjamin and asked him to stand guard while Ryder drove home. In his parents' three-story mansion, he heard the sound of showers running, the opening and closing of closet doors, and the sound of hairdryers. Everybody was home.

Ryder entered his room and headed for the shower. Given that his parents and siblings were in the midst of getting ready for the evening, the water would be cold, or tepid at best, but he didn't mind. Maybe a cold shower was just what he needed.

Ryder started undressing. He took his shoes and socks off, then unbuttoned his shirt and draped it over a rail. He glanced in the mirror and noticed that his pants looked tighter than usual. Had they shrunk in the last wash? He popped the button open and lowered the zipper, then freed himself of them. When he hooked his thumbs into the waistband of his boxer briefs, he felt something different from this morning. He pushed his underwear down, and stared at himself in shock.

His heart skipped a beat, then another one. His eyes went wide. No, that couldn't be. It was impossible.

He stared at the evidence of his metamorphosis in the mirror. It had happened. The deformity above his cock had grown into a perfect second cock, one that was only marginally smaller than his original one.

The realization of what this meant hit him like a freight train. Scarlet had triggered his transformation. It was irrefutable evidence that she was his mate. There was no doubt about it. A storm of emotions hit him all at once. What the hell would he do now? Already, their relationship was complicated by the fact that he was now her bodyguard. A bodyguard she barely tolerated and avoided as much as she could. How was he going to fight against that kind of insurmountable obstacle? And even if she'd felt the same attraction and connection he'd felt the night before, he still had two more obstacles to overcome: tell her that he was part satyr and had two cocks, and that he was a vampire who wanted to drink her blood.

"Hey, Ryder, can you—"

Ryder spun around to see his brother appear in the open bathroom door. He reached for a towel to cover his groin, but it was too late.

"Oh my God!" Ethan blurted.

"Don't you ever knock? Get the fuck out!" Ryder yelled.

But Ethan didn't leave. "You've got your second cock! I can't believe it."

"Get out!"

"Nessie, Mom, Dad! You've gotta see this," Ethan called out over his shoulder. "Ryder's got his second cock!"

Furious, Ryder snatched his brother by the throat and pinned him against the wall. His hands were already turning into claws, and his fangs were descending.

"If you ever enter my room again without knocking, I'm gonna throttle you," Ryder ground out between clenched teeth. "Now get the fuck out, or I'll toss you out the window."

"Ryder?"

At the sound of his sister's voice, Ryder whirled his head toward her. Her gaze was directed at his groin, her mouth open. Only now Ryder realized that he'd dropped the towel when he'd attacked Ethan. In vampire speed, he released his brother, snatched another towel from the rack, and wrapped it around his midsection.

"Nessie, get the fuck out!"

"But I wanna see it close up," she insisted. "I barely got a glimpse."

While Ethan retreated into the bedroom rubbing his neck, he didn't leave, neither did Vanessa.

"And that's a glimpse too much. Some privacy, now, both of you!"

Ryder stepped through the bathroom door into his bedroom. From the hallway, he already heard hurried steps. That's just what he needed: his parents. They entered his bedroom and stared at him. His mother was still in her bathrobe, his father wearing only a pair of pants, his chest bare.

"Can nobody in this house respect my privacy?" Ryder grumbled.

Vanessa smirked. "You can't expect us to just ignore that you got your second cock. It's a big deal."

Ethan elbowed his sister in the ribs. "Yeah, pretty big from what I saw."

"Ethan, Nessie, enough!" Gabriel commanded. "Leave, now!"

Reluctantly Ethan and Vanessa left the room.

"And close the damn door!" Gabriel added.

When his siblings finally shut the door, his mother approached him. "I'm so happy for you, Ryder." She practically beamed as if he'd won a trophy. "Now let me see it."

"Mom!" Ryder reared back from her. "I'm not gonna let you see it."

"I'm a doctor. It's nothing I haven't seen before." She cast a sideways look at Gabriel. "As you well know."

"You're my mother, and I'm not five years old anymore." He gripped the towel at the spot where he'd fastened it, making sure that it wouldn't slip in his mother's presence.

"I just want to make sure it all looks good," Maya insisted.

"Trust me, it looks like it's supposed to look. So would you please stop embarrassing me, Mom?"

"There's nothing to be embarrassed about, son," Gabriel said with a proud smile.

Then he looked at Maya and added, "Why don't you give us a moment, baby?"

"Of course," Maya said, then smiled at Ryder. "I'm so happy for you."

She left the room and closed the door behind her.

Gabriel let out a long breath. "The day is finally here." Then he grinned. "And don't worry, son, I don't need to take a look. I know that it's an unusual feeling at the beginning."

"Thanks, Dad." At least one person understood what was going on inside him.

"I always thought Ethan would be the first to find his mate." Gabriel smirked. "Given his quest to sleep with every available woman in this city, be it human, witch, or vampire. But you? I didn't realize you were seeing anybody."

For a moment, Ryder remained silent. "I'm not."

Surprise registered on his father's face. "But then how… I mean, we both know the only way for your second cock to form, is if you have sex with your intended mate."

Ryder nodded. He was aware that it could take as little as two hours and as long as twenty-four for the transformation to be complete, for the deformity to turn into a second cock. "I had sex. Last night."

"But you're not dating her? I'm not judging, you know, but…"

Ryder knew that he had to give his father an explanation, but he couldn't tell him the truth.

"I went to the Mezzanine last night. I met her there, and we hit it off…" He shrugged. "I don't know who she is. I've never seen her before."

Gabriel ran a hand through his long hair, which was loose. Whenever he left the house, however, he tied it back in a ponytail. "Well, don't worry. We can work with that. We'll find her. There are security cameras at all entrances and exits. I'll get Damian on it to send us the security tapes from last night, and we'll go through them to find her."

Ryder was afraid his father would say something like that. But he had to stop him, or he'd find out that he'd lied about not knowing who the woman was. He hated lying to his father. They'd always had a close relationship, and trusted each other, but for now, he had to hide that he knew who his mate was, and that she wanted nothing to do with him.

"What if she doesn't want to be found?" Ryder asked. "What if she doesn't like me?"

Gabriel threw his head back and laughed.

"How's that funny, Dad?"

"Ryder, you slept with her the first time you met her. I'd say it's pretty evident that she likes you."

"She could have been drunk."

"She wasn't. And you know how I know that?"

"Enlighten me," Ryder said.

"Because, you, my son, are an honorable man. You would never take advantage of a woman when she's in no state to make an informed decision."

"But—"

"I know you too well," Gabriel interrupted. "If you thought a woman was in danger of being taken advantage of because she was inebriated, you would drive her home personally and make sure she's all right."

Ryder sighed. What if his father was wrong? What if he had taken advantage of Scarlet last night? Doubts kept invading his thoughts. Had he misinterpreted her actions?

"Let's find her," Gabriel said. "I'll call Damian."

"Don't, Dad. I want to do this myself. She's my mate, my responsibility. I won't need your help."

Gabriel nodded. "I know that, son, but if you're hitting a dead end, you only have to say the word, and I'll help you."

"I have a question," Ryder started, though he wasn't quite sure how to approach this.

"Sure, what about?"

Ryder hesitated. "What if we're not compatible?"

"What do you mean?"

"Well, what if she doesn't feel the same for me as I feel for her? What if my mate rejects me for whatever reason? Does that mean I'll never find another one to share my life with?"

Gabriel put his hand on Ryder's shoulder. "Don't trouble yourself with thoughts like that."

"Please answer the question, Dad. Will I be alone if it doesn't work out with her?"

Gabriel sighed. "No, you won't. You can always find somebody else who will love you, and whom you'll love back, because in the end, even mates meant for one another have free will. But before you give up, know this: only a union with your intended mate will truly fulfill you. If you take another woman as your wife, you'll always feel that something is missing from your life."

Slowly Ryder nodded. "Thank you, Dad. Thanks for being honest."

He had to make this work with Scarlet, which meant he had to spend more time with her to figure out what he had to do for her to accept him.

"Anytime, son."

"I should get showered and dressed. It's been a trying day. My new charge is difficult."

Gabriel furrowed his forehead. "Don't tell me Grayson was right about her. That would be a first."

"Occasionally he's on the money, though I don't agree with him on everything. Scarlet is headstrong and cunning. But don't worry, I'll watch her like a hawk. That's what her father pays us for."

Ryder hated deceiving his father, but right now he had no choice. Knowing how many rules his own father had broken to woo his mate, Ryder was confident that he would understand his actions when the truth came out—which it ultimately would. But the *when* was up in the air.

"I know you can do it. Scanguards can count on you always giving your best."

He hoped that Scarlet would see it the same way. Over time, he'd wear down her resistance. He just needed to keep a cool head, and use his charm to make Scarlet see that they were good together, and that their night together hadn't been a mistake but the beginning of something special.

11

Tired from working on her thesis all afternoon and evening, Scarlet shut down her computer. She'd taken only a short dinner break—Thai food delivered by a restaurant only three blocks away. Just after finishing her dinner in the kitchen, while Ryder had remained in the living room reading, she'd overheard him talking to Benjamin on the phone, asking him to relieve him for the night.

From her bedroom on the second floor, she'd watched him leave a minute after Benjamin parked his black Porsche on the other side of the street. She'd seen them exchange a few words, and Scarlet wondered what kind of gossip the two had shared. She shuddered at the thought that Ryder had told Benjamin—and maybe some of his other friends and colleagues too—that he'd fucked her in a storage room the previous night.

She'd done everything to distract herself from the memories of her sexual encounter with Ryder, but even going over her paper for the umpteenth time hadn't stopped the images from invading her thoughts. She felt heat build up inside her and knew she had to do something to avert the feverish episode she felt coming on.

She took a shower, careful not to get her hair wet, and the cold water helped cool her down. After drying off, she slipped into her bathrobe, and brushed her teeth. It was time for bed. Tomorrow, she had an important meeting with her professor regarding the progress she was making toward her doctorate in psychology. She felt confident that she was on track. At least one thing in her life seemed to go her way.

Scarlet switched on her bedside lamp and pulled back the duvet cover. Beneath it, she kept her pajamas, a pink ensemble of a pair of loose-fitting shorts and a light, sleeveless top. But before she could put it on, she heard a sound from downstairs.

Scarlet stilled, listening intently. Had Benjamin entered the house to use the bathroom? Scarlet walked to the window that overlooked the street, pulled the curtains apart a little and looked outside.

Benjamin's black Porsche was gone. She knew he wouldn't leave unless somebody else was taking over for him. She looked for her cell phone. It should be on her nightstand, but it wasn't there. Damn it, where had she left it? She quickly walked into her ensuite bathroom and flipped on the light. But it wasn't there either. Then she remembered. The battery had been low, and she'd plugged it into an outlet in the kitchen while she'd eaten her dinner. She had forgotten to bring it with her when she'd returned to her room to continue working.

Her heartbeat accelerated. After her half-brother, Joshua, had died in a shooting at a nightclub several years earlier when he'd been only twenty-four, her father had become overprotective of her. The man suspected of killing her brother and wounding several other nightclub patrons, had been found dead the next day. Her father still suspected that the murderer was a contract killer, and that one of his enemies was behind it. But no proof of that theory was ever found.

What if her father was right after all? What if somebody was trying to kill her too? Perhaps somebody had killed her bodyguard and driven the body away in his Porsche, then returned to the house to finish her off? She had to do something. But what? The smartest thing was to call 9-1-1. Yes, that's what she had to do. But the only phones in the house were on the first floor: a landline nobody ever used was located in the living room, and her own cell phone was in the kitchen. Neither would be easy to get to.

Another sound from downstairs made her heart jump into her throat. Shit! She'd watched enough horror movies to know how this could end. If only she had something to defend herself with. Maybe something to knock the intruder over the head with.

Scarlet glanced around her room, but there was nothing suitable. She wasn't going to use her laptop, no, that was out of the question. Plus it was too bulky anyway. She needed something she could hold in one hand.

Frantically, she let her gaze roam, when her eyes fell on the open bathroom door. She rushed toward it, glad that she was barefoot, and the lush rug underneath her feet swallowed the sound of her footfalls.

In the bathroom, she opened the cabinet below the sink and pulled out her hairdryer. It would have to do. She put her hand around the thick shaft and turned off the lights again. She did the same in her bedroom, not wanting any light to warn the intruder that she was on to him. With light feet she walked to the door and turned the knob very gently. She eased the door open, when she heard a floorboard creak farther down the hall.

Scarlet held her breath. It appeared that the intruder was already on the second floor. But if she was quick and quiet, she could make it to the stairs without him noticing her. And once arrived at the bottom of the stairs, she could run out onto the street and flag down a car before he could catch up with her. If he caught her in the house, she would try to hit him over the head with the hairdryer or throttle him with the electric cord if need be.

Scarlet collected all her courage and slipped out of her room. The second-floor hallway was dark. She stalked along the wall in the direction of the stairs. She spotted a faint light coming from downstairs as if the intruder had switched on the light in the downstairs foyer. Or had Ryder left it on when he'd left earlier in the evening?

At the other end of the hallway, where the master bedroom and two more bedrooms were located, she heard the sound of a door, but she couldn't tell whether it was being opened or closed. She knew it then: the intruder was looking for her, checking all the rooms until he found hers. Her window of escaping was narrowing. But she only needed to bridge a distance of a few more feet until she would reach the top of the stairs.

As quickly as she could, Scarlet made two steps forward then three more to her right, bringing her to the top of the stairs, when the electric cord from the hairdryer unfurled and hit the banister. The sound reverberated in the empty hallway, and her heart stopped. Before she could set a foot on the first step, somebody rushed toward her, grabbed her from behind and jerked her back with such force, that all air rushed from her lungs. The assailant's grip was like an iron vice around her midsection. She gasped for air to scream, but didn't even get that far.

"What the—?" He loosened the grip around her waist somewhat. "Scarlet?"

Stunned at recognizing Ryder's voice, she kicked her foot back to hit him in the shin. Her arms were imprisoned by him, preventing her from using the hairdryer.

"Ouch!" he let out before he set her back down on her feet and turned her to face him. "What are you kicking me for?"

"What the fuck are you doing up here?" she yelled.

A moment later, the lights came on. Ryder had flipped the switch.

She glared at him. "You scared the living daylights out of me." She lifted her hand with the hairdryer, which was still shaking from the fright he'd caused her.

"You thought I was a burglar?" He shook his head. "Nobody gets in here without either me or Benjamin knowing about it."

"Well, Benjamin is gone. And you left earlier. How the fuck was I to know that you would come back?"

"I texted you! But no, you ignored me like a spoilt little brat! When I said that you can pretend that I'm not even here, I didn't mean that to include that you can ignore messages pertaining to your safety!"

"My phone was in the damn kitchen, charging!" she yelled back. "And don't take that tone with me."

"What tone?"

"That self-righteous I'm-the-boss-and-you-listen-to-me-tone! You're not even supposed to be on this floor! Only the bedrooms are up here. And there's no way I'm letting you come into mine. So you might as well get your ass downstairs." She clenched her jaw, furious.

"You think I was trying to sneak into your bedroom?" Ryder huffed. "Trust me, I don't need to force myself on a woman who doesn't want my attention." He pointed his hand toward the other end of the corridor. "I was heading for the guest room."

"To do what?"

"To sleep."

Her mouth gaped open. For a long second, she was speechless. But then she found her voice again. "You can't sleep here. I can't allow that. My father would never condone it."

"I've already cleared it with him."

She hadn't expected that. But there was no way she would admit it. "He would never!"

"Yeah, and why wouldn't he?" Ryder moved closer, bringing them almost nose to nose. "Is it because he knows that his precious daughter can't keep her hands off strangers?" He looked down at her for a moment. "And do you have to run around the house half naked?"

Only now she realized that the belt of her robe had loosened and the garment had fallen open in the front, revealing that she wasn't wearing anything underneath. At the same time she noticed that Ryder's breathing had changed, and that her own heart was racing.

"Christ, Scarlet, please, cover up, or…"

Before he could turn away, she dropped the hairdryer to the floor and grabbed Ryder by his shirt, pulling him even closer. "Or what?"

"Or this," he rasped.

His hungry lips were on hers an instant later, and she welcomed his kiss like a person lost in the desert welcomed a glass of water.

12

Ryder was losing his mind. One minute they'd argued like cats and dogs, the next Scarlet had pulled him to her in an unmistakable way, and he'd been unable to keep his animal lust leashed. He should have turned the other way the moment he'd noticed that she wore nothing underneath her gaping robe. But he hadn't listened to his rational side. No, once again, the satyr and vampire in him had taken over. Scarlet had provoked him, and he'd swallowed the bait hook, line, and sinker.

The moment Scarlet parted her lips to invite him to explore her, Ryder realized that all resistance was futile. All rational thought went out the window, and he was reduced to his animal urges. He'd always believed himself to be more in control than some of his fellow vampires, but clearly, he was only fooling himself. He was no different from Benjamin, or Grayson, or his own brother. He just hid his desires better. Even from himself.

He intensified the kiss. Scarlet's hands were on his chest, touching him through his shirt, while Ryder slid his hand underneath her robe and touched her naked skin. The previous night, she hadn't been naked, but now he reveled in the softness and warmth of her skin. With his hands, he explored her, mapped every curve and every valley, while he pressed her against the wall behind her, imprisoning her with his lips on hers. She moaned into his mouth and pressed her breasts into his hands, demanding a firmer touch. He complied with her unspoken request and kneaded the supple flesh until her nipples turned into stiff peaks.

Her breathing was ragged, their kiss only interrupted by their moans and muttered exclamations of words professing the pleasure they were giving each other. Scarlet's hands were on his naked chest now. He had no idea how and when she'd managed to strip him of his shirt, too engrossed in exploring her body, finding out what he'd missed the night before. He slid one hand down to her pussy, through the thatch of hair at the apex of her thighs.

She greeted him with a loud moan, her sex warm and wet. He stroked his finger along her cleft, and felt her gasp at the touch, her fingernails digging into his shoulders now, holding on to him as if holding on to a life raft. He could feel her heart race, her blood rushing through her veins, her arousal spiking, her blood calling to him. The vampire in him was tempted, the taste of her blood within easy reach. But Ryder pushed him back. Instead, he thrust his finger into her, rubbed his thumb over her clit, and made her ride his hand. She didn't protest and moved her hips, undulating her pelvis to create more friction on every descent and every withdrawal.

He'd never thought himself to be a selfless lover, but he couldn't get enough of watching her as he pleasured her. She was without inhibitions, had no self-control, no restraints. All she demanded was pleasure, and he was happy to oblige her for as long as he could. Feeling her chest press against his now, her breasts molded to his muscles, he knew she was close to her climax.

"Ryder, please…" she begged.

He strummed her clit faster and with more pressure, his middle finger plunging deep and hard. She was so wet he felt her juices dripping on his hand and his pants.

"Please, fuck me. Your cock, I need your cock."

Scarlet suddenly put her hands on the waistband of his pants and opened the button. Her hands were on his zipper, before he could take a breath. Another second, and his two cocks would burst from their prison. He grabbed one of her hands to try to stop her, but she continued working his zipper. He had no choice, but to pull his finger from the tight sheath and use both his hands to stop her from undressing him.

"No!" he said harshly and imprisoned her hands.

She stared at him, confused. "I need you to fuck me."

"But I *am* fucking you." He took both her hands into one and brought his right hand back to her pussy.

She protested. "I want your cock, Ryder, now!"

"I can't, please, Scarlet, I can't."

"Don't you want me?"

He wanted her more than anything, but he wasn't ready to show her his two cocks. She would look at him and think him a freak. No, she had to get to know him and like him first before he could spring this on her. Before he could reveal his secrets.

"I do, I want you. But I can't."

Her facial expression suddenly changed to one of anger. "Why are you doing this to me? Do you enjoy torturing me? Do you?"

Ryder saw the unshed tears that now rimmed her eyes, and felt his heart clench with pain.

"No, I have no intention of torturing you. I would never hurt you," he professed.

Scarlet pushed him away from her so unexpectedly that he lost his balance for a second. As he caught himself, she pulled her bathrobe around her and tightened the belt.

With a clenched jaw she glared at him. "I don't know what kind of sick game you're playing, but I'm done playing it. Go and find somebody who's as cruel as you. I wish I'd never met you!"

She spun around and rushed back to her bedroom. When she jerked the door open, Ryder heard a stifled sob rip from her throat, before she slammed the door so hard that the entire house seemed to shake.

Ryder let out a shaky breath and ran a trembling hand through his hair. Fuck! This couldn't have gone any worse if he'd tried. He should have never even kissed her tonight, but stuck to his plan to win her over with small gestures of kindness. Instead, he'd behaved like a caveman, destroying everything in his wake. Maybe he didn't deserve a mate when he clearly had no idea how to treat the woman he wanted to spend the rest of his immortal life with.

That thought shook him to his core. He wanted Scarlet. He didn't know how and when it had happened, but he remembered what his father had told him when Gabriel had first laid eyes on his mate.

"I looked at her, and knew that there would never be another woman for me, whether she would have me or not," Gabriel had said, a moist sheen covering his eyes. "I had a snowball's chance in hell. I saw myself as a monster, but your mother saw past all that. Because we were meant for each other."

If his father had succeeded so could Ryder. He couldn't allow himself to give up so quickly. He had to win Scarlet's love, no matter how hopeless the situation looked right now.

13

Ryder hadn't slept well. In fact, he'd been up half the night trying to formulate a plan of how to win Scarlet over after the disastrous event from earlier. But that wasn't the only reason he hadn't been able to sleep. Both his cocks had been rock-hard for hours after he'd nearly fucked Scarlet in the hallway. When he realized that they wouldn't return to their relaxed state on their own, he'd given in to his needs, and masturbated to visions of Scarlet playing in his mind. He'd climaxed with both his cocks simultaneously, and the experience had blown his mind, and further cemented his determination to make Scarlet his.

Before dawn, he called Wesley, Scanguards' resident witch.

Wesley picked up after several rings, sounding sleepy. "This had better be important."

Through the line, Ryder heard a soft female voice ask, "Who is it, babe?" Ryder recognized Virginia's voice.

"Ryder," Wesley said.

"Hey, Wes, sorry to disturb you so early, but I'm in a bind. I messed up. I need to smooth things over with a girl."

Wes chuckled. "You've gotta be kidding me. Mr. Cool-as-a-cucumber screwed up? What happened? Did you bite a girl without her permission?"

"Of course not!" Ryder ground out. He wasn't a cad. "But she's mad at me, and I want her to like me again."

"The answer is no," Wes said firmly.

"You don't even know what I want your help with," Ryder said, stunned at Wesley's instant refusal.

"I'm not making you a love potion. It's unethical. Bye, Ryder."

"Don't hang up!" Ryder said quickly. "I'm not asking for a love potion."

"What do you want then?"

"Your recipe for your famous coconut pancakes."

"Why didn't you say so immediately?"

"You didn't let me get a word in edgewise."

"Fair enough. So you're trying to win her back the old-fashioned way? Good, 'cause a love potion isn't permanent. I take it you really like her then?" Wes fished.

Ryder ignored his questions. If he told Wes anything, all of Scanguards would know it minutes later. "So you'll send it to me?"

"Texting it to you in a moment."

"Thanks."

"And Ryder?"

"Yes?"

"Good luck!"

"Thanks, bro."

A few seconds later, the text message with Wesley's recipe arrived, and Ryder got to work on preparing what he needed.

By the time Scarlet came down the stairs, dressed in jeans and a dark sweater that reached down to the middle of her thighs, obscuring her delectable figure, the whole house smelled of coffee and pancakes. She looked a little pale this morning, her hair tied back in a ponytail again, her facial expression distant and reserved. She barely looked at him.

"Morning," he said, deciding that saying *good* morning would only invite a snide remark. He wasn't going to give Scarlet a reason to start an argument. "I don't know whether you like pancakes, but I made plenty."

"Hmm."

Well, at least she wasn't completely silent. A *hmm* hardly qualified as a word, though apparently in Scrabble it counted.

Ryder turned back to the oven and pulled out the casserole where he'd kept the pancakes warm. He placed the dish on the table he'd set for one person only. He wasn't planning on joining her for breakfast, not because he wasn't hungry, but because he knew she didn't want his company.

"I'll be in the living room," he said, and left the kitchen.

He heard Scarlet pull the chair out from under the table to sit down. At least, she wasn't rejecting his peace offering outright. It was a start.

In the living room, Ryder settled in an armchair and stared out the window. He'd have to learn to be patient. Rome wasn't won in a day either. Neither would Scarlet.

His cell phone rang. He looked at the number and picked it up. "Hey, Damian, what's up?"

Damian chuckled. "Heard you were at the Mezzanine two nights ago. Quite something that happened there…"

Ryder sat up, rigid like a lamppost. Had somebody seen him and Scarlet together and told Damian? Fuck, this wasn't good.

"Just as well that we got those new cameras. It's all on tape. I'm not gonna let that happen again."

Fuck! Ryder's heart pounded. Damian had recorded him and Scarlet during sex? Christ! What else could go wrong? This was a disaster. Once in his life he did something crazy, and everybody would find out about it? Why was this happening?

"Uhm…" He searched for words but had none.

"I've decided to post the recording online."

Ryder jumped up. "Damian, please don't do that. I'm in enough hot water already."

"Huh?"

"Please, she doesn't deserve that. It was my fault. Don't release the sex tape. She'll never forgive me if you do. I'll do anything to make this go away," Ryder pleaded.

"Sex tape?" Damian shot back. There was a short pause, then he said, "OH MY GOD! You had sex in my club!"

Raucous laughter nearly pierced Ryder's eardrum.

"You dog!" It wasn't an admonishment, rather a compliment. Figured! Damian was just as over-sexed as his twin. And the nightclub he ran with Patrick, Samson's youngest son, provided the perfect outlet for him.

"Fuck," Ryder let out, realizing his mistake. "We're not talking about a sex tape…"

"We are now!" Damian said, chuckling. "Cause a guy getting his dick stuck in a beer keg isn't half as interesting as you having sex in my club. I've gotta tell Patrick!"

"You can't tell anybody, do you hear me?"

"Oh, come on. Finally you do something reckless, and the rest of us can't even hear about it? So where did you fuck her? In the restrooms?"

"I'm not gonna answer that question."

"Not in the restrooms then. You're right, that's kinda gross. Maybe in one of the corners with the comfy seating areas? I told Patrick that we should have gone with leather. Easier to wipe off, you know. I've gotta talk to him about that."

"Please…" Ryder let out a breath and ran a hand through his hair. "I can't talk about it."

"Don't be so sensitive. We've all had one-nighters in the oddest places. Some chicks are just so horny and drunk they can barely wait for you to pull your dick out. No harm in that."

"It wasn't like that!" Ryder growled. "Don't talk about her like that. She wasn't drunk." He was pretty sure about that. Scarlet had known exactly what she was doing. And so had he.

Damian let out a gasp. "Are you saying you're in a relationship? You're dating? Since when?"

Ryder hesitated.

"Come on, bro. If this is serious, then of course I won't blab to anybody about it. You should know that. I've watched plenty of vampires turn all protective and possessive when they find the one to know not to joke about something like that. So, is that it? Is she the one?"

Ryder knew exactly what Damian meant by his question. "Yes."

"Good for you. So when can we all meet her?"

"When I'm back in her good graces." Which right now didn't look so good.

"Hey, I feel you. If there's anything I can—"

"There isn't. But thanks. Talk later."

"Chin up!"

Ryder disconnected the call and listened for sounds from the kitchen. Scarlet was still in there, and judging by the sound of cutlery scraping against porcelain she was enjoying more of the pancakes.

His cell phone rang again. This time it was his sister.

"Nessie?"

"Hey, are you busy right now?"

"Kinda. I have to drive my charge to an appointment at the university in a short while. Why?"

"Thank God you have time. I need to talk to you. It's important."

He listened carefully. Her voice sounded different this morning.

"Is something wrong, sweetie?"

"Well, nothing's wrong per se, but…" She hesitated.

"Come on, you know you can tell me anything."

"You're always so nice, even when I piss you off."

"Piss me off about what?"

"When I charged into your room yesterday and wanted to see your two cocks."

"Oh that."

"I'm really sorry about that."

He sighed. If he was honest with himself, he had to admit that he wasn't mad at her. He'd simply been stunned and shocked when Ethan and Vanessa had barged in. "And I'm sorry that I screamed at you, sweetie. I shouldn't have. I should have more self-control. It's just, there's a lot going on with me right now."

"I get it. That's why I wanted to talk to you. I really can't talk to anybody else about it. My girlfriends wouldn't understand. They're vampires, not part satyr. And I can't talk to Mom about it. It would be too embarrassing."

"Why?"

"It's about sex."

"Oh." He wasn't sure he wanted to have this kind of conversation with his little sister. "I'm not sure I—"

"Please, Ryder, I need to know."

"Okay?"

"We both know what a satyr's second cock is for," she started. "I like regular sex just fine, you know, but what… you know, what if I don't like *that*?"

"Nessie, are you afraid of having anal sex? It's nothing to be scared of."

"Easy for you to say. You're a man. What if it hurts?"

"It won't hurt. I promise you that. It's pleasurable, for both the man and the woman."

He knew it instinctively judging by the way Scarlet had reacted when he'd fucked her with his finger in her anus. And he knew with certainty that he would enjoy her tight muscles clamping around his cock. He couldn't wait for that to happen.

Ryder cleared his throat, trying to push the thoughts from his mind, or he'd have another pair of raging hard-ons. "You'll see." He heard the creaking of the floorboards outside the living room. "Nessie, I've gotta go. Talk about it more later?"

"Thanks, Ryder. And please, don't mention this to Mom or Dad, okay?"

"Okay." He disconnected the call and turned around.

Scarlet stood in the open door and stared at him, her jaw clenched tightly. "I need to be at my professor's office in twenty minutes."

The tone of her voice was icy with a side of hailstorm. It appeared that the pancake breakfast hadn't done anything to lift her mood.

14

If she hadn't had an appointment with her professor, Scarlet would have gone back to her room and cried her eyes out. But she had to pull herself together. She couldn't give Ryder the satisfaction of knowing that he'd hurt her. No wonder he hadn't wanted to sleep with her last night. He had a girlfriend! *Nessie.* He'd probably come straight from her bed, and knew he couldn't perform again so soon. And from what she'd picked up from their lovey-dovey conversation, Ryder was talking her into having anal sex with him.

Scarlet had no idea how she made it through her conference with the head of the psychology department, during which Ryder had waited outside the office. Because of the additional pointers her professor had given her, Scarlet had to spend several hours in the university library to do research. By the time they left, it was past five o'clock in the evening. During the drive back to the house, Ryder attempted to make conversation, but she ignored him.

The moment he parked the car outside her home, Scarlet jumped out and crossed the street. At the entrance door he caught up with her. She pulled out her house key, but he was faster. However, the door opened inward before Ryder could put the key in the lock.

Claudia greeted them and ushered them inside. "There you are, Scarlet. Hi, Ryder."

"Mrs. King," Ryder said, while Scarlet greeted her stepmother with a quick "You're here."

Claudia put her hand on Scarlet's arm. "My nephew arrived on an earlier flight. Come and let me introduce you."

Even though Scarlet wasn't in the mood to make polite conversation with a stranger, she allowed Claudia to lead her into the living room, where a young man rose from the couch and turned toward them.

"This is Derek, my nephew," Claudia beamed. "Derek, this is my dear stepdaughter Scarlet."

Derek, who looked like he was about five to eight years older than Scarlet, approached her. He was a little shorter than six feet, with short dark hair and light brown eyes. He was slim, but didn't look like he worked out. His muscles were nowhere near as defined as Ryder's. Damn it, she shouldn't compare everybody to him.

"Aunt Claudia has told me so much about you," Derek said with a wide smile. "Though she forgot to mention how beautiful you are."

Scarlet forced herself to smile and offered her hand in greeting. "Nice to meet you too."

Instead of taking her hand, Derek kissed her on both cheeks. She froze, and Claudia laughed.

"Sorry, Scarlet, I should have warned you that Derek spent a few years in Paris, and that's how the French greet each other."

Scarlet nodded, and from the corner of her eye she saw Ryder stare at Derek as if he was about to pounce. His reaction gave her an idea.

"That's actually a nice way of greeting somebody. We should do this more often in the States. It breaks the ice." Scarlet tossed Derek a flirtatious smile. "Tell me more about your time in Paris."

She didn't give a fig about Derek or his time in France, but if by flirting with him she could get back at Ryder, then that's what she would do.

"Of course," he said with a charming grin. Then his gaze veered to Ryder. "But where are my manners? You must be a friend of Scarlet's."

"I'm Ryder, her bodyguard," Ryder answered stiffly.

"Nice to meet you, Ryder." Then he turned his gaze back to Scarlet. "So you want to know more about Paris?"

"Absolutely. I've always wanted to go, but so far there's never been the right time, or the right person to go with." She smiled at him sweetly, knowing that Ryder was watching them like a hawk.

"I have an idea," Derek announced. "Why don't the three of us go to that charming little French bistro I read so much about? There's nothing better than to tell stories about Paris over French food."

"That sounds perfect," Scarlet said quickly. She was hungry anyway, so why not kill two birds with one stone? Fill her belly with delicious food, and get back at Ryder for hurting her by flirting with Derek. That would show him that what had happened between them meant nothing to her.

"Then it's settled," Derek said. "Claudia? You know the restaurant I'm talking about, right?"

"Yes, of course, *Bistro Tartin*. But you two will have to go alone. I have to review a contract for Brandon, and he wanted to get feedback on that tonight while he's with his client in Phoenix."

"That's not a problem," Derek said. "Do you want us to bring you back some food?"

She made a dismissive hand movement. "No, please don't. I want to keep my figure, and just looking at French food makes me gain a pound. But you and Scarlet have fun."

Derek looked at Scarlet. "Guess you're stuck with me. I'd better get us an Uber to pick us up. I didn't rent a car. Claudia warned me that parking in San Francisco is notoriously difficult."

"We can take my car," Scarlet offered. "It's in the garage. I don't use it much but—"

"I'll drive you," Ryder interrupted.

"There's no need," Derek said. "Scarlet will be perfectly safe with me."

"I'll drive you," Ryder insisted. "It's my job. And don't worry, I won't be sitting at your table. But Mr. King hired me to protect his daughter. And that's what I'll do."

Scarlet noticed how the two men stared at each other like two bulls sizing each other up before a fight.

There was a sudden tension in the room. Claudia broke it. "Of course, Ryder. Thanks for offering to drive them." She smiled. "I'll see you all when you come back after dinner. Oh, and, Ryder, after you bring them back, why don't you take the rest of the night off since I'll be here? You're working long enough hours as is."

"Of course, Mrs. King," Ryder said.

Scarlet looked down at herself. "Do I have time to get changed? I think I need to put on something a little fancier for a French restaurant." And for her flirtation to have the desired affect: to show Ryder what he was missing, and to pretend that she was interested in another man, a good looking one at that.

Derek was handsome and had an easy smile. He oozed charm and was dressed fashionably like someone who'd just stepped out of GQ Magazine. However, despite all his good attributes, nothing inside her stirred when she looked at him. When he'd kissed her on the cheek, her body hadn't reacted at all. Her heart wasn't beating any faster either. He didn't excite her, and under normal circumstances she would have found him boring. But these weren't normal circumstances.

She regretted that she had to use him for her own selfish purpose, but in love and war, everything was allowed. And this was war.

Liar.

She tried to silence her inner voice, but the damn thing continued.

It's not war. It's love.

She turned on her heels and hurried up the stairs. In her room, she grabbed a pillow, held it to her face, and screamed into it. Then she dropped it, feeling marginally better. She marched to her walk-in closet and entered, flipping on the light.

What should she wear? Tight pants? A low-cut dress? A short skirt? The choices were endless.

15

Ryder leaned against his SUV in the no-parking zone right outside the French bistro where he'd dropped Scarlet and Derek off. No meter maid would bother him, because his car sported a special decal on the license plate, marking it as a vehicle with special parking privileges thanks to Scanguards' close ties to SFPD. From his position only a few yards away from the outside dining area, he watched Derek and Scarlet enjoy their dinner. They sat under a heat lamp that made the area comfortable for the diners, despite the cool evening air.

Just as well that Scarlet sat right beneath the warming lamp, because her skimpy clothes certainly didn't provide her with much warmth. If vampires could get heart attacks, Ryder would have been struck dead the moment Scarlet had descended the stairs in her home. Even her stepmother had raised a stunned eyebrow, but had made no comment.

Scarlet wore the exact same outfit she'd worn the night Ryder had met her at the Mezzanine. That was no coincidence. It was provocation. Ryder's blood was reaching its boiling point. She was flaunting her sexuality. The only concession she'd made was draping a light wrap over her shoulders, which did nothing to hide her curves or her flesh. Or the fact that Derek could ogle the mounds of her breasts whenever he wanted to.

She'd tossed him a triumphant look before letting Derek help her into the car. Did she not see how that guy was leering at her? Ryder was in the right mood to kick Derek in the balls for looking at her with such undisguised lust. And Scarlet pretended that she didn't even notice it. She continued hanging on his every word as he droned on about his time in Paris, laughing at the stupidest of jokes. Even from this distance, Ryder could pick up fragments of their conversation thanks to his superior vampire hearing.

It didn't escape Ryder either that Derek used every occasion to put his paws on Scarlet, ever so often touching her arm while talking, or using the old you-have-something-on-your-face trick to touch her face as if removing some imaginary hair or food particle. Ryder had to keep his anger tightly leashed, or he would go to their table and give the jerk a thorough thrashing. But he couldn't, or Scarlet would have good reason to demand that Ryder be fired.

That, he couldn't risk. Because being pulled off Scarlet's protection detail while a predator like Derek was moving in on his territory, was the worst thing that could happen to him right now.

The dinner dragged on, trying Ryder's patience. It seemed like an eternity, until Derek finally called for the check and settled the bill. Moments later, they were back at the car. This time, Ryder blocked Derek and helped Scarlet into the back seat of the SUV himself.

"What do you think you're playing at?" Ryder whispered under his breath as he leaned in, pretending to adjust Scarlet's seatbelt.

"None of your business," she replied just as quietly.

The evening traffic in San Francisco had picked up and the ride back to the house took almost half an hour. When Ryder stopped the SUV outside the King residence, Scarlet leaned forward.

"Thanks, Ryder," she said in a soft voice, which she probably only employed for Derek's benefit. "Enjoy your evening off. I'll see you in the morning."

Scarlet and Derek got out of the car, and there was nothing Ryder could do or say. Claudia had confirmed that she would be staying overnight, and had given him the night off.

Ryder slammed his hands against the steering wheel. "Fuck!"

He was at his wit's end. He needed advice from the only person he knew who'd understand what he was going through. Even if it meant that he had to admit to him that he'd lied.

Ryder pulled out his cell, then made the call.

"What's up, son?"

"Dad, I need to talk to you. It's important."

"I'm on my way to Scanguards," he said. "Just come by. I should be there in twenty minutes."

"No. Not at Scanguards. Somewhere more private."

"Should I worry about you?"

"No, Dad, but meet me where we can't be overheard by any vampires, and that includes Mom."

"Okay, I can meet you outside Grace Cathedral in ten minutes."

"Thanks, Dad. I'll see you there."

Ryder arrived outside of Grace Cathedral, which sat on the top of Nob Hill just opposite the famed Fairmont Hotel, a minute before his father pulled up in his black BMW M760i. It was a special edition, retrofitted with UV-protective windows in case he got caught outside during daylight.

Ryder walked to his father's car and opened the passenger side door. He hopped in and closed the door. Inside the car it was almost eerily quiet.

"Talk to me," Gabriel said.

Ryder came straight to the point. He figured it was best to get something important off his chest first. "I lied to you about the woman I had sex with, Dad."

"I know."

Ryder stared at him, stunned. "How do you know?"

"I'm your father, Ryder. I just know."

"So then you know what predicament I'm in." Ryder sighed.

"Not exactly. But when I asked you if you wanted help finding her, I could tell that the reason you didn't want my help was because you'd already found her. But that's all I know. So I guess she didn't turn out the way you imagined your future mate to be?"

Ryder took a deep breath. "She's everything I ever wanted. I would blood-bond with her tomorrow if I could, but… but…" Ryder looked down, unable to find the right words.

"She rejected you when you told her what you are?" Gabriel asked, his voice kind and gentle.

Ryder shook his head. "I haven't told her yet."

"But why not?"

"Because… because she's my charge. She's Scarlet King."

Gabriel let out a gasp. "Oh boy."

"Yeah. You could say that."

"Did you know before you took the assignment?"

Ryder shook his head. "No, I recognized her when I showed up to take over for Grayson. I know I should have told you and Samson immediately. It's unethical to be on her protection detail with what's happened between us, but... but... I can't think rationally when I'm around her. I know what the rules are, and I broke them nevertheless."

"Let's not talk about rules right now. I broke plenty of them where it concerned your mother. I believe you know the story about her craving my blood just after her turning?"

"After she was attacked and turned, and Scanguards found her? Yes, I know that Mom hated drinking human blood."

"Yes, and she would have died, had she not fed. She was drawn to my blood, and I gave it to her. But I wanted something in return: a kiss for each feeding. I knew it was wrong, but I demanded it anyway, because I wanted her to be mine. It was unethical, but I did it anyway." He smiled. "So you see, something can be unethical, yet be right nevertheless." He gripped Ryder's shoulder and squeezed it. "I won't tell Samson. You will continue as Scarlet's bodyguard."

"Thank you, Dad." Ryder forced a smile. "Unfortunately that's not the only problem between us."

"Go on."

"Last night when I went back to stay at the house, it came to an... an incident. We had an argument, and then suddenly we were kissing, and before I knew it, she was trying to undress me. And I stopped her." He looked straight into his father's eyes. "I was afraid of how she would react when she saw my two cocks."

"Hold it," Gabriel interrupted. "She slept with you when you still had the mass above your cock, and you were worried she would be shocked to see two cocks instead?"

Ryder sighed. "She never saw the deformity."

"But you had sex with her. How did she not—" Gabriel stopped himself. "Oh, I get it. You, uhm... okay. Continue."

"So you see, I was worried that she would reject me, so last night I told her I couldn't have sex with her. She was furious."

Gabriel laughed out loud. "Oh, denying a woman sex when she really wants it. Big mistake!"

"It's not funny, Dad! And then she accused me of playing some sick game with her, and now she's giving me the cold shoulder. And I just had to sit through two hours of her shamelessly flirting with a guy she's just met, and you should have seen what she was wearing! It leaves practically nothing to the imagination!" Conjuring up the image made his rage rise to the surface once more.

"Way I see it, there's the good news and the bad news."

"What's the good news?"

"She wants you."

"Did you not just hear what I said? She told me she's sick of me, and that guy was practically pawing her over dinner."

"Trust me on that. Women do crazy things when they feel wronged. Time to apologize."

"I'm assuming that's the bad news."

"No, the bad news is that you're gonna have to man up and explain to her why you didn't want to sleep with her. Admit to her that you're scared to be rejected because of your two cocks. That's a risk you have to take."

"And what about telling her that I'm also a vampire?"

He shrugged. "Cross that bridge when you get to it."

Ryder forced a smile. He knew his father was right, but that didn't make it any easier. "Wish me luck."

"You've got this, son."

Ryder wished he had his father's confidence.

16

Scarlet had to realize that flirting with a guy in whom she wasn't even remotely interested turned tedious very quickly. Particularly when the reason why she was flirting with him in the first place was gone. All the fun of it was over when the audience she'd performed for was gone.

The moment Scarlet returned home, she wanted to go to her room and call it a night. Claudia was coming down the stairs, dressed in casual pants and a sweater, her handbag slung over her arm, her car keys in her hand.

"Are you going somewhere?" Scarlet asked.

"I'm sorry," Claudia said with a regretful look, "but I just spoke to your dad, and the document he needs for his meeting first thing tomorrow morning is in his home office in Palo Alto. I have to drive down there and scan it in for him so I can email it to him, or he can't finish the deal he's working on." She cast a look at Derek. "Sorry, Derek, I know we haven't had any time to catch up yet, but I'll be back first thing tomorrow morning. I promise."

"I totally understand," Derek said with a smile. "I'm sure Scarlet and I can keep each other company, right Scarlet?"

Scarlet forced a smile. Crap! She would be alone with Derek overnight? She hoped he didn't expect her to stay up half the night entertaining him. Listening to his mundane stories about life in Paris while feigning interest had been exhausting enough. She was beat and needed to get a good night's sleep.

"Yeah, sure," Scarlet replied. "Though I've gotta work on my thesis all day tomorrow. My professor had some issues with it, so I need to fix them."

"You're working too much," Claudia said. "Take a couple of days off while Derek is here." She walked to the entrance door, and smiled back at Scarlet and Derek. "I'll see you both tomorrow."

A moment later, the heavy door fell shut behind her.

"Well, how about a drink?" Derek asked.

"I'm not a big drinker, and—"

"Oh come on, just one," he said with a charming smile. "It's still early. Only old people go to sleep this early. And I don't want this nice evening to end yet."

He was already heading into the living room where he opened a cabinet. Scarlet eyed him, surprised. How did he know where her father kept the liquor? She watched him as he poured himself whiskey then looked over his shoulder.

"Same for you?"

"No. I'll have port." Whiskey was too strong for her. But a few sips of port she could handle.

When Derek handed her the glass and clinked his to hers, he looked into her eyes. "I had a really nice time at dinner. You're an extraordinary young woman."

How would he know that when he'd been the one talking continuously? He hadn't asked her a single question, clearly too enamored with his own voice.

"Thanks." She sipped on her port while he took a big gulp of his whiskey. She set the glass down on the coffee table. "Oh, you know I just remembered that I have to upload a document for the university, or I'll miss the midnight deadline."

She didn't care if he knew that this was an excuse. She wanted to be alone. She made a few steps toward the door, but he followed her.

"You've still got a couple of hours until midnight," Derek said.

When she looked over her shoulder, he stepped closer and chuckled. "There's no need to play hard to get."

Scarlet reared back. "What?" Her heartbeat suddenly accelerated.

He put his hand on her arm, and the unwelcome touch made her take a step back. In an attempt to put as much distance between them as possible, she hit a standing lamp behind her.

"You don't have to play coy with me, Scarlet. You can't deny that we hit it off tonight. No reason to stop now."

Scarlet made a step sideways toward the door, but he cut off her escape route, trapping her.

Derek leaned in. "I've wanted to kiss you ever since you came down the stairs, dressed like this for me."

"I'm sorry if I gave you the wrong impression, but I'm not interested in you." Not even if he were the last man on earth and the survival of the human race depended on her sleeping with Derek.

He ignored her protest and braced his hands to either side of her head, his palms on the wall. "No woman dresses like that unless she wants to attract a man's attention. Well, you've got my attention. But if you want to, we can play this little game. I'm up for it."

"Let me go!" she demanded, this time firmer. "I'd like to go to bed now. Alone."

Derek didn't move. "I'm getting a lot of mixed signals here, Scarlet. Maybe you're just shy when it comes to sex. Don't worry. I've got experience. I can teach you."

Not in a million years!

Besides, she had enough experience.

He dipped his head, but she pushed against his chest with all her strength. "Stop! Get off of me!" When he didn't let her go, she reminded herself of the self-defense class her father had made her take. Which of the maneuvers she'd learned would work in her current position?

Derek glared at her. He made a motion to immobilize her arms so she wouldn't be able to defend herself, but before his hands could wrap around her wrists, he was jerked back and flung against an armchair, making it turn over.

Ryder!

Stunned, Scarlet watched as Derek found his balance again, but Ryder didn't give him a chance to defend himself.

"She said no! What part of *no* don't you get?" Ryder yelled at Derek before he punched him in the face.

Derek's head whipped back, and he stumbled backward, but before he could crash to the ground, Ryder snatched him by the collar of his shirt and jerked him back.

"Oh, no, you're not getting away that easily!" Ryder ground out, the chords in his neck bulging, his muscles flexing under his shirt.

Again, Ryder punched him, and Derek yelped in pain, blood running from his nose now.

"Get the fuck out, before I have to call the coroner," Ryder ground out between clenched teeth and catapulted him through the door into the hallway, where Derek landed hard on the wooden floor.

"You can't throw me out. It's not your house!" Derek yelled back.

Scarlet marched through the door. "No, he can't." She paused for effect. "But I can. Get out!"

Ryder stepped next to her, but remained silent. She appreciated him letting her have this moment, while she suppressed the urge to kick Derek while she had the chance. But she wouldn't sink this low. He didn't deserve it.

Derek scrambled to his feet. "This is not over. I'm Claudia's guest. Wait until she hears about this."

Was he trying to threaten her? "Wait until I tell my father."

With a glare, Derek moved his gaze from her to Ryder. "I'll get you for assault."

"Yeah, not in this town, you won't," Ryder replied. "Or would you like me to have a chat with the Chief of Police and tell him that you were attempting to rape Scarlet?"

With a defiant lift of his chin, Derek spun around and left the house, slamming the door shut behind him.

Ryder walked to it and flipped the deadbolt shut, before turning back to Scarlet. "Does he have a house key?"

"I don't know. It's possible that Claudia gave him one." Though she hoped not.

"And where is your stepmother? The whole reason for giving me the night off was because she was staying here."

"She had to drive back to Palo Alto for some papers for Dad."

"And leave you alone with a man you've only just met?" Ryder growled in displeasure.

Ryder was one to talk. He, too, was a man she'd only just met. But she decided not to point this out. Instead she said, "Do you think Derek will come back?"

"Jerks like him don't learn from their mistakes."

Scarlet nodded. "I'm assuming you're staying overnight."

"Yes." Then he ran his eyes over her. "Did he hurt you?"

"No. He didn't get a chance." She'd been incredibly lucky. Her stupid idea of flirting with him to get back at Ryder had nearly backfired in a bad way. Scarlet took a breath. "How did you know to come back?"

Ryder hesitated, then gave her a regretful look. "I didn't. I should have known he would try something like that, but the reason I came back had nothing to do with Derek. I wanted to speak to you about what happened last night. I wanted to explain why—"

"There's nothing to explain." She tried to keep all her emotions in check, but wasn't sure she succeeded. "Thank you for helping me just now, but it doesn't change what happened between you and me. I know why you rejected me last night."

He looked at her, seemingly baffled. "What? How?"

"Oh please!" she huffed. "You have a girlfriend! By the sounds of it, last night you came straight from her bed to mine. Of course you couldn't have sex with me. You were already… well, uh, depleted."

"I don't have a girlfriend!" Ryder protested. "And I certainly wasn't depleted as you put it. I didn't have sex with anybody last night."

"Don't deny it. You spoke to her this morning. *Sweetheart, Nessie,*" Scarlet said imitating his inflection.

"That wasn't my girlfriend. Nessie is my sister."

"And why would I believe you?"

Ryder pulled his cell phone from his pocket and selected a contact, then put the call on speaker and let it ring. He showed her the display so she could see that the contact's name was indeed *Nessie.*

"Hey, what's up?" a young woman answered.

"Nessie, you're on speaker with me and the girl you asked me about yesterday."

"Oh my God! You found her? I wanna meet her! When are you bringing her home?"

"Soon," Ryder said with a smile, "I hope. But could you please clear something up for her? Would you please tell her how you and I are related?"

"What kind of question is that?"

"Just answer it."

"You're my big brother. How else would we be related?"

"And could you please tell her if I'm in a relationship."

"You mean like a girlfriend? Hell, no. Though it's not for a lack of Ethan and me trying to set you up."

"Thanks, Nessie, talk later," Ryder said and disconnected the call. He remained silent for a few seconds. "Do you believe me now?"

The call had sounded genuine, and she believed Nessie. But there were several things that were surprising.

"You told her about me?"

Ryder nodded.

"She asked you whether you found me. Does that mean you were looking for me?"

"Yes. After you disappeared from the club, I tried to find you, but I had no luck until I got assigned to your security detail."

"Why were you looking for me?"

"Isn't that obvious?" He shook his head lightly. "I want to be with you."

"Hmm." She wasn't ready to believe that. Just proving that he spoke to his sister and not a girlfriend didn't explain everything. She recalled the part of the telephone conversation she'd overheard in the morning. It was the oddest conversation between a brother and sister Scarlet could imagine. "You and Nessie spoke about anal sex. I find that odd. Did you tell her about what we did at the nightclub?" The thought alone made her feel flushed.

"No, of course I didn't tell her about that. Just that I met someone."

She raised an eyebrow. Could she trust him not to have told everybody about their sexual encounter?

"I can see that you're not satisfied with my explanation yet. There's more. But it's not something I can tell you."

"Figures," she interrupted him. What kind of excuse would he use now?

"I have to show it to you." He paused. "There's a reason why I couldn't sleep with you last night. I was scared to let you see me naked."

"What the—"

"Please, Scarlet. I was worried that you would reject me once you saw me…"

"Why?" She couldn't imagine why somebody like Ryder could possibly have body image issues.

"I'll show you, but"—he pointed to the living room window—"I'd rather not have an audience."

Scarlet contemplated his words for a long few seconds.

"Fine. We'll go upstairs. But if this is a trick—"

"It's not."

17

Upstairs, Ryder pulled the curtains in Scarlet's bedroom shut, then turned back to her. The room was flooded in light, and for a moment Ryder wished that only the bedside lamps were lit. They would be less harsh.

Never before in his life had he ever felt more nervous than under Scarlet's scrutiny.

"Okay, we don't have an audience," Scarlet said, arms crossed over her chest. She tilted her chin in his direction. "Go ahead."

"Before I get undressed, I wanted you to know that what you'll see is…" He couldn't find the right words.

"You're stalling."

"This isn't easy for me. Please promise to keep an open mind."

"Strip," she demanded. "Or you might as well leave now, and never come back."

The challenge was clear. He was out of time. Ryder pulled his shirt over his head and tossed it on a chair, while Scarlet watched his every move.

"Looks like you don't have a third nipple," she said. "I guess then it can't be too bad after all."

"Trust me if it was just a third nipple, we wouldn't be in this situation."

Ryder kicked his shoes off, then put his hand on the button of his pants, hesitating. His heart was pounding now, and his hands were trembling. He opened the button, then lowered the zipper. Quickly, before his courage could desert him, he pushed down his pants and rid himself of them. He now wore only his boxer briefs. Swallowing hard, he hooked his thumbs into the waistband and dragged them down. As he straightened to give Scarlet a full view of his twin appendages, he cast his gaze downward, avoiding meeting her eyes.

A gasp tore from Scarlet's throat, and he steeled himself for the coming rejection. But Scarlet remained silent. Why didn't she say anything? Or react by throwing something at him? Anything would be better than this silence. He'd scared her speechless. And that was never a good sign. Insults he could handle. But knowing that she was horrified by the sight of his two cocks felt like a hot knife was slicing his heart in two.

This had been a colossal failure.

"I'm sorry," he said, barely getting the words out. "Now you know why I couldn't let you see me naked." At least she knew now that he hadn't been playing sadistic games with her like she'd accused him of the night before.

Without looking at Scarlet, Ryder snatched his boxer briefs, pants, and shirt from the chair, and held them in front of his groin, then reached for his shoes, before turning toward the door.

"Where do you think you're going?"

"To the guest room."

"No, you're not!"

Fuck! She wouldn't even let him stay in the house to protect her? That's how disgusted she was with him?

"At least give me a half hour so Benjamin can take over for me," Ryder begged.

"I don't want Benjamin here."

Ryder growled. "You can't be alone in the house, not with Derek out there planning God-knows-what."

"I'm not alone in the house, you're here."

"You just told me to leave, and I understand it, I do. I look like a monster, and what woman in her right mind would want to have to deal with that?" He still couldn't look directly at her, not wanting to see the disgust in her eyes. It would have been better if she were hurling insults or heavy items at him, or having an emotional outbreak.

"I know you're angry with me for hiding this from you," Ryder said. "My only excuse is that when I met you in the club, I realized you were everything I ever wanted, and I couldn't resist the draw you had on me. I never wanted to hurt you or betray you."

He walked toward the door, his heart breaking more with each step. He'd taken a risk, and it hadn't turned out the way he'd hoped. "I just hope you do me the curtesy to keep my secret."

"I'll keep your secret, under one condition."

He froze.

"Don't leave."

At the unexpected words, Ryder turned slowly, hesitantly. Had he heard right, or was his mind playing tricks on him? Was he hearing what he wanted to hear?

For the first time since he'd exposed himself in front of her, he met Scarlet's gaze. There was no disgust in her eyes, no fear either. Rather, she looked curious.

"And drop your clothes. I want to look at you."

He dropped his shoes and clothes right where he stood, then slowly walked toward her, and stopped a few feet away from her. When he noticed her curious gaze on his cocks, he felt blood rush from the rest of his body to his groin. Both his cocks started to harden.

Scarlet lifted her head, and when he looked into her eyes, he saw something he hadn't expected: desire.

~ ~ ~

Scarlet couldn't take her eyes off Ryder's cocks. Everything made sense now. Why he'd taken her from behind that night in the club, and not gotten undressed. Why he'd touched her and almost made her climax the previous night outside in the hallway, yet resisted her demand to fuck her, even though his arousal was evident.

She should be feeling disgust at the sight in front of her. But she didn't. She'd read about this condition. It was called Diphallia, a male with two phalluses, two cocks. Only a hundred people in the entire world had ever been reported suffering from this condition, and while many of those men had misshapen cocks, Ryder didn't.

Both were beautiful, and perfect. And now hardening in tandem. She licked her lips, wondering whether this meant that they were both fully functioning.

"Do they both work?"

There was a hesitation in Ryder, but then he replied, "Yes. They both get hard, and they both…uhm… they both ejaculate."

Scarlet's pulse ticked up at the welcome news. "May I touch them?"

She met Ryder's gaze, and saw his apprehension melt away. She understood now, why he'd not told her about this earlier. How many women had rejected him the moment he undressed? How many disappointments did he have to swallow? How much heartbreak? How much loneliness? And she hadn't made it easy for him either, making wrong assumptions and false accusations.

"You sure about it?" he asked, his voice raspy now.

"Please."

She sat down on the edge of her bed and beckoned him to approach. His erections jutted out in front of him, hard and heavy, as he bridged the distance between them with several steps. When he stopped in front of her, she reached out and stroked her hand over his upper cock, which was slightly smaller than his lower one.

Ryder hissed in a breath.

"So sensitive," she murmured and used both hands now to touch both cocks at the same time.

"Fuck!"

Scarlet chuckled at his curse. "You're perfect." She lifted her eyes up to his face and noticed him watching her in fascination.

"I don't disgust you?"

"Does that look like disgust?" she asked and brought her lips to his upper cock, parted them and licked over the bulbous head.

Ryder gasped in surprise, and his eyes seemed to flicker, the light in the room reflecting in them. His reaction made her feel powerful. He'd shared his secret with her, and the knowledge that he'd taken this risk confirmed that his claim that he wanted her was true. Were it not, he could have simply let her believe that he had a girlfriend, and their night at the nightclub was just casual, anonymous sex that meant nothing.

"Scarlet," he murmured.

"Hmm?"

"May I make a request?"

"What is it?"

"Take your clothes off."

She smiled at him. "Only if you promise me that this time you won't deny me your cock...or rather, your cocks." Because the sight of his virile erections made her want to do all kinds of taboo things.

"That'll be an easy promise to keep," he said with a grin. "Now strip for me, before I have to go all caveman on you."

18

Ryder felt a weight lift off his shoulders. He'd hit the jackpot: Scarlet wasn't disgusted by his two cocks. On the contrary, she seemed to be delighted and rather eager to explore his naked body. In anticipation of burying himself in her sweet body, his cocks were already harder than a crowbar, or rather *two* crowbars.

Scarlet rose from the bed and reached behind her to open her bustier.

"Take your time," Ryder said, letting his eyes roam over her curves. "I wanna enjoy this."

She smiled at him. "Well, in that case…" She bent down to kick off her high heels one by one, then turned around. "Why don't you give me a hand with it?"

She stepped back so she brushed against his cocks, making Ryder hiss in a breath.

"You're literally a cock-tease," he said, gripping her hips and pulling her against his body, his cocks between them, the contact driving him half insane.

After a second, he stepped back, then released her hips and found the zipper of her bustier. Slowly, he pulled it down, and the garment fell to the floor. From behind her, Ryder slid his arms around Scarlet, and covered her breasts with his palms. Stiff nipples greeted him, and he kneaded her supple flesh, loving how she yielded to his touch.

Ryder dipped his head to her neck and pressed his mouth to her warm skin, inhaling her female scent. Scarlet's carotid artery pulsed against his lips, tempting the vampire in him to taste her. One day soon, he hoped, but not tonight. One step at a time, one secret at a time.

Scarlet leaned back against him, but he stopped her from pressing her delectable ass into his groin by sliding his hands back down to her hips.

"The skirt," he demanded, his heart thundering, his cocks twitching in excitement. "Open the zipper."

She reached to her right and slowly lowered the zipper of her tight skirt. Then she wiggled out of it, until it pooled around her feet. She stepped out of it. She wore a thong tonight, a black lace thong with barely enough fabric to qualify as an item of clothing.

"Fuck, Scarlet," he growled. "That's how you left the house tonight?" He gripped her hips. "Had I known, I would have bent you over my knees the moment you came downstairs."

Scarlet turned her head to look over her shoulder, an innocent expression on her face. "Would you like to do that now?"

Before he could react, she bent forward, resting her head and arms on the edge of her bed, her ass pointed at him like an offering. He nearly lost it right there. He'd never slapped a woman, not during sex, not in anger, and not even in play. But right now, the thought of his palm connecting with the soft skin of her exposed ass cheeks sent a shudder down his spine and into his balls.

"Christ, Scarlet! Are you trying to make me lose the last bit of my self-control?"

"Is it working?"

"What do you think?" he replied, and slapped her white flesh, eliciting a moan to roll over her lips.

"Again," she demanded.

"You like that?" he asked in surprise.

"Don't you?"

He slapped her other cheek, then laid both his hands on her ass to calm her skin. He had no intention of hurting her. "Maybe another day, we'll explore how far you want to go with this. But tonight"—he gripped her thong and pulled it off her with such force that the skimpy garment ripped—"I wanna make love to you."

She spread her legs, her chest now fully resting on the bed, but he wasn't ready to subject her to the satyr way of sex.

"Turn around, Scarlet. I want to look into your eyes. And I want you to see me this time. No more hiding."

Scarlet rose and turned to him. Her gaze roamed from his face down to his groin and lower, when she suddenly chuckled.

For an instant he feared the worst: that she was playing with him.

"You're still wearing socks."

He followed her gaze to his feet. Scarlet was right. How could he have missed that? "I had no idea." He grinned.

"Apparently that sort of thing happens when all the blood leaves the brain to support…" She chuckled. "… two cocks."

"Are you making fun of me?" he asked, while he rid himself of his socks, enjoying this newfound playfulness.

"I wouldn't dare," she replied with a chuckle. "Or you might bend me over your knees and slap me as punishment."

Ryder put one arm around her waist and drew her to him, their bodies connecting skin to skin. Her breasts molded to his hard chest, and his cocks were crushed against her stomach.

"Something tells me that you wouldn't consider that a punishment." He dipped his head to hers. "Besides, I have no intention of punishing you. If anything, I should be the one to be punished. I should have told you right away why I was apprehensive about you finding out—"

Scarlet put a finger over his lips. "It's all forgotten now." She slipped her other hand onto his butt and drew him closer. "Do you think we could…" She tipped her head toward the bed. "Given that we're already naked, and your cocks are hard, and—"

Ryder chuckled. "I get the drift. No more delays." Knowing that Scarlet was just as eager to have sex as he was, made him feel ecstatic.

He lifted her off her feet and laid her down on the bed. For a moment, he feasted his eyes on her. How had he gotten so lucky that the universe had bestowed him with such a beautiful mate? Tonight he'd worship her body like a temple, and then soon, very soon, he would tell her who he really was. Judging by how quickly she'd accepted his two cocks, her mind was open to things that fell outside the realm of the ordinary. If he played his cards right, she would soon accept that he was a vampire satyr hybrid.

Ryder joined Scarlet on the bed and rolled over her. He looked at her face and saw only excitement and acceptance there, no apprehension, no fear.

"Thank you, Scarlet," he murmured, "thank you for not running away, screaming."

She smiled up at him. "And miss out on this?" She tilted her pelvis up to rub herself against his cocks.

Ryder dipped his head to hers and captured her lips, kissing her softly, drinking in her scent and her taste. Scarlet parted her lips to respond to him, to invite him to dance with her tongue. There was no rush tonight. They were alone, and they had all night to explore each other. He wanted this to be perfect, because what happened tonight would become the foundation of their trust in each other.

Ryder intensified the kiss, and Scarlet mirrored him. She put one hand on his nape to hold him close. The touch made him shudder with pleasure, sending a bolt of fire down his spine into his tailbone. Her other hand slid onto his butt to press him more firmly down on her. He reveled in her eagerness and ground his groin into her, indicating to her that he too couldn't wait until their bodies were joined.

He let go of her lips and drew his head back a few inches so he could see her face. Her lashes lifted, and her blue eyes looked back at him, arousal evident in them.

"Patience, baby," he murmured with a smile, "you'll get what you need tonight." And every night thereafter, because he would never be able to deny her anything.

"Promises, promises," she replied with a chuckle. She opened her legs wider and suddenly wrapped them around his lower body, her ankles crossing just below his butt.

"I see you're a little impatient," he said. "And there I was planning on taking my time."

"I've been patient enough," Scarlet said. "I've been waiting since last night."

"Well, if that's the case, then maybe I should do this, before you lose your patience with me."

He lifted himself off her and slid farther down her body, until he was settled between her legs, his head at her pussy. He inhaled the scent of her arousal, before sliding his hands underneath her ass and tilting her toward him. Eager to taste her, Ryder brought his lips to her pussy and licked over the rosy flesh.

A gasp tore from her throat. "Ryder! Oh!"

Knowing that Scarlet enjoyed the touch of his lips and tongue, filled him with male satisfaction. Her juices tasted like fresh morning dew, and her flesh was responsive and soft. He licked her cleft, then ran his tongue farther up to where her clit was hiding beneath a tiny hood. When he touched the engorged organ with the tip of his tongue, Scarlet almost lifted off the mattress. She moaned, and gripped the duvet beneath her with both hands.

Her pelvis rocked back and forth in an attempt to force him to give her more, but Ryder held her tightly. He knew she would come soon, but he wanted to prolong her pleasure, because once he was inside her, he couldn't guarantee that she would orgasm, because he wouldn't last more than a minute. His cocks were already too hard, and he couldn't stop himself from grinding them against the duvet to take off the edge. He could feel pre-cum oozing from their tips.

"Please, Ryder!" Scarlet begged. "I need to feel your cocks."

He lifted his face from her pussy. "Soon, baby, soon."

"Now, Ryder," she insisted.

"Let me make you come first."

"No, I want to come with you inside me."

He met her gaze, and knew he couldn't say no. He would never be able to say no to her.

Without another word, he crawled up to her, adjusted himself, so his lower cock was poised at the entrance to her pussy, and his upper one just above. He thrust into Scarlet, and all breath rushed from her lungs. She pressed her head back into the pillow and arched her back. Her breasts were like an offering, and he kissed first one nipple, then the other, while farther below, he continued plunging into her, hard and fast, while his second cock slid over her clit with every descent and every withdrawal.

Scarlet panted, her body glistening now, her lips parted, her pulse racing.

"This what you wanted?" Ryder asked, his voice raspy, his breath hitching.

Her eyes flew open, and she pinned him with them. "Your cocks… they're perfect."

"So are you," he said and kissed her, letting her taste herself on his tongue.

She didn't pull back, but kissed him back, her hands now on his ass, forcing him to fuck her harder and plunging his cock deeper into her, just like she'd demanded at the nightclub.

"You want it that rough?" Ryder asked, because he realized just how frantically he fucked her.

"Harder!" she demanded.

"Fuck, baby!"

He doubled his efforts, surprised that he still had enough restraint to stop himself from coming too quickly. Her pussy was warm and drenched in her juices, her muscles tight and clamping around his erection ready to milk him. Every time their bodies came together, it felt like a spear of fire raced into Ryder's balls, until suddenly, Scarlet's interior muscles spasmed around him.

She let out a cry of release. Ryder felt her shudder as she climaxed, and let go of the last thread of his self-control and came. He felt seed shoot from his main cock and fill Scarlet's pussy, making every subsequent plunge into her even smoother. Almost simultaneously, his upper cock spilled its seed onto Scarlet's belly. His double orgasm was even more powerful than when he'd masturbated to memories of Scarlet the night before. Nothing had ever felt this amazing.

Ryder knew right there and then that he would never want another woman but Scarlet, no matter how long he would live.

19

Scarlet felt the waves of her orgasm reverberating in all her cells. Her entire body felt as if she were a ragdoll. She'd never felt so satisfied in her entire life. Ryder had surprised her. She'd expected that he would penetrate her with both his cocks, one in her pussy, the other in her anus, but he'd instead used his second cock to stimulate her clitoris so that she climaxed longer and harder than she ever had.

Ryder slowly lifted himself of her, and cool air blew against her heated body.

"Are you leaving?" she asked, suddenly panicked.

He chuckled and pressed a kiss to her lips. "Of course not. I'm not leaving your bed tonight. But I'd better get us cleaned up." He pointed to the semen that was pooling on her stomach.

She suddenly felt silly that she'd worried about Ryder leaving. Relieved, she followed him with her eyes as he walked into her ensuite bathroom. His butt muscles flexed as he walked, and his legs looked just as muscular and strong. Ryder had a body to die for. She couldn't believe he was single. How could other women have rejected him, when everything about him was perfect? He was as good looking as any male model, well-spoken, educated, and on top of it a considerate and experienced lover. And he was strong and protective.

Ryder interrupted her thoughts, when he returned with a wet washcloth in his hand. Scarlet's eyes fell to his cocks. Both of them looked relaxed now, but still big and beautiful. She licked her lips, when she heard Ryder chuckle softly. Scarlet lifted her eyes.

"You look as if you want more," he said as he leaned over her and used the warm, wet cloth to clean her stomach and her pussy.

Without inhibition, she said, "I want both your cocks inside me at the same time."

Ryder's lips parted, and she noticed that his cocks twitched all of a sudden. But a regretful look crossed his face.

"I'm afraid I didn't find any lubricant in your bathroom."

A protest already rolled over her lips. "I don't mind—"

Ryder put his finger over her lips. "I do. I don't want you to feel any discomfort or pain. I want this to be perfect. This will be our first time, and I want you to enjoy it as much as I will enjoy it. Even if that means I have to wait."

Excitement filled her chest. "But you will take me with both…"

"… with both my cocks inside you? Oh yes, I promise. I can barely wait."

He glanced down to his cocks. She followed his gaze and noticed that both were already rock hard and standing to attention, the bulbous heads glistening.

"How are you already hard again?"

"That's your doing."

"But I didn't do anything."

"You were talking about wanting me to take you with both cocks. With one in your pussy, and the other in your delectable ass. That kind of talk gets me hard in an instant."

He tossed the washcloth on the bedside table, then lifted the duvet and helped Scarlet crawl underneath it, before he joined her.

"But I'll let you recover a little first," Ryder said and pulled her into his arms. "I took you hard. You're probably sore."

"I'm not."

He laughed softly. "Don't you want to cuddle a bit, or do you only want me for sex?"

"Are you for real?" she asked, amazed that he would suggest to cuddle when he was already hard again, and clearly ready for more sex. "Most other men would—"

"I'm not most other men," Ryder replied.

She smiled. "You're right." She slid her hand down his body and touched his cocks. "You're not like other men. Far from it."

Ryder tucked her against his body, spooning her, his cocks wedged against her backside. "Tell me about yourself, Scarlet. You're obviously not just the studious young woman you pretend to be. There seems to be so much more to you. Why do you hide those parts of you?"

Ryder was right. She was hiding parts of herself. "Same reason as you. I don't want to get hurt."

He pressed a kiss into her hair. "I would never hurt you."

"I know that now." How she'd come to this conclusion, Scarlet didn't really know. But she knew what she felt. "When I'm with you, I feel safe."

"I *am* your bodyguard, you know," he said with a smile in his voice.

She laughed, but then turned more serious. She wanted him to know that being with him was different, special. "When I'm with you, I feel like I belong."

"What do you mean?"

"You know, my whole life… it always felt somehow disjointed. My family is like a patchwork. This is my father's third marriage. I guess he was never very lucky with women, until now, until he married Claudia."

"What about your mother?" Ryder asked.

"She died when I was fourteen."

"I'm sorry. That must have been hard. How did it happen?"

"Heart attack. She was only forty."

"She must have had a heart condition then. In general, it's rare for women your mother's age to have a heart attack. That's tragic."

Scarlet sighed. "I never knew about a heart condition. I was still a kid and probably too self-absorbed to notice. Though I remember that she was sick on and off, but I never knew it had anything to do with her heart. Dad was crushed after her death. We all were. Joshua too."

"Joshua?"

"My half-brother. He's my dad's son from his first marriage."

"Did his first wife die too?" Ryder asked.

Scarlet shook her head. "No. She left him when Joshua was only a year old. She divorced him and left Joshua with him. She had no interest in children, never even wrote him a single birthday card. Luckily, Joshua was too young to remember her, and when my dad married my mom, she became his mother. And when I came along shortly afterwards, we were a real family for a while. Joshua would have been twenty-seven next month."

Ryder squeezed her tightly. "He passed away? Oh, Scarlet, I can't even imagine how I would feel if I lost my mother and my siblings. I would be devastated."

"It was hard for Dad and me. Claudia was a rock for Dad to lean on. They'd gotten married only four years before Joshua was killed. I remember where I was when I heard of the shooting."

"The shooting?"

"Yes. It happened just outside a nightclub. A man pulled a gun without provocation and shot Joshua. A couple of other people were injured too, but they survived. Joshua didn't. He died right there outside the club. The paramedics tried to revive him, but they couldn't." She felt tears well up in her eyes at the awful memories.

"Shhh, baby, I'm here for you. You don't have to tell me more if it's too painful for you."

She turned her head halfway so she could look at him. "I want to tell you about it. Because all these events, my mother's death, my half-brother's murder, they turned me into who I am today."

Ryder stroked his knuckles over her cheek. "You're a strong woman."

"I wasn't always. But I had to become strong. After Joshua died, everything changed for me. Dad became overprotective. He believed, and still does, that Joshua's death wasn't the result of a random shooting. He thinks that Joshua was targeted because of him. Dad has made many enemies over the years with the business decisions he made."

"So they never found the shooter?" Ryder asked with interest.

"They did. They found him a day after the shooting. He was dead. A self-inflicted gunshot wound to the head."

"Did he have connections to your father? Is that it?"

"No. The police couldn't find any connection to Joshua or my father or any of his business associates. Dad believes that he was a contract killer, and that the real culprit is still out there. That's why he made sure that I got into Stanford, so I could live at home under his watchful eye. And when I transferred to the University of San Francisco last year, he insisted on a bodyguard. Had I said no, he would have never let me move into our house in Pacific Heights. But I wanted some freedom, you know, some autonomy."

"Of course you did," Ryder said. "Everybody your age wants that. It's part of being an adult. We all have to stand up for ourselves."

"Yes, but it's not always easy. I don't want to hurt my father by pushing back too hard, but I don't think he understands what I'm going through. I feel trapped."

"I'm sorry. I know that overprotective parents can be difficult to deal with."

"Are yours like that too?"

Ryder chuckled. "In some ways, but not in others."

"What do you mean by that?"

"As part of my training at Scanguards, I went to Baltimore for a few years, learning everything I could from a great group of, uhm, other bodyguards. My parents trusted me enough never to worry about me, or to demand that I come home more often to visit. They let me find my own way. And now that I'm back, I'm spending more time with my family again. I know it may sound odd to you, but I actually like living with them again. Granted, at thirty, that may sound like I'm not independent—"

"You're thirty?" She turned in his arms. "You look way younger."

He laughed. "Family genes. We all look younger than we are."

"And you don't mind living with your parents? Aren't they constantly checking up on what you're doing?"

"They don't really have the time or the inclination to do that. They both work. Dad's a director at Scanguards, and Mom's a physician."

"Is that why you work for Scanguards? Because your dad works there?"

"I can't imagine doing anything else. Guess I was born to protect others. We all were."

"You mean Nessie? Is she a bodyguard too?"

"No, but she works for Scanguards too. Community outreach, and a few other pet projects. But Ethan, my younger brother works as a bodyguard too."

Scarlet now remembered that Nessie had mentioned her brother's name. "All five of you live in the same house?"

"Yep, not far from here actually. Mom and Dad converted a huge Edwardian house so that we all have our own private space. Mom and Dad have their own little love nest on the top floor, and Nessie, Ethan, and I share the second floor. And the first floor is for everybody. It works just fine. We get time as a family, and time alone when we need it."

Scarlet smiled. "It must be nice to be a real family."

"It is. You'll see."

Her heart skipped a beat. "You're planning to introduce me to them?"

"Well, you heard my sister. She wants to meet you. And since she can't keep a secret to save her life, I'm sure the rest of my family is already aware that I'm in... that I've met someone."

It didn't escape Scarlet that Ryder had wanted to finish the sentence differently. What had he wanted to say before correcting himself?

That I'm in *a relationship*?

Or that I'm in *love*?

Scarlet tamped down her excitement. She didn't want to expect too much. They'd only known each other for a few days. Time would tell if they were really made for each other, or if the explosive attraction between them would fizzle out quickly.

20

Scarlet stirred, but didn't open her eyes, not wanting her dream to vanish in daylight. The warm body pressed to her back felt comforting, and the arm slung across her front was muscular. She felt hot breath at her nape, and something hard against her backside.

"I know you're awake."

In a split-second everything came back to her. "Ryder." She turned in his arms. "I was afraid that I only dreamed this."

He chuckled and lifted the duvet. "You mean this?"

His twin cocks were as hard as the night before.

"Yes, this, you." She smiled. "You're still here."

"Of course I am. I'm doing my job: guarding your body." Ryder dipped his head to her breasts and began licking them, while his hand already swept down to the juncture of her thighs, where her sex still pulsed with the memory of their lovemaking.

He bathed his fingers in her pussy, which was already drenched with her juices.

"Is that part of your job?"

He lifted his head a fraction. "I take my job very seriously."

She smirked, and Ryder suddenly pulled her on top of him so she straddled him before she even knew what he intended.

"But if you'd like to take the lead, I'm game."

Scarlet lifted herself onto her knees, while she looked at his two cocks. "I never thought I'd have to say this, but I'm having a hard time choosing. They're both equally perfect."

"Take the bigger one," Ryder said with a grin. "And if you're a good girl, I'll let you have both of them later when I've gotten us the lubricant."

"And what if I'm a bad girl?"

With both hands he gripped her backside, before he slipped one finger, still wet from her juices, down her crack. "Oh, then I'll have to tie you up and punish you before I take you with both cocks."

"Then maybe I should be bad," she murmured and pushed against his finger, until he slipped inside her anus one knuckle deep. The feeling was exhilarating.

Ryder looked at her, his eyes shimmering almost golden again. "Have you ever had a cock inside here?" He pushed his finger deeper by another knuckle as if to emphasize his words.

Heat charged through her, and she closed her eyes and tilted her head back. "No, never. Nor any fingers."

"Good," he said, and she could hear male satisfaction in the tone of his voice. "Because I want to be the only one who takes you like that."

His possessive statement sent a shiver down her spine, and a moment later, Ryder was pumping his finger in and out of her anus in a steady, slow rhythm, his eyes locking with hers now.

"It feels good," she admitted and took hold of Ryder's larger cock, adjusted the position and impaled herself on him.

"Fuck!" Ryder cursed, and thrust his finger deep.

"Oh my God," Scarlet let out, her breath rushing from her lungs. "That's even better... oh... oh!"

"Wait until I replace my finger with my second cock."

She bent forward, bringing her face to his. "I can't wait."

He captured her lips and kissed her, while he continued thrusting in and out of her. She was so close, her orgasm already on the horizon. Just a few more seconds, a few more thrusts and—

Ryder suddenly stilled and took his lips from hers. "Do you hear that?"

Dazed, she shook her head. "Hear what?"

"Damn it! The garage door. Somebody is opening the garage door."

Frozen in place, Scarlet listened. Now she could hear it too.

"Crap!" Scarlet cursed.

"Nobody can find me in your bedroom," Ryder said and pulled himself out of her. "Or they have a valid reason for taking me off your security detail."

Scarlet nodded. "I know."

Ryder kissed her on the lips. "Take a shower and get dressed. Stay in your room, until I know who it is."

"What about you?"

"Don't worry, I can get ready in less than three minutes, and that includes a shower." He grabbed his clothes and shoes from the floor and rushed to the door. He opened it quietly, then listened, before leaving the room and closing the door behind him.

Scarlet jumped out of bed the moment he was gone, then raced to the door and locked it. If Derek was back, she didn't want him to be able to barge into her room. She equally dreaded seeing Claudia. By now Derek had probably told her that Ryder had beaten him up and had the evidence to back it up: a bloodied nose and probably other bruises too.

On her way to the bathroom, Scarlet glanced at the clock. It was shortly before eleven o'clock. She had to do a double-take, but she'd read the time correctly. She and Ryder had slept for far too long. She would have to use her trusted excuse that she'd studied all night to explain why she'd overslept.

She jumped into the shower, and allowed the warm water to caress her skin reminding her of how Ryder had touched her and made her feel loved and wanted.

~ ~ ~

Ryder chucked a bottle of blood, which he'd kept in a small thermos in his overnight bag, before taking a thirty-second shower. Three minutes after hearing the garage door for the first time, he walked down the stairs into the foyer, fully dressed and looking impeccable, expecting to see Scarlet's stepmother. Instead, a man was walking down the corridor toward the kitchen. Or rather, he limped slightly. A small suitcase stood in the foyer.

"Scarlet? Honey, are you home?" he called out.

Ryder cleared his throat, making the man pivot. He looked younger than he was, despite the gray at his temples. He was handsome and fairly slim. Ryder could guess who this was. "You must be Mr. King."

Brandon King nodded and walked toward him.

"I'm Ryder Giles, your daughter's bodyguard. Are you all right, sir?" he asked pointing to King's ankle, which he now saw had a bandage around it.

"Slipped in the bathroom a few days ago," he said.

"Sorry to hear that. Pleased to meet you, sir." Ryder extended his hand in greeting, and King shook it.

"I wish I could say I'm pleased to meet you too," King said. "Where's Scarlet?"

"Upstairs. I believe she's studying."

"Good." He motioned to the living room. "You and I need to have a word."

In the living room, King turned to him, his expression stern. "I've been made aware of your behavior."

Shit! Had somebody seen him and Scarlet together? Impossible. "Sir?"

"My wife's nephew made a complaint about you. You assaulted him. In my house, and without provocation! I can't tolerate somebody like you in my—"

"Without provocation? There was plenty of provocation!" Ryder growled.

"Then you don't deny that you broke his nose."

"Is that all I broke? I rather hoped that he had more injuries after the thrashing I gave him."

"Mr. Giles! How dare you? You're lucky he's not pressing charges. But under these circumstances, I can't allow you to remain in charge of my daughter's security. Pack your things and leave!"

Ryder didn't move. "I can't do that, sir!"

"What the—"

"I was doing my job, sir, protecting your daughter. Had I not interfered, he would have raped Scarlet! Right here, in this room."

Stunned, King stared at him. "That's… that can't be. Claudia told me herself that Derek and Scarlet went on a date and that my daughter flirted with him."

"Oh, yeah? And in which book does it say it's okay to rape a woman if she flirted with the guy before?" Furious now, Ryder took a step toward King.

"There must have been a misunderstanding," King claimed.

"Scarlet said *no*. I don't know how you interpret that word, Mr. King, but in my book, *no* is *no*. It's immaterial if your daughter flirted or not. He put his hands on her despite her protests. I heard her scream from my post outside." While this wasn't technically true, because he'd entered the house for another reason, it was the gist of it.

King ran a hand through his hair clearly trying to digest the news. "You don't know my daughter the way I do."

Ryder doubted that, but he didn't interrupt.

"She's not stable…"

"What do you mean?" Ryder asked, surprised at the statement.

"Scarlet has episodes during which she doesn't know what she's doing. Maybe that should have been made clear to you before you got this assignment."

"Are you saying she's schizophrenic?" Ryder shook his head in disbelief. There was no way Scarlet wasn't of sound mind. There was nothing wrong with her, absolutely nothing. She was perfect in every way. "Scarlet is as sane as you and I."

"I'm afraid she isn't. The doctors have never been able to diagnose her, but just because there's no label for it, doesn't mean that she's not sick. She is." King looked to the picture of a woman on the mantlepiece, then back to Ryder. "Just like her mother. She too had these episodes where she would get violent and unpredictable. So, Mr. Giles, perhaps you saw what you saw, Derek putting his hands on her, but he may have simply tried to defend himself during one of her episodes. It's not the first time that she's acted hysterical. And my wife assures me that Derek is a gentle young man who would never—"

"You believe your wife and her nephew rather than your daughter?" Ryder was outraged. "Your daughter needs our protection. Derek made threats toward her. I was there. I saw what he did. Your wife wasn't even in the house! She gave me the night off, making me believe she would be staying here in the house to watch over Scarlet."

King let out a harsh breath. "How dare you speak about my wife like that! She cares for my daughter. She's been by Scarlet's side for the last six years, helping her through these episodes, despite Scarlet's emotional outbreaks. Mr. Giles, my daughter is sick and at risk of hurting herself and others. Her episodes are getting worse every month, and it was a mistake to even let her live on her own here. That's gonna change. Immediately! Scarlet's mental health is clearly taking a turn for the worse. She needs professional help, and not a bodyguard who feeds into her delusions."

"Delusions?"

Ryder spun around to see Scarlet at the door to the living room, staring at her father. Her hair was in a strict ponytail again, and she wore a pair of jeans and a casual shirt. Disappointment and rage were brimming in her eyes.

"How could you, Dad? How could you tell him?" Scarlet's voice cracked.

Ryder would have loved nothing more than to put his arms around Scarlet and console her. But he couldn't, not in front of her father.

"Mr. Giles, leave us. And while you're at it, pack your things and leave my house. We won't need your services anymore. Scarlet will return to Palo Alto with me."

Without a word, Ryder walked toward the door, where Scarlet still stood frozen. He met her eyes, wanting to convey a silent promise that he wouldn't give up on her. But there was so much pain and anger in her eyes that he wasn't sure she even saw him.

Walking past her, Ryder whispered low only for Scarlet to hear, "I won't leave you." Slowly he turned to the stairs and walked up to the second floor.

21

Scarlet had listened to the voices coming from downstairs and recognized her father's. And by the sound of it, neither Claudia nor Derek were with him. She was surprised that he was here, since Claudia had told her that he had an important business meeting in Phoenix this morning. It was the reason Claudia had had to return to Palo Alto the previous night to get him a document he needed. Curious why her father was suddenly showing up in San Francisco, Scarlet had quietly made her way downstairs.

She hadn't had any intention of listening in on her father's conversation with Ryder, but when she'd heard her father tell Ryder that she was mentally ill, she'd frozen in shock. Every word out of her father's mouth had been another slap in the face. He was making her sound like a lunatic. And not only that. He wanted to take her back to Palo Alto to live with him and Claudia, robbing her of her freedom. And of Ryder, whom he'd fired unceremoniously.

"I'm not mentally ill!" she cried out, glaring at her father. Her hands balled into fists. "How could you lie to Ryder like that? How could you embarrass me like that?"

"Scarlet, honey, it's for your own good. You need help."

Her father made a few steps toward her, and she noticed that he favored his right leg, a bandage peeking out from underneath his pants. His sprained ankle had still not healed, but she was too angry to ask about his wellbeing right now.

Scarlet moved her gaze back to his face. "What I need is to be allowed to live my life without interference."

"We've tried that, Scarlet," her father said. "But it's obviously not working. Your behavior toward Derek is inexcusable. And as a result, your bodyguard hurt him. Is that really what you want?"

"My behavior toward Derek?" She almost yelled the words, but she didn't care that she sounded like a fury. "He attacked me! He didn't want to take no for an answer. He almost raped me."

"You're hysterical, Scarlet, calm down."

"Calm down? You believe Derek over me? Ryder was there. He saw what Derek tried to do!"

Her father sighed. "Please, honey, it's time you face the facts. I've let you get away with too much ever since your mother died. Because I love you. But that approach didn't work. It's my fault. I should have been firmer with you, and gotten you help earlier."

"I don't need help! I need to live my life the way I decide. I'm an adult."

"You're not behaving like one. You're throwing another one of your tantrums. Claudia was right. You're not well. Your condition is getting worse. I didn't want to see it, but—"

"My condition?" She huffed angrily. "I have PMS, but since you're a man, you clearly don't understand what that means. I'm not the only woman who has to deal with it. And it doesn't make me mentally ill!"

Her heart thundered, the sound so loud, it echoed in her ears.

"It's more than just PMS," her father claimed.

"What? Are you a doctor now? You forget that I'm the one studying psychology, not you. And trust me, I don't have a mental disorder. I have a physical issue. That's all it is. P. M. fucking S."

"Don't you take that tone with me! I'm still your father!" His face turned red with anger.

"Then act like it! Trust me instead of a jerk who tried to rape me!"

"Don't be so dramatic. Derek didn't try to rape you. You were having one of your episodes, and were coming on to him. And just because you regret it now, doesn't mean you can besmirch a young man's reputation by claiming he wanted to rape you. You'll apologize to him, and to Claudia!"

"I won't! And you can't make me!"

"Goddamn it! You're just like your mother. You're showing the same symptoms as her. I hoped for so long that you didn't suffer from the same ailment, but I can't turn a blind eye to it any longer, or you'll end up like your mother!"

"What? End up how? I don't have a heart condition! So leave Mom out of this. This isn't about Mom. It's about you! You not believing in me. You throttling me with your protectiveness! I can't breathe! Don't you understand that? You're suffocating me."

Her father clenched his jaw. "I'm doing it for your protection."

"That's not protection!" she cried out. "That's control!"

"You need a firm hand. I made a mistake with your mother. I let her get away with everything, and it only got worse. I saw it coming, just like I see it in you now. I know how this will end."

"Now who's being dramatic? I can take care of myself."

Furious, her father gripped her biceps. "No, you can't. Just like your mother couldn't. And now she's gone."

"Because she had a heart attack! There's nothing wrong with my heart," Scarlet protested while she tried to free herself from her father's grip.

"Damn it, Scarlet! She didn't die of a heart attack. She killed herself!"

Stunned disbelief paralyzed her.

"And you're showing all the signs that you'll do the same thing. And I can't lose you too. Not after losing her and then Joshua."

Her pulse pounding in her veins, her breath trapped in her lungs, Scarlet felt as if she stood outside of her body, watching herself and her father. As if this was a nightmare, not reality.

"No," she pressed out on a tiny breath. It couldn't be true. "She died of a sudden heart attack." She looked in her father's face, and saw the truth there as clearly as if it had been written in ink. "Why?"

Her father let go of Scarlet's arm. "She had one of her episodes. She was delirious. I don't think she even knew what she was doing."

But Scarlet barely heard the words. Her mother had left her voluntarily. She'd killed herself not caring what it would do to her daughter. But that wasn't all.

"You lied to me. You lied to me all my life. How could you?" Tears welled up in her eyes, and she tried to push them back down.

"All I wanted was to protect you. So you wouldn't meet your mother's fate."

Scarlet shook her head. Her father believed her to be crazy and a suicide risk. "If you'd ever bothered to talk to me about all this, you would have realized that I'm not like that at all. I'm not crazy, and I would never dream of taking my own life." She tipped her chin up in defiance. "But you never even tried to understand me."

"Please, Scarlet. You need help, before it's too late," he pleaded.

"I don't need your help." She turned on her heel and marched out into the hallway.

At the stairs, she stopped for a long second. But she couldn't set a foot on the stairs. It would mean defeat, giving in to her father's wishes, and accepting that he was right in his assumptions, when she knew he was wrong. If she wanted a life of her own, one in which she made her own decisions, no matter the consequences, then she couldn't stay here. She turned and directed her gaze to the entrance door. Her mind was made up.

She bridged the distance to the door with a few steps, and opened it. Without looking back, she stepped outside and ran. Tears were now streaming down her cheeks, but she didn't care if anybody saw her crying. She just had to get away. She felt betrayed by her father as well as her mother. Scarlet had only been fourteen when her mother had committed suicide. Soon after that, her episodes had started. And now her father claimed that the unexplained symptoms Scarlet suffered from were the reason her mother had killed herself? She didn't want to believe it. Instead, she channeled all her anger and disappointment toward her father. Not only had he lied to her about her mother's death, he believed Derek's version of the events of the previous night instead of hers.

And Ryder? What if he wanted nothing to do with her now that her father had told him that she was mentally ill? That she was crazy? And her father firing him now gave him the perfect reason to never have to see her again.

Never in her life had she felt so alone as in this moment. Had her mother felt like this too, before she'd chosen the easy way out by ending her life? Had her father betrayed her too by not listening to her, simply assuming that her ailment was mental not physical? Was there nobody her mother could have turned to for help? Nobody who would have understood what she was going through?

"Scarlet! Come back!" her father called out after her, but she didn't look back. She knew he wouldn't be able to catch up with her, not with his injured ankle.

22

Ryder collected his toiletries from the ensuite guest bathroom, then tossed them into his overnight bag together with the few clothes and the book he'd brought. He was still fuming, still enraged about the way Brandon King had spoken about his daughter. Scarlet had been assaulted, and her father made excuses for the would-be rapist, claiming that it was all Scarlet's fault? What kind of father did that? This would have never happened in the Giles family. His parents and siblings would always have his back, and so would everybody at Scanguards, no matter the minor rivalries that existed among the hybrids and some of the more seasoned vampires.

Ryder didn't care that King had dressed him down and fired him. It wouldn't stop him from looking out for Scarlet. She was his mate, and nothing would change that. He would protect her, and when she was ready, he would make her his. And Brandon King couldn't do anything about it.

With a look toward Scarlet's room, Ryder walked to the stairs, when he heard the front door being slammed.

"Mr. Giles? Ryder?" King called out.

Ryder hurried down the stairs and found King looking distraught and breathing hard. Sweat was on his brow, and he used the banister as support.

"What is it?"

"I need your help."

"You just fired me. And after the way you treated your daughter, I'm not—"

"Scarlet's gone. We argued, and she ran off. I couldn't run after her." He motioned to his ankle.

"Fuck!" Ryder cursed and dropped his bag, already charging toward the door.

"Find her, please!" King begged.

Ryder didn't bother replying. From the raised entry level of the house, he looked up and down the street, but he couldn't see Scarlet anywhere. She'd probably already turned a corner. He picked up her scent, but was unable to figure out from where it came. The wind was dispersing it into different directions.

"Fuck!"

He pulled his phone out of his pocket, and clicked on the app to trace the location of Scarlet's cell phone. When the dot appeared on the display, he breathed a sigh of relief. She hadn't left her cell phone at home. But she was already farther away than he'd expected. He raced to his car on the other side of the street and jumped inside, but a traffic light changing at that moment sent a whole bunch of cars down the street, preventing him from pulling out of his parking spot.

"Move, for fuck's sake!" Ryder yelled, frustrated.

Finally, there was a gap in the traffic, and he charged out, engine revving. He made a U-turn, tires burning on the asphalt, the SUV swerving, and kicked the gas pedal down. One eye on the traffic, one eye on the dot on his cell phone, he took the next turn barely slowing down. A few more blocks, and he would be able to see her.

At the next intersection, he raced through it when the light was already turning red again. One driver honked angrily, but Ryder ignored him and made an illegal left turn at the end of the block. That's when he saw her. Scarlet was running down the narrow street not looking right or left. Ryder shot past her with the car, screeched to a halt a few yards ahead of her and jumped out of the SUV.

He almost collided with her a moment later. He wrapped his arms around her, but Scarlet hammered her fists against him, not even looking at him.

"Scarlet! I'm here now. Scarlet."

She finally lifted her eyes, the skin around them puffy and red and still wet from her tears. "Ryder."

She stopped fighting against him, and he just held her. "I've got you, baby, you're with me now."

"I won't go home," Scarlet said with a determined look.

"You don't have to, I promise." He tipped his chin in the direction of the car. "Please get in my car, so I don't block traffic, and then we can talk, okay?"

"Okay."

Ryder led her to the passenger side and helped her inside. Behind him, another car was already honking at him. Ryder made a sign to apologize, and hopped in on the driver's side. Moments later, he drove off.

He glanced at Scarlet, who sat there and stared at her hands in her lap. Ryder reached over and squeezed them, and she jolted. Their eyes met, and he let go of her hands.

"I'm sorry," she murmured.

"There's nothing to be sorry about," he assured her. "Let's get you somewhere safe."

"My father... he thinks I made it all up... he believes that Derek never tried to rape me... and what he said about me... about me being mentally ill—"

"It's not true," Ryder interrupted. "You don't suffer from any mental disorder. I can assure you. So don't even think about that. And we both know what Derek did. I was there. I should have known that he would poison your father against you."

"Thank you... thank you for believing me. I wouldn't know what to do if you sided with my father..." She reached for his hand, and he took it, and held it.

"I'll always believe you," he promised, before he stopped the SUV and switched off the engine.

"Where are we?"

"This is where I live."

He parked in the driveway, blocking access to the garage. As a rule, his parents' cars were parked in the garage underneath the house, so that they could get into their cars via the house and never be exposed to sunlight. He and his siblings had to park outside, either in the driveway, or on the street. The fact that neither Nessie's nor Ethan's car was parked in the driveway, told him that his siblings weren't home. And his parents would be sleeping. Nobody would disturb Scarlet and him.

"Come," he said, and they got out of the car.

Ryder took Scarlet's hand to lead her up the stairs to the front door, unlocked it, and ushered her inside. It was quiet in the house just as he'd expected.

They walked past the open plan living and dining area that led to the kitchen. Beyond it was a small office, as well as a powder room. At the back of the house a door led downstairs into the garage, and a small workout room that used to be his mother's clinic before Scanguards had installed a mini medical center for her at headquarters.

"Do you want something to drink or to eat?" Ryder asked.

She shook her head.

"Okay," he said softly, "let's go to my room. Nobody will disturb us there."

On the second floor, Ryder turned toward the back of the house. He opened the door to his room, and ushered Scarlet inside, while he listened for any sounds from the third floor. He heard none. His parents were sleeping. He entered his room behind Scarlet, then closed the door quietly. For the first time in years, he locked the door. It was one thing for his siblings to walk in on him constantly, it was another to subject Scarlet to the same breach of privacy.

"You have a lot of space here. Even a living area," Scarlet said and pointed to the comfortable couch.

"We all have similar rooms. That was the deal with my parents for me and my siblings to agree to keep living at home."

He led her to the couch, and she sat down. Ryder took a seat next to her and held her hand. "I understand that you're upset about your father believing Derek and not you. I tried to make him see reason, but whatever Derek and Claudia said to him convinced your father that Derek told the truth."

Scarlet sniffled. "And that's not even the worst." Her hand trembled.

"We both know you're not mentally ill. You're perfect."

She lifted her head and gave him a brief smile. "I wish I could be as certain as you. But after what my father told me today, I don't know."

There was a resignation in her voice that Ryder didn't like. "Don't listen to him about that. He's wrong."

"But what if he's not? What if he's right and I'm like my mother? What if I'm crazy like her, and will commit suicide too?"

Ryder's heart stopped for a second. "What? You told me that your mother died of a heart attack."

Scarlet nodded. "That's what I believed until today when Dad told me the truth. That she killed herself because she was crazy." Tears ran down her cheeks.

Ryder pulled her into his arms, and rocked her softly. "Scarlet, I'm so sorry."

"He lied to me all these years. And Mom, she just left me by killing herself as if she never even loved me."

He pulled her into his lap, holding her tightly, and allowed her to cry for as long as she needed to, while his heart ached for her. To believe that her own mother didn't love her enough to want to stay alive, was heartbreaking. And for her father to claim that Scarlet was heading toward the same fate, wasn't just irresponsible, but cruel.

Now Ryder understood why Scarlet had run away, and why she didn't want to return home. He wouldn't force her to, but he had to inform her father that he'd found her and that she was safe—without disclosing where she was.

"I have to call your father," Ryder said.

Scarlet lifted her head. "Please don't make me go back there."

"I won't. And I won't tell him where you are, just that you're safe. I know you might think that he doesn't deserve to know that you're all right, but he's still your father, and despite everything that passed between you today, he loves you. Okay?" He pulled his cell phone from his pocket.

Scarlet nodded.

"I'll put it on speaker."

"I don't want to talk to him."

"I know, and right now, you shouldn't. But I want you to hear what he says. Okay? Just keep quiet so he won't know that you're listening in."

A moment later, the call connected.

"Ryder?" King asked in a rushed tone. "Have you found her?"

"Yes, sir. She's safe."

"Oh God, thank you. Bring her back, and we'll talk."

"I'm afraid I can't do that, sir."

"But—"

"Scarlet doesn't want to see you right now. She needs time to process what happened."

"Uhm—"

But Ryder interrupted him again. "I'll keep her at a safe place. I guarantee you that. But she needs time away from you and the rest of your family."

After a long audible exhale, King replied, "Fine. As long as she's safe. I'll return to Palo Alto later today. I've got work to do. But Claudia has some meetings in the city this week, so she'll stay at the house for a couple of nights."

"And Derek?" Ryder asked.

"I can't just tell him… I mean…"

Ryder noticed how Scarlet pressed her lips together, disappointment and anger rising again.

"As long as Derek is here, Scarlet won't feel safe," Ryder said firmly. "Particularly not in her own home. If he doesn't leave San Francisco, I can guarantee you that your daughter won't come home."

"Fine. I'll talk to Claudia so he'll cut his visit short."

"I'll be in touch," Ryder said curtly, then disconnected the call.

"Thank you," Scarlet said.

Ryder leaned in and kissed her gently on the cheek when he noticed how hot her skin was. He touched her cheeks and forehead with the back of his hand. "You're burning up."

"I'm fine."

"I'll get my mother. She's a physician. She can check you out."

"No!" Scarlet shot up from his lap. "I'm not sick! I wish everybody would just stop treating me like an invalid!"

"I'm not. I'm concerned, because you seem to be running a fever. Mom can give you something for it."

"It won't work," Scarlet said.

"But—"

"There's only one thing that works."

"Tell me, and I'll get it for you."

She hesitated.

"Please, Scarlet, what can I do?"

"Have sex with me."

23

"You wanna have sex?" Ryder asked, stunned. He'd expected Scarlet to say she needed to drink something cold, or rest, but not sex.

"Please don't say no…"

Involuntarily he smiled. "I love the way you pout…" He kissed her gently.

"I don't pout."

"Yes, you do. And it's incredibly sexy. How could I ever say no to you?"

He pulled her head to his and slanted his mouth over hers, kissing her. Scarlet instantly put her arms around him, shifting and wiggling on his lap until she was straddling him. With surprising strength, she pressed him back to lean against the sofa's backrest. Ryder gripped her hips and jerked her pelvis toward his so her pussy aligned with his cocks.

Even through her jeans and his pants, Ryder felt Scarlet's heat and wetness. The aroma of her arousal rose into his nostrils, making him even harder than he already was. And another scent drifted to him: the sweet scent of her blood. It made his fangs itch with the need to descend and taste her. But he resisted this urge, knowing that he couldn't allow himself to give in to his need, when Scarlet wasn't ready for it.

One step at a time, he cautioned himself.

Scarlet's kiss was different this time, more heated, more intense. Hungrier. He welcomed her passion that matched his own. With eager hands she tugged at his shirt, pushing it up, so she could put her hands on his naked skin. Her touch was scorching like lava, her hands hot like a blacksmith's iron, stoking the fire inside him higher, sending flames through his body.

For a brief moment, he released her lips, and pulled his shirt over his head. Scarlet let out a moan, before she dipped her face to his neck and kissed him where his carotid artery pulsed. He knew then with absolute certainty that a blood-bond with her was inevitable. He wanted her to drink his blood so they became one.

Breathing raggedly, Ryder grabbed the seam of her T-shirt and ripped it down the middle. Scarlet yelped in surprise and reared back, but there was no admonishment in her gaze. Instead, she hurriedly freed her arms from the ripped shirt, and thrust her naked breasts toward him.

"Fuck!" he cursed and brought his lips to her bosom, covering her supple flesh with kisses. He held on to her waist, and Scarlet arched back, her pussy grinding against his cocks, and her breasts offered like a sacrifice. He took what she gave him so willingly, using his hands to draw her closer to his groin, while he captured one breast with his mouth, licking over her hard nipple until her gasps and moans drowned out the world around him.

"Ryder," she begged, "please fuck me."

He lifted his head from her breasts, and looked at her. The desire he saw in her beautiful blue eyes made his cocks twitch in anticipation of what was to come.

"With both my cocks this time?" he asked, though he already knew the answer. But he wanted to hear her say it.

A flicker of excitement flashed in Scarlet's eyes, and her heart now beat so loudly, his vampire senses had no trouble picking up the thrilled drumming of her pulse.

"Yes, I want both of them."

He needed no further confirmation. "Then that's what you'll get. Inch-by-rock-hard-inch."

The thought alone nearly brought him to a climax. Fuck!

With Scarlet still straddling him, he rose, holding her tightly, and carried her to his bed. There, he placed her on the duvet. Her hands were already on the button of her jeans, but he swatted them away.

"I need to do that," he said harshly, the need to be in control even stronger now.

She let herself fall back, and Ryder stripped her of her jeans and shoes in one fell swoop. Then, slower this time, he pulled her panties down her legs, and freed her of them too. He raked a long look over her naked body. Her skin was flushed.

"Now you," she demanded.

He took off his pants, and shoes, not forgetting his socks this time, before he hooked his thumbs into the waistband of his boxer briefs and freed his eager cocks. Released from their prison, they jutted out, hard and heavy, the blood inside them turning them almost purple in color, veins snaking around the shafts like vines.

Scarlet licked her lips, her eyes focused on his twin erections. "Don't make me wait," she murmured.

"I won't," he said, just as eager as she. "Give me a second." He marched into his bathroom, opened the drawers of his vanity and removed the tube of lubricant. Moments later, he was back in his bedroom. At the foot of his bed, he stopped.

"On your hands and knees, baby," he demanded. A shiver of excitement went through his body when she eagerly complied with his wish.

"Like this?" she asked, her voice teasing now, her heart-shaped ass pointed at him without inhibition.

His breath was choppy now, his balls pulling up tightly, the tips of his cocks already oozing pre-cum. "Yes, just like that."

He unscrewed the tube of lubricant and pressed a dollop on his right hand. First, he lubricated his upper cock with it, until every inch of it was covered, the action making him harder, if that was even possible. Then he took a second dollop and brought his hand to her ass and slid it along her crack until he reached the puckered hole.

Scarlet gasped at the contact, but didn't shy away. Slowly, he rimmed the tight ring with his wet fingers, gently testing Scarlet's readiness to allow him inside. He slowly eased the tip of his finger past the gate, the lubricant making the entry smooth.

"You okay?" he rasped.

"Yes," she said on a moan. "Give me more."

Without hesitation, he complied with her demand and drove his finger into her, until it could go no farther. Then he withdrew just as slowly, and added more lubricant to his finger, before repeating the same action. He wanted to make sure that she wouldn't feel any pain when he thrust his cock into her anus, aware that this would be her first time.

On the next descent of his finger, Scarlet pushed against him, making his finger slide into her harder and faster. A loud moan dislodged from her throat. "Oh God, yes!"

With his other hand, he found her pussy. He rubbed a finger along her cleft and found it drenched in her juices. She was ready for him. Eager to take her with both his cocks, Ryder used his hands to position his two hard-ons, the lower one at the entrance to her pussy, the upper and slightly smaller one at her virgin hole. He put his hands on her hips and held on to them tightly, immobilizing her so he could control the tempo and the intensity of his first thrust.

Ryder's heart thundered as his twin erections slid into their respective caves as if gliding into custom-made sheaths. Tight muscles clamped down on them, imprisoning them in their warm depths. Buried in Scarlet's hot body, Ryder shut his eyes and clenched his jaw, the pressure around his cocks so intense, he feared he would come instantly. The bliss of being encased in her silken depths was greater than he'd imagined, and he hadn't even moved yet.

"Christ!" he let out on a breath. "You're so tight."

Even her pussy felt tighter now than before, his second cock pressing against the membrane that separated the two hard-ons inside Scarlet's body. He didn't dare move, simply allowed Scarlet's body to adjust to the fullness.

"Are you okay?" he asked.

Scarlet let out a breath. "Oh my God."

"Am I hurting you?" he asked, worried that this was too much for her after all.

"No." She exhaled slowly. "It's good... your cocks... they fit perfectly..."

"As if they were made for you?"

She turned her head to look over her shoulder. Ryder saw a glint of desire flash in her eyes. "Would you do me a favor, Ryder?"

"Anything."

"Fuck me. Fuck me hard."

Her words sent a jolt through his body. "Hard?"

"Yes. I need it," she murmured. "Fuck me as hard as you can. And even once I come, don't stop. Just keep fucking me for as long as you can."

Ryder couldn't believe he heard right, but there was no doubt about it. Scarlet wanted him to take her hard even though this was her first time with two cocks inside her. How had he gotten so lucky?

"Do it!" she demanded.

He withdrew from her sheaths until only the two bulbous heads were still inside her, before he thrust back into her. A moan ripped from her lips and bounced off the walls of his bedroom. He gripped her hips tightly, making sure his thrusts didn't catapult her against the headboard, while he continued standing behind her, his feet firmly planted on the floor, his hips thrusting back and forth.

The feeling of both his cocks plunging into Scarlet's body, making her moan and writhe with each movement, was intoxicating. Every time he thrust forward, Scarlet pushed her ass back toward him, doubling the impact of their bodies slamming together. He tried to restrain himself from using too much force, worried about hurting her, but in light of Scarlet's own actions, he was unable to hold back. He was fucking her harder than he'd ever fucked any vampire female, and he did it with two cocks. Yet Scarlet showed no signs of pain or discomfort, but continued demanding he plunge his twin erections into her with full force.

Beneath him, Scarlet suddenly shuddered, and he felt the ripples of her orgasm race through her body, her muscles spasming around his cocks. The sensation nearly robbed him of his self-control, but he wasn't going to disappoint Scarlet, and continued thrusting into her. His hard-ons complied with Scarlet's wish as if they knew what she wanted and needed. As if she commanded them. He didn't question it, didn't fight against it. Instead, he worked his hips, and allowed the two beasts inside him to take over.

The satyr in him relished the knowledge that his future mate welcomed his second cock wholeheartedly without inhibition or reservation. By taking her like this, his second cock deep inside her, the satyr claimed what was his, even if Scarlet didn't know it yet. But her body did. Her body knew that it belonged to him now. The way she welcomed him, the way she offered herself to him was how a satyr's mate reacted instinctively to her mate's lovemaking.

Ryder looked down to where his cocks plunged into Scarlet's beautiful body, when he felt her body spasm again. She was climaxing again.

"Fuck, baby! That feels so good." The ripples her orgasm sent through her body and engulfed his cocks made his heart skip a beat.

"More," she cried out. "Ryder, please, take me…"

"You're mine now," he vowed. "I'm never gonna let another man touch you." The possessiveness that took hold of him was new to him. But it felt right.

"Only you," she murmured, moaning again.

"You like to be fucked liked that, don't you?"

"Yes!"

"Tell me you love my cock in your ass," he demanded.

"I love it."

"Say it."

"I love your cock in my ass and the other one in my pussy."

Ryder continued thrusting hard and fast. Hearing her words sent his arousal into the stratosphere. He'd never been one for talking dirty during sex, but he needed to hear Scarlet affirming that she loved the way he fucked her. Everything male in him needed to hear her submitting to him in every way.

"Tell me, are you ever gonna let another man fuck you?"

"No!"

"Good! Cause I'll never allow it. From now on, I'm the only one who gets to give you this pleasure, the only one who'll make you come."

"Yes, you'll be the only one…" Her breath came in ragged pants now, her body perspiring, her pulse racing.

"Then say it, say what I want to hear. Say that you're mine." He abruptly stilled, his cocks halfway outside her body.

"I'm yours."

The last word had barely rolled over her lips, when he thrust back into her and let go of the leash with which he'd held himself in check. Two more thrusts, and he felt Scarlet orgasm a third time. This time, her climax ignited his cocks, and hot semen shot through them and exploded from their tips. His orgasm was so intense that he thought he'd expire right there. His knees buckled, and he collapsed on her. In the last moment, he braced himself and rolled them sideways on the bed, so they lay on their sides, spooning, his cocks still inside her.

He wrapped his arm around her, tucking her close to his chest, exhaling sharply. "Scarlet, baby, I've never felt like this. Never before."

"Not with any of the women you had before me?"

"I've never taken a woman like I took you. Never with my two cocks. This was a first for me too." And he was glad for it, glad for the fact that a satyr received his second cock only when he'd met his mate. Because the way they'd made love, the intimacy they were sharing was only meant for a couple destined to mate.

Scarlet looked over her shoulder and smiled. "I'm glad. I've never felt anything so… so satisfying."

He pressed a kiss on her lips. "Neither have I." He smiled at her. "You're beautiful in every way. Looking at you, watching my cocks thrust into you, I've never seen a more erotic sight. I wish you could have seen what I saw."

"Maybe you should take me in front of a mirror next time," she suggested. "That is, if you want to do it again."

"I'm floored," Ryder admitted. "I fucked you so hard that you'll probably be sore for days, and you're wondering if I want to do it again?" He took her chin between thumb and forefinger. "If it were up to me, we wouldn't be talking right now, but making love again. But it's not up to me. It's up to you."

A slow smile spread on her lips. "I noticed a large mirror on your closet door when we came in."

Ryder felt his heartbeat kick up. Was she serious?

"Maybe you want to bend me over that armchair over there so we can both see our reflection in the mirror? Unless you weren't serious when you said that it's up to me…"

"Oh, I was serious…" He kissed her hard and deep, before releasing her. "Now get that sweet ass of yours over there to the armchair, and bend over for me."

24

The sun was already low on the horizon when Scarlet opened her eyes. A look at the clock next to the bed confirmed that it was late afternoon. She'd dozed off after she and Ryder had made love a second time, and by the looks of it, Ryder was spent too. He lay on his stomach, his eyes closed, his face looking peaceful.

She felt better than she ever had. Making love to Ryder had given her a deep sense of belonging and satisfaction. Ryder was an amazing lover, wild, passionate, and skilled. And she had surprised herself by how uninhibited she'd been, spurring him on to take her without holding back. It had been liberating. She felt every cell of her body now as if she'd woken up from a long sleep like Sleeping Beauty.

And Sleeping Beauty was thirsty. Scarlet sat up and swung her legs out of bed. She didn't want to wake Ryder. Upon entering his room, she'd seen a small refrigerator next to the sofa. Maybe he kept water in there. She walked over to it and bent down. When she opened the mini-fridge, the door made a sound. She looked inside, but instead of bottles of water she only saw two bottles with red liquid. Tomato juice? Yuck. She caught a glimpse of the label. *AB+ provided by Scanguards* it said. She shook her head. Scanguards bottled tomato juice? Odd for a security company.

She had no choice but to go downstairs to the kitchen to get herself something to drink. Scarlet saw a bathrobe hanging over a chair and slipped into it. It was way too big, but it would do. When she opened the door and listened, she didn't hear anything. It appeared that Ryder's parents weren't home yet. Nobody would see her.

Barefoot, she walked downstairs, the old wooden staircase creaking under her feet. She went into the kitchen. It was modern, bright, and made for a large family. She could imagine how Ryder, his siblings, and his parents sat around the huge kitchen island, enjoying dinner together, talking and laughing, and sharing stories. She envied Ryder for his family.

Her own family had never been like that. Even before her death, her mother had often been absent, not physically, but emotionally and mentally. Scarlet finally understood why. Her mother had suffered from depression. Why else had she committed suicide?

Not wanting to take away from the happiness she felt with Ryder, she pushed the thoughts about her mother away. Instead, she walked to the large stainless-steel refrigerator, and opened it—apparently with a little too much force, because a bottle of white wine clanged against a shelf and fell toward her. Luckily, she caught it just before it could fall to the floor.

"Whoa!" she said under her breath.

That was lucky! Making a mess in her boyfriend's parents' house on her first visit wasn't the way to make a good impression. Boyfriend? She smiled to herself. Yes, this was not just casual sex. Not anymore. Particularly not after the things he'd said to her, words he'd asked her to repeat: that she was his, that he wouldn't allow any other man to touch her ever again. It was possessive, and didn't really match with her determination of being an independent woman, but she couldn't help it: when Ryder had said it, she'd felt a pleasant shiver race through her body. His possessiveness had aroused her. Nobody had ever desired her like this. She felt the same possessiveness in response. She didn't want Ryder to ever touch another woman.

Scarlet sighed contentedly and stared back into the refrigerator. In the door, she saw several small bottles of water. She snatched one, unscrewed the lid and led the bottle to her lips, while she closed the refrigerator door.

Scarlet choked on the water, and it spewed out of her mouth and onto the man who suddenly stood only a few feet away from her. He was a little taller and broader than Ryder, his shoulder-length dark-brown hair loose. She estimated his age somewhere in the mid-thirties. He wore only a pair of jeans, and was bare-chested. Water was currently dripping from said chest, water she'd spewed at him because he'd startled her. But she wasn't staring at his chest for long, because the scar on the left side of his face drew her attention to it. It reached from his eye down to his chin, and it looked as if it pulsed angrily.

Her heart was racing. Who was this man, and what was he doing here?

He let his eyes roam over her robe, then looked straight at her face. "I didn't realize Ryder brought a guest."

"Sorry, yes, Ryder invited me. I'm—"

"Scarlet King, I recognize you."

She raised her eyebrows.

"From your file at Scanguards. I should introduce myself. I'm Ryder's father, Gabriel Giles." He offered his hand. A smile suddenly lightened up his face and made him look more approachable.

She shook his hand, stunned. He looked at least fifteen years too young to have a son Ryder's age. "Mr. Giles, nice to meet you."

"Gabriel, please. I have the feeling we'll see you here quite frequently." His gaze drifted to the robe she wore.

It wasn't difficult to see what Ryder's father was thinking. He knew she'd just had sex with his son. His son who had two cocks. She felt heat rise into her cheeks. Embarrassment flooded her. Gabriel Giles might as well have walked in on Scarlet and Ryder having sex. She desperately searched for something to say, but her mind went blank.

"I didn't mean to make you feel uncomfortable. That wasn't my intention. I only meant to say that—"

"What my husband is trying to say is," a woman said, appearing from the hallway, "that Ryder is a lucky man to have found you."

The woman was beautiful with the figure of a model, and hair as black as a raven. She, too, looked like she was in her early thirties. She wore a red silk robe that reached to just above her knees.

"I'm Maya, Ryder's mom."

"Nice to meet you, Mrs. Giles," Scarlet said and shook her proffered hand.

"Call me Maya please."

"Thank you," Scarlet replied, "I'm sorry, uhm…" She pointed to the refrigerator. "I just wanted to get some water. I didn't realize you were home. And Ryder didn't mention—"

"Don't apologize," Maya said softly. "Of course, you can help yourself to anything in the fridge. But Ryder normally has better manners than to have you fend for yourself."

"It's not his fault. He's sleeping," Scarlet said.

"Not anymore," Gabriel said and turned toward the hallway, where at that moment, Ryder appeared, barefoot, and dressed in shorts.

"Are you giving Scarlet the third degree?" Ryder asked, though there was no malice in his voice. He looked relaxed and not at all embarrassed that everybody looked like they'd just gotten out of bed.

"I think your father startled her," Maya said, then she winked at Scarlet. "Don't let the scar fool you. He's like a teddy bear, big and soft."

Scarlet noticed the tender look Maya and Gabriel exchanged.

"Are you trying to ruin my hard-won reputation as a tough guy, woman?" Gabriel asked with a smirk at his wife.

"I wouldn't dare." Then she glanced at the window. "We'd better get showered and dressed. I have appointments in the clinic."

"You work at night?" Scarlet asked politely.

Maya nodded. "We both do."

"I'm sorry if I woke you with all the noise," Scarlet said.

"We were already awake," Maya said.

Then she turned to the hallway, and Gabriel followed her.

"Oh, Mom!" Ryder called out. "A favor." He followed her, and Scarlet heard him lower his voice and exchange a few words with her.

"No problem. Just come by HQ later," Maya replied to whatever Ryder had asked.

A moment later, Ryder appeared in the kitchen. He walked straight to Scarlet and drew her into his arms.

"You should have woken me. I could have gotten you something to drink."

"You looked exhausted."

Ryder chuckled. "Your fault." He kissed her softly. "I'm sure I can come up with a way for you to make it up to me." He ground his pelvis against her stomach.

"Shhhh! Your parents!" She motioned to the ceiling. "Why didn't you tell me that they were home? I thought we were alone in the house. They probably heard us having… making… I mean, you know…"

"God, you're adorable when you blush." He kissed her on the nose. "As for my parents hearing us having sex: serves them right. You know how many times my siblings and I had to listen to them making love? We made them move to the third floor because of it."

She couldn't suppress a chuckle. "Ryder! You're terrible."

"It was traumatizing when I was a teenager."

Scarlet shook her head trying very hard not to laugh. "They look so young. I can't believe they're your parents. I mean your mom can't be older than thirty. And your dad, he definitely looks way younger than forty."

Ryder shrugged. "Good genes." Then he changed the subject. "How about we shower, and then I'll make us dinner?"

"That sounds great. I'm famished."

"Me too."

He raked a hungry look over her that made her knees wobble.

"You're insatiable."

Ryder grinned. "Look at the pot calling the kettle black."

25

"That was delicious," Scarlet said and wiped her lips with a napkin. "Did your mother teach you how to cook?"

"I taught myself. My mother doesn't cook."

And why would she? She didn't eat. She only drank Gabriel's blood. And though his father also drank Maya's blood—most likely whenever they had sex, which was often—he had to drink human blood to sustain him. One day soon, Ryder would drink Scarlet's blood—and hers exclusively—once they were blood-bonded. The prospect of making Scarlet his made his heart beat excitedly. But there were still hurdles to jump over, before it could happen.

Ryder took the empty plates, walked around the kitchen island, and placed them in the sink to rinse them. They'd been sitting at the kitchen island, enjoying a leisurely meal alone. Neither Ethan nor Vanessa had returned home, and Gabriel and Maya had left a little earlier for work.

"I'm surprised your parents didn't stay for dinner. They missed out on the best pasta carbonara," Scarlet raved.

"It's actually breakfast for them," he deflected. "They normally eat at Scanguards. There's a lounge there with free food for all employees."

"Free? Wow, that's generous. And that would explain the tomato juice in your little fridge."

Ryder nearly dropped the plate in his hand. "Tomato juice?"

"Yeah. Sorry, I was looking for water, but you only had a couple of bottles of tomato juice in it, and I noticed that the label said it was bottled by Scanguards."

Ryder forced his heart to beat normally again. Luckily, Scarlet hadn't looked close enough at the bottles, or she would have realized that the liquid wasn't tomato juice but blood. Human blood.

"Sorry, I'll make sure to stock up on water for you," he said with a smile. "Can't get you all dehydrated with all the physical exertion I'm putting you through…"

Scarlet's cheeks turned a pretty pink. He walked around the island and stopped next to the barstool she sat on, turning it, so he could step between her legs and put his arms around her.

"Why are you blushing?"

She shrugged. "It's just… what we've been doing… I always thought it wasn't something a nice girl did… you know. Do you think I'm shameless?"

"Oh, for sure you are." When she gasped, he added, "I love shameless. I love that you have no inhibitions, and that you accept me the way I am. Do you regret having allowed me to take you with both my cocks?"

"No," she said without hesitation.

He smiled. "Then there's nothing to be ashamed of. All that matters is that you and I enjoy it. Nobody will judge you for it."

"It's just, your parents… you know, they obviously know that you have two cocks. I mean, you said you were born like that… so they probably know what we did… I want to make a good impression. I don't want them to think that I'm… uhm… you know… slutty."

Ryder put one hand under Scarlet's chin and tipped it up so she had to look at him. "Would it make you feel any better to know that I'm not the only one in this family who has two cocks?"

Her eyes widened. "Are you saying that your father…"

Ryder nodded. "And my brother. It's hereditary." Then he smiled. "So if you think you're slutty because you enjoy both my cocks inside you, then the same would go for my mother. You see, nobody in this family would ever judge you for enjoying what nature gave me. On the contrary. My parents are delighted that I found you, and that you didn't reject me for something that I had no say in."

Scarlet put her arms around him and brought her face within inches of his. "I love feeling both your cocks inside me at the same time. It makes me feel complete."

"That's what I like to hear, 'cause I can't think of anything more enjoyable than making love to you like that. The feeling of your muscles contracting around me when you come is better than everything I've ever experienced."

"You're making me hot, talking like that," she said, her breath suddenly hitching.

"Good, 'cause you make me so fucking horny that I want to bend you over right here, right now, and fuck you until neither of us can move another limb."

He pressed his lips to her and kissed her passionately, his hands already on the T-shirt he'd taken from Vanessa's closet since he'd ripped hers earlier.

His cell phone rang. He recognized the ringtone as that assigned to his sister's number, and ripped his lips from Scarlet's. "Damn it, that's Nessie. I've gotta take this."

He answered the call and pressed the cell phone to his ear. "Yeah?"

"I need your help. There's been an attack."

Alarmed, he asked, "Are you all right?"

"I'm fine, but somebody else wasn't as lucky. A girl is badly wounded. She was attacked by a vampire. He fled when he saw me."

"Shit! One of ours?"

"No. Never seen him before."

"Did you call HQ?"

"I did. Nobody's close enough. I'm in the Marina. You're the closest."

"Send me your location."

"Thanks, Ryder."

He disconnected the call, and a moment later, his cell phone pinged. Vanessa had sent him her location.

"What's wrong?" Scarlet said, concern flickering in her eyes.

"Somebody was assaulted."

"Your sister? Oh my God!"

"She's fine, but I have to help the girl that's with her."

"Has she called 9-1-1?"

Ryder hesitated for an instant. Scarlet wouldn't understand why they couldn't just call an ambulance. A vampire attack had to be dealt with by

Scanguards directly. No outsider could find out what had really happened, or their secret would be exposed. It would create a widespread panic in the city.

"The girl is under Scanguards' protection. We can't involve the police or bring her to a hospital."

"But—"

"It's complicated. I will explain later." Once he'd come up with a believable cover story. "Let's go." He lifted Scarlet off the bar stool and set her on her feet.

"I'm coming with you?"

"Yeah. I'm still your bodyguard. I can't leave your side."

It was true, though there was very little chance that anybody would find her and harm her at his home. But she'd already found his stash of blood—although she'd mistaken it for tomato juice—and he couldn't afford for her to stumble upon anything else that she might find odd in his home. The tinted windows came to mind. All windows in the house were covered with a special film that filtered out the UV rays of the sun that would burn and ultimately kill a vampire. The invention enabled vampires to live virtually normal lives in their own homes.

"Okay," she agreed.

"Let me get you one of Nessie's jackets," Ryder said and went to the hall closet where he chose a jacket that would protect Scarlet from the cool San Francisco night air. "Here."

She slipped into it, and moments later, they left and hopped into Ryder's SUV. He'd already memorized Vanessa's location and was headed down one of the steepest streets in the city, Divisadero.

"So if you're not planning to bring the injured girl to a hospital, what are you gonna do?" Scarlet asked, casting him a sideways look.

"My mom will take care of her at Scanguards. I told you she's a doctor."

"A surgeon?"

He evaded the question. "She's treated all kinds of injuries in the last two decades: anything from gunshot wounds, to knife wounds, infections, and bite wounds."

"Bite wounds?"

"Yeah, from animals," he lied. The bite wounds had been inflicted by vampires.

"I'm amazed. I mean she's so young. Training as a doctor takes years. How did she even have time to have three children on top of going through medical training and gaining experience in trauma medicine?"

Scarlet was smart, and while he loved the fact that his future mate was intelligent and had a healthy dose of curiosity, it also meant Scarlet would soon figure out the truth about his family and Scanguards. He had to reveal his secrets very soon, before she stumbled on them by herself, but right now wasn't the right time. He hated having to lie to her, but he had no choice.

"She's a great multi-tasker," Ryder claimed. "And as I said, she's not as young as she looks."

"How old is she?"

He chuckled. "I can't tell you that." She'd been in her early thirties when she'd been attacked and turned into a vampire by her stalker, an incident which lay more than thirty years in the past.

"You don't know?" Scarlet asked, her forehead furrowing.

"Of course I know, but Mom is of the belief that no woman should ever have to reveal her true age." He shrugged. "Sorry."

"She's beautiful," Scarlet said.

Ryder looked at Scarlet for a moment, before turning his attention back to the road. "You're just as beautiful. If not more so. Especially with your hair loose like this."

She laughed softly, her long hair caressing her face. "A ponytail is practical."

"And the glasses you don't really need?"

"How do you know I don't need them?"

"Because you're not wearing them now, and you're not wearing contacts either. Let me guess: you want everybody to believe that you're a studious little mouse rather than the hotblooded vixen you really are."

"You think I'm a hotblooded vixen?"

He put his hand on her thigh. "Yes. But I'm okay with you hiding behind this librarian façade you've got going."

"Because having a vixen as your girlfriend would be embarrassing?"

He laughed. "Not in the least. But once my friends discover what you're hiding behind your demure front, I'm gonna have to beat them all off with a stick."

Scarlet reached over to him, and placed her hand on his crotch. The touch made him jerk the wheel for a second, before he got his composure back.

"They're not gonna have a chance," she murmured. "I've found what I want."

"These two cocks do come with an attachment," he said, "me. I hope that's not a problem."

"I wouldn't have it any other way."

He pressed his hand over hers, making sure she felt how his twin cocks were filling with blood, getting hard because of her touch.

Moments later, he turned into a small alley and stopped the car. "We're here."

26

Ryder parked the car in a dark alley behind a row of restaurants in the fashionable and expensive Marina district. When he hopped out of it, Scarlet followed him. Perhaps she could lend a hand. She walked around the SUV, and felt chilled all of a sudden. Despite the nice weather during the day, nights in San Francisco were always cool. She was glad that Ryder had given her a jacket to wear.

The moment Scarlet stepped around the SUV, she saw a young woman crouched down next to another woman. Even though there were no streetlights, light from the buildings backing up to the alley provided sufficient illumination for her to see that both women were covered in blood. Shock raced through her body.

"Nessie," Ryder called out and joined them.

"Thank God you're here," Vanessa said. "I can't stop the bleed. I've already given her my—" She stopped abruptly, her gaze landing on Scarlet.

Ryder looked over his shoulder. "Scarlet, please stay in the car."

"I can help." And by the looks of it, the injured woman needed all the help she could get.

"Is that her?" Vanessa asked her brother.

"Yes, that's Scarlet."

"You brought her? Are you insane?" Vanessa ground out under her breath, but Scarlet heard it nevertheless.

Ryder shot her a scolding look. "Nessie!"

Vanessa met Scarlet's eyes. "Nothing personal, Scarlet, but this is not for the faint of heart."

"If you can handle it, so can I," Scarlet said. After all, Ryder's sister couldn't be any older than herself. And Scarlet had never been squeamish around blood.

The injured woman moaned in pain.

"We've got you, Lizzy," Vanessa said. "We'll take care of you."

Scarlet stepped closer, and watched as the two siblings put pressure on the woman's wounds and applied tourniquets with strips of ripped fabric. From what Scarlet could see in the dim light, she was bleeding profusely from her neck and her chest. Her hands, lying by her sides, were bloody too as if she'd fought with her attacker. Scarlet's eyes fell on the woman's clothes and shoes: a hyper-short skirt, high heels, and stockings. Her top, which was soaked in blood was low cut. She didn't want to judge, but if her clothes were anything to go by, then this woman was a prostitute.

Scarlet guessed that a potential customer had done this to her. A fucking psychopath! As part of her undergraduate degree, she'd studied the profiles of men who attacked prostitutes. Psychopaths who found pleasure in hurting women who were already down on their luck. Her heart went out to the girl.

"She needs an ER. Now, or she's gonna bleed out," Scarlet said, concerned. Nobody deserved that, no matter how they made their living.

"No," Ryder said firmly. Then he looked at his sister. "Did you call ahead?"

"Mom is waiting at HQ for us. She's prepping for surgery."

"Then let's get her in the car. You drive," Ryder said. "I'll stay in the back with her to keep pressure on her wounds."

Scarlet watched how Vanessa and Ryder carried the gravely injured woman to the car and put her on the back seat with her head on Ryder's lap, while he pressed his hand on Lizzy's neck wound.

Vanessa slammed the door shut, then nodded to Scarlet. "Let's go."

The moment Scarlet sat in the passenger seat and closed the car door, Vanessa was already stepping on the gas. Scarlet didn't even have time to put her seatbelt on. Vanessa was driving just as fast as Ryder had on the way here. At the next intersection the signal was turning red, but Vanessa didn't slow down. Instead she hit a button on the dashboard, and a police siren sounded, accompanied by flashing blue and red lights. Scarlet was stunned by it. She'd had no idea that Ryder's car practically turned in to a police cruiser.

"Nessie!" Ryder called out from the back seat. "Don't drive like an old lady. Step on it!"

Finally, Scarlet managed to click the seatbelt in. Just in time, because now Vanessa raced through the streets, dodging obstacles with such skill that Scarlet wondered if Vanessa was a professional race car driver. Vanessa's reaction speed was something Scarlet had never seen in anybody before.

Scarlet was glad to be strapped into the passenger seat now, or she would be in danger of flying through the windshield when Vanessa hit the brakes and then made a ninety-degree turn.

"How's she holding on?" Vanessa asked.

"Barely," Ryder said. "Her pulse is getting weaker. How much did you give her?"

"A couple of ounces," Vanessa replied with a quick sideways glance at Scarlet.

"She needs more," Ryder said.

"More of what?" Scarlet asked, looking over her shoulder.

"Keep your eyes on the road, Scarlet, please," Ryder ordered. "Help Vanessa navigate."

Even though Scarlet knew that Vanessa didn't need her help, she followed Ryder's command. He probably didn't want her to have to look at the terrible injuries for fear that she would get nauseous from the sight.

"Easy, Lizzy," Ryder now murmured in the backseat. "Don't try to speak."

"Two more minutes," Vanessa said.

They were already in the Mission. Scarlet knew that Scanguards' headquarters was located somewhere in this neighborhood, though she'd never been there herself.

Finally, Vanessa slowed the SUV sufficiently so she could turn into the entry of an underground garage. The tag reader which was probably attached somewhere to the front of the car, recognized the SUV, and the gate opened. Vanessa drove in, and Scarlet heard the gate come down behind them. In the large garage, Vanessa stopped on the first level right outside an elevator. In front of it, Maya, dressed in blue scrubs and a white doctor's coat, her hair in a bun, waited with a gurney, ready to receive her patient.

Vanessa jumped out of the SUV, while Maya already opened the door to the backseat.

"How's she doing?" Maya asked.

"Pulse is in the 50s, stabilizing. Pressure is still dropping. She lost a lot of blood," Ryder replied, sounding like an experienced EMT, even though he didn't have any instruments to help him determine Lizzy's blood pressure.

"Okay," Maya said. "Vanessa, help me get her on the gurney."

Scarlet hopped out of the SUV, and watched mother and daughter put Lizzy on the gurney, while Ryder continued to press down on her neck wound.

"Lizzy, I'm Maya," Maya said. "I'll take care of you. You're gonna be just fine."

Scarlet let out a breath, relieved that Maya felt confident.

Maya whirled her head toward her, noticing her only now. Then she looked at Ryder. "Scarlet shouldn't be here."

"Can't change that now," Ryder said, staring back at his mother.

"Fine. You know what to do."

Scarlet felt taken aback by Maya's frosty greeting. She swallowed hard. "I can wait in the car."

"No!" all three members of the Giles family said in unison, while they pushed the gurney into the large elevator.

"Come, Scarlet," Ryder said and motioned for her to step into the elevator next to him.

A second later, the doors closed, and the elevator descended. The ride was smooth and fast.

When the elevator stopped and the doors opened, they all hurried out, and ran down the long corridor, pushing the gurney. The double doors at the end of the corridor opened inward just before they reached them.

Scarlet followed them inside. The large room looked like a state-of-the-art emergency room with different treatment bays, crash carts, ventilators, imaging machines, and many other things that Scarlet didn't know the names of. Several people sat in a glass-enclosed waiting room, and one man lay on one of the beds, an IV in his arm, receiving a blood transfusion. There was only one other medical staff member, a woman in a nurse's uniform.

"The OR is prepped," the nurse said.

"Vanessa and Ryder, you're with me," Maya ordered. "Jenny, have Scarlet wait in waiting room H."

Then they disappeared through another set of double doors, and silence descended on the room.

Scarlet took a breath, trying to calm herself down. She hoped that Maya could save the young woman. Her eyes fell on the people in the waiting room. Several had blood on them, either on their clothing or their faces or hands. Scarlet guessed that they'd all been in an accident.

Jenny, who looked slightly older than Scarlet, smiled at her. "Well, Scarlet, let me show you to the waiting room. And I can get you something to drink or to eat while you wait."

"I don't need anything, but thanks."

"All right then," Jenny said. Instead of leading her to the glass-enclosed waiting room, Jenny opened the door to another corridor and motioned her to follow. At the first door on the left, she stopped, and opened it. It was a comfortable room with a large sitting area, a TV, and lots of magazines to read. It was empty. Scarlet entered.

"Make yourself at home. I'll let you know when they're coming out. And if you need anything, there's a call button." She pointed to a red button on the wall.

"Thank you."

Jenny left and pulled the door shut behind her. Scarlet was alone.

The events of the last hours replayed in her mind. She was sure that Maya was a capable doctor and would be able to help Lizzy, but Scarlet still couldn't figure out why Vanessa hadn't called an ambulance instead of calling Ryder and bringing the injured woman here. Something didn't add up. The woman had clearly been attacked by somebody. So why was Vanessa keeping this from the police? Did she know who'd attacked Lizzy, and wanted to protect that person?

27

Scarlet yawned and looked at her cell phone. She'd been waiting in this room for almost an hour. And she urgently needed to go to the bathroom. There had to be a restroom somewhere. She rose and opened the door to the hallway and stepped outside. On the way from the medical suite to this waiting room, she hadn't seen any signs for bathrooms, so she decided to head in the other direction, farther down the corridor. When it turned, she followed it, but none of the doors she encountered on the left or the right were bathrooms.

The corridor ended at a door. She pushed it open, and stepped through it. Behind it were stairs. Clearly, there were no bathrooms in this direction either. She should have asked Nurse Jenny to direct her to the restrooms. Scarlet pivoted to put her hand on the door handle, but there was none. The door couldn't be opened from this side, at least not without an access card. A card reader was affixed next to the door. Probably a security measure so nobody unauthorized could enter the medical floor from this staircase.

Scarlet had locked herself out.

"Crap!" she cursed.

Now she had no choice but to walk up a floor. To her relief, the door she reached was unlocked. Scarlet pushed it open and looked around. She was in another corridor and decided to try to find a bathroom to her right. She finally found a door with the sign of a woman on it, and opened it. The restroom was clean and large, with several stalls and multiple wash basins. She used one of the stalls, then washed her hands and dried them and checked her face in the mirror. Happy with her reflection, she turned around.

She almost collided with an older woman and froze, her heart pounding. "I'm sorry, ma'am!" Scarlet hadn't seen her when she'd looked in the mirror. She let out a breath, trying to calm herself.

"No problem." The woman looked her up and down. "Are you supposed to be on this floor?"

Scarlet sighed. "No, I think I got lost. I was in the medical center, and then I was looking for a restroom, and I locked myself out, and the only place I could go to was up a flight of stairs. Maybe you could help me find my way back?"

"Sure, just turn left out the door, take the second corridor to the right, and it'll lead you back to the elevator."

"Thank you, ma'am, I appreciate it."

Scarlet turned, and left the restroom. She followed the woman's instructions and made it back to the elevator. Relieved, she pressed the button, when she heard footsteps coming from behind her. She glanced over her shoulder.

Benjamin was walking toward her, his eyes narrowed. "What the hell?"

"Oh, hey, I got totally turned around. Can you help me get back to the medical center, please?"

He stopped in front of her, glaring at her. "Who the fuck are you? And what are you doing on a restricted access floor?"

"It's me, Scarlet. Why are you pretending not to know me?"

The elevator doors opened.

"Because I don't know you." He grabbed her arm and dragged her into the elevator with him, then pressed a button.

"Let go of me. Why are you such an asshole?" The few interactions she'd had with Benjamin when he'd guarded her house had always been pleasant. Clearly the guy was in a bad mood.

"Because we don't tolerate intruders. What are you trying to do here, huh? What's your plan?"

"I don't have a fucking plan! I was looking for a restroom!"

"Not a very original excuse. I've heard better ones."

She tried to free herself from his iron grip on her biceps. "Damn it, Benjamin! You're hurting me."

He stared at her, his expression changing. "Oh for fuck's sake! My brother let you in here? I'm not Benjamin, I'm Damian, his twin."

He finally let go of her arm. She rubbed it.

"I didn't know Benjamin had a twin." Benjamin had never mentioned it. Not that they'd exchanged much more than a few pleasantries.

"Yeah, well, he likes to pretend he's unique. He's not."

"Hmm. Are you always this unfriendly when somebody is asking for directions?"

"It's part of my job. You're not supposed to be on this floor."

"Duh! I told you I was looking for a restroom and got lost."

"Benjamin knows better than to let his girlfriends run loose at Scanguards."

"I didn't come with Benjamin." She grunted in frustration. "And I'm not his girlfriend."

The elevator pinged, and the doors parted.

"So you snuck in, just like I thought!" Damian growled.

The open doors suddenly revealed Grayson standing in front of the elevator, staring at her.

"Scarlet! What are you doing here?"

"Grayson," she said, surprised at seeing him.

"So you're not here for Benjamin? You were looking for Grayson?" Damian asked.

"No, I'm not!" Scarlet protested.

"Maybe next time," Damian said talking over her, addressing Grayson, "you'll tell your hum—"

"Zip it, Damian!" Grayson interrupted with a raised voice.

There was a moment's pause, where neither of the three said anything.

"And she's not my girlfriend, she's my charge. Or rather was. And she's not supposed to be here." Grayson looked directly at her. "So what the fuck are you up to this time? Who the fuck let you in here? And where is your visitor's badge?"

Grayson's bossy tone pissed her off. "Well if somebody would let me get a word in edgewise, then I could explain what happened!" She put her hands on her hips and glared at Grayson. "So am I allowed to talk now or not?"

From somewhere down the hallway somebody approached and chuckled. Scarlet turned her head to look. A young man who looked somehow familiar was watching them and grinned.

"Finally somebody who gives you lip. How refreshing!" the guy said.

"Shut it, Ethan!" Grayson growled.

"Ethan?" Scarlet repeated. "Are you Ethan Giles? Ryder's brother?"

"Yeah, that's me." He approached, looking curious now. "Have we met?"

No wonder he looked familiar. There was definitely a family resemblance.

"I'm… uhm… Ryder's girlfriend."

Ethan stared at her, mouth gaping open, eyes roaming over her as if she was a unicorn, or something else so rare he'd never seen it.

"Ryder is dating a client?" Grayson asked, sounding annoyed. "That's—"

"You're his girlfriend?" Ethan asked though it sounded more like a statement. "You're the one." Then he looked at Grayson and Damian. "She's the one."

Scarlet watched the three stare at her in silence. Now all three had the same look as Ethan had when she'd told him she was Ryder's girlfriend. "Did I do something wrong? I'm sorry for being on this floor if I shouldn't be on it, but I got lost when I was looking for a bathroom. I need to get back and find Ryder."

"Where did you last see Ryder?" Ethan asked.

"He was with your mother and your sister. We brought in an injured woman, and they all went into the OR."

"I'll take you down there," Ethan offered. "Before he goes berserk when he can't find you."

"Yeah, that would be ugly," Damian said with a nod. "And, Scarlet, maybe don't mention to him that I grabbed your arm, okay? I mean, no harm, no foul, right?"

"It's fine," she said, not really understanding why he made an issue out of this.

"No, really," Damian insisted.

"Come," Ethan said and led her into the elevator.

He swiped his ID over the card reader before pressing a button. When the doors finally closed, and the elevator descended, he smiled at her.

"So you're Scarlet."

"Is there something I'm missing? I mean, is it really that unusual that I'm dating your brother?"

"No, no, of course not. Though he's not had a lot of girlfriends. And certainly none like you."

She found his words odd, but didn't get a chance to reply, because the elevator had already stopped, and the doors were opening.

"Scarlet!" Ryder fairly jumped into the elevator and pulled her into his arms. "I looked everywhere for you. Thank God, you're okay." He kissed her as if they were alone, and not standing right next to Ethan.

"I got lost trying to find a bathroom. No big deal," she said, although she liked knowing that Ryder had been looking for her. And judging by the intensity of his kiss, he was relieved to have her back. "I ran into your brother."

"Thanks, bro," Ryder said and patted Ethan on the shoulder. "I owe you one."

"Wouldn't want to lose her now, would we?" Ethan said.

Scarlet stepped out of the elevator with Ryder's arm around her waist, while Ethan pushed the button for the doors to close.

"Thanks, Ethan!" she said before the elevator departed.

"I was worried when I couldn't find you," Ryder said.

"With so many bodyguards all in one spot, what could possibly have happened to me? I'm safe." She changed the subject. "How's the injured woman? Lizzy?"

"She's doing great. Mom is just doing the last sutures. She'll be done in a few minutes. We'll keep Lizzy here until she's fully recovered."

"I'm so glad. When I saw how much blood there was, I didn't think she'd make it," Scarlet said. "Your mother must be an amazing physician."

"She is."

"And I'm sorry that I made her angry."

Ryder furrowed his brow. "Angry? What do you mean?"

"When she met us in the garage. She didn't want me here."

"She wasn't angry at you. She was just surprised, and I guess a little worried that what you saw here would upset you."

"Are you sure? I mean, maybe it was a little much, you know, me sneaking around their house, practically half naked."

Ryder laughed softly. "You wore my robe, that's hardly half naked."

"Does nothing faze you?"

"Since you're bringing it up, there is something I'm a little worried about."

She knew it. She'd done something wrong.

"It's about what your father told me. That you're ill. That you have episodes of—"

"I don't wanna talk about it." So her father had managed to plant seeds of doubt in Ryder after all. She should have known this would happen.

"Scarlet, baby." He took both her hands and kissed her knuckles. "Whatever it is, it won't change how I feel about you. All I want is for my mother to ask you a few questions about your symptoms, and to draw some blood."

"But what would be the use in that? It's just really bad PMS. Lots of women have that. My mother had it."

"I don't want you to do anything you don't want to do, but my mother is a great doctor. She might be able to help you figure out why you go through this. Earlier today, before we had sex, your body was burning up. At least talk to her, tell her about your symptoms. I would never forgive myself if I didn't make sure you're all right."

His eyes were kind, and she saw affection shining from them. "All right, I'll talk to her."

"Thank you." He pressed his lips on hers and kissed her deeply, reigniting the flames of lust she'd felt when they'd made love earlier in the day.

When he released her lips, she said, "But afterwards, can we go back to your place?"

His eyes seemed to shimmer golden all of a sudden. "Are you tired?"

"No."

"Yeah, me neither."

"Good," she rasped, her heart beating violently. "'Cause I need to feel you again." She pressed her pelvis against him.

"Baby, I'm already hard. Let's get you to talk to Mom, so we can get outta here before I have to find us a broom closet."

"A broom closet sounds pretty good right now."

"Don't tempt me."

28

Ryder waited in the V Lounge until his mother was done talking to Scarlet and drawing her blood. No humans other than the blood-bonded mates of Scanguards personnel were allowed in the V lounge, which looked like a VIP lounge in a five-diamond hotel with comfortable seating areas, soft music, a bar, and a fireplace. There was a good reason why humans weren't allowed to enter: the lounge served human blood on tap. And Ryder needed it.

In the darkness on the backseat of his SUV, he'd given Lizzy some of his own blood, or she would have died on the way to Scanguards' headquarters. He'd been as clandestine about it as possible, making sure that Scarlet couldn't see what he was doing. When he'd returned from the OR and gone to fetch Scarlet from the waiting room reserved for humans, he'd feared the worst: that she'd seen a vampire and fled. It wasn't an unrealistic worry. After all, on the medical floor, it happened frequently that injured vampires would be in such a state that their fangs showed, and their eyes glowed red. It couldn't be avoided, particularly when a vampire was in pain, or hungry, or sometimes simply couldn't control his urges around human blood. And this wasn't how he wanted Scarlet to find out that vampires existed, and that he and his family weren't human.

While waiting for Scarlet, Ryder ordered a tall glass of AB positive blood from the tap and gulped it down, feeling his strength slowly return. He ordered another one, when the door opened, and Luther entered.

Luther was a big vampire, broad-shouldered, tall, with a commanding personality. He hadn't always been one of the good guys. Everybody at Scanguards knew his story. Over three decades ago, he'd made an attempt to kill Delilah and Nina, Samson's and Amaury's mates. For his crimes, he was sentenced to twenty years in the vampire prison in the foothills of the Sierra Nevada. Upon his release, he'd been instrumental in saving Isabelle, Samson and Delilah's daughter, from a vampire associated with the prison, and earned Samson's forgiveness. He'd joined Scanguards shortly after that, and was splitting his time between San Francisco and the vampire prison, where he worked as a security consultant.

"Hey, Luther, it's been a while," Ryder greeted him.

Luther approached and greeted him with a pat on the shoulder, then pointed at the blood on his clothing. "Been playing with your food?"

"Yeah, not so much. Nessie and I brought in a girl. She was attacked by a vampire."

"Fuck! Did you get him?"

"Not yet."

"Who's the victim, another prostitute?"

"Yes, but what do you mean by another?"

"You hadn't heard? There've been several attacks on prostitutes all the way from Grass Valley to San Francisco. I've reason to believe that a guy we recently released from prison may be behind it."

"Is that why you're here?" Ryder asked and took a sip of his second glass of blood.

Luther didn't order any blood. As a vampire blood-bonded to a human, he only drank from his human mate, Katie. Were he to drink blood from any other human, it would make him violently ill. Only vampires bonded to other vampires could drink any human's blood.

"Among other things," he said evasively.

The door suddenly opened, and Haven entered.

"There you are," Luther said to his brother-in-law.

Katie's oldest brother, Haven, was a vampire like Luther. Their brother Wesley was an accomplished witch. The three siblings had been destined to become the most powerful witches ever to walk the earth, but when a rival witch had attempted to steal the power for herself, Haven had sacrificed his mortal life to prevent the evil witch from reaching her goal. Dying, he'd been turned into a vampire by Yvette, the vampire female who'd fallen in love with the dashing former vampire hunter.

"Hey, bro," Haven said and embraced his brother-in-law. "I came as soon as they told me you were here. What's up?" With a sideways glance at Ryder, he added, "Hey, Ryder."

"Haven," Ryder responded. "I'll give you guys some privacy."

"Not necessary," Luther said. "You might as well listen in. It concerns us all."

Curious, Ryder remained standing where he was.

"We have a problem at the prison," Luther said. "Two V-CONs"—short for vampire convicts—"have shown signs of an unexplained illness."

"Vampires can't get sick," Haven said.

"I know," Luther said. "That's why I'm worried. Something is making these men sick, and we've checked everything and everyone in the prison. Our blood supply is clean, and we haven't found any contraband either."

"That leaves only the women who're being ferried into the prison," Haven said with a contemplating look.

"You're still bringing prostitutes into the prison?" Ryder asked, surprised. "I thought that was done away with when you got rid of the corrupt guards."

Luther shrugged. "It works as an incentive. Weekly visits by the prostitutes keep quite a few of the V-CONs in check. Makes 'em more docile. But over a week ago we suspended the program until we can figure out why these inmates are getting sick. We don't want any of them to infect the prostitutes, if it's something contagious."

"And? Has this illness spread to other V-CONs or guards? Or any other visitors?" Ryder asked.

"No, but the two V-CONs have gotten worse. We've put them on extra rations of blood, but it's not helping." Luther sighed. "That's why I brought them here. My guards are installing them in the medical center downstairs right now." He looked at Ryder. "We're hoping your mother can figure out what's wrong with them."

"You're bringing two dangerous V-CONs here? What the fuck!" Ryder growled.

"I had no choice. And Samson approved it. They're guarded at all times. I can assure you that Maya will never be alone in a room with them."

"If anything happens to her—"

"It won't," Luther interrupted. "I'm not suicidal. Gabriel would kill me without hesitation if any of them harmed Maya. So pipe down, Ryder. We're taking every precaution."

"You'd better."

Ryder's cell phone chimed. He looked at the display. It was a text message from his mother that Scarlet was ready.

"Gotta go," Ryder said, then cast a last look at Luther. "I hope you know what you're doing."

He left the V lounge, and made his way back down to the medical center. At the elevators, Vanessa was waiting with Scarlet.

"Thanks, Nessie," he said and reached for Scarlet's hand. "Do you need a ride home?"

"No, I'll stay here with Lizzy for a while."

Once back in the SUV on their way home, Ryder gave Scarlet a sideways look.

"Everything okay?"

She smiled. "Your mother is a good doctor. In fact, she's the first doctor who ever truly listened to me, without dismissing my symptoms as made-up or psychosomatic."

"That's good."

"She said the results of the blood tests will be ready tomorrow night. She said she has a good idea of what the underlying cause of my severe PMS is."

"She did?"

Scarlet nodded. "But she didn't want to speculate, and said she needed the blood tests to confirm her hunch."

Ryder smiled. He had a hunch himself about why Scarlet had felt so feverish earlier in the day, particularly since it had subsided quickly when they began to make love.

"How are you feeling now?" he asked instead of sharing his thoughts with her.

"Better." She sighed. "That was quite something tonight. You and your sister seemed so calm. You knew exactly what to do. But I still don't understand why you couldn't bring Lizzy to a hospital. You said you'd explain it to me."

Ryder contemplated his answer for a moment, deciding to stick to the truth as much as he could, so his lies wouldn't trip him up later.

"Scanguards has a contract with the mayor's office. We take care of certain people that, shall we say, don't always get the right care because of what they do."

"You mean prostitutes?"

"Yes, sex workers. They live a dangerous life, and take up valuable police resources. So the city contracted with Scanguards to take care of them when they're being assaulted, threatened, or in any other way harmed. I've seen plenty of violence directed toward sex workers, but it never gets easier. Tonight, we were able to save Lizzy's life, but some other night we won't be so lucky. But we do what we can."

It was mostly the truth. Scanguards took care of a certain segment of the population, and yes, it was mostly sex workers who benefited from it, but what he'd left out was that Scanguards also took charge of all crimes in which vampires were involved, either as the perpetrators or the victims. And the person who'd hurt Lizzy was a vampire. Ryder wondered whether Luther was right, and the vampire who'd attacked her was an ex-V-CON. If it was, at least it would make it easier to find the bastard, since he was in the database Scanguards kept of all known vampires including those in prison.

"That's very admirable but also very sad," Scarlet said.

"Hmm." He reached for Scarlet's hand and squeezed it. "I'm sorry you had to see all that."

"I'm not that squeamish. It's not like I'm gonna faint at the sight of blood." She shrugged and pointed at his shirt. "Your shirt is ruined. I don't think the bloodstains will come out in the wash."

"Occupational hazard," he said lightly. "I'll jump in the shower when we get home. We're almost there."

A few minutes later, Ryder parked the car on the street, keeping the driveway free so his parents would be able to get into the garage when they returned just before sunrise. Inside the house it was dark and quiet. They were alone. He led Scarlet up to his room, and closed the door behind them.

"You must be tired," he said with a look at the clock on his bedside table. It was almost 3a.m.

"I think I'm getting a second wind," she replied and yawned.

Ryder chuckled. "Go to bed. I'll take a quick shower."

He walked into the bathroom, undressed and placed his blood-stained clothes in the hamper. Then he turned on the water and stepped into the shower. The warm water ran over his skin, and the blood that had soaked through his shirt washed down the drain. His nerves calmed under the spray of the water, relaxing him.

His thoughts went back to his conversation with Luther and Haven. He'd never heard of vampires getting sick. It just wasn't possible. They could get injured, yes, and those were the cases his mother treated in her medical suite, mostly by stemming blood loss and giving them transfusions of human blood. But a mysterious illness where vampires got sick and human blood couldn't make them better, when in fact, human blood was the cure-all for a vampire, was simply out of the question. Something wasn't right.

29

Scarlet took off her clothes, and put them on a chair in Ryder's bedroom. She knew she should go to bed and sleep, but Ryder taking a shower, was too tempting to miss out on. She just couldn't get enough of him. By now, the fact that he had two cocks felt completely natural to her. As did their lovemaking. She felt closer to him than she'd ever felt to anybody. Was this love? She made no effort to answer this question. They'd only known each other for a few short days, although so much had happened in this short time span. She didn't want to jinx what she had with Ryder by putting a label on it.

The water in the shower was still running. She walked toward the open door to the bathroom and looked inside. Ryder stood under the spray of the water, his back to her, his hands braced against the tiles. The water ran down his muscled shoulders and back, and over his firm ass. She'd never seen anything more erotic. Ryder was a beautiful male specimen. Looking at him made her hungry for sex.

"You just gonna stare at me, or are you gonna come in?" he asked without looking over his shoulder.

"Well, since you're inviting me…" She opened the glass door and stepped inside.

"You don't need an invitation," he said on a chuckle. "I'm yours for whatever you want."

"Well, in that case…" Scarlet put her hands on his shoulders, caressing the hard muscles there, before sliding her fingers down his back. "Do you have any idea how sexy you are?"

She moved her hands farther down to touch his firm butt.

Ryder inhaled sharply. "I'm glad you like what you're seeing."

She squeezed him before she slid her hands around his hips to his groin and found his cocks fully erect. "I like the way you get hard so quickly."

"I have to in order to keep up with your sexual appetite."

"Keep up with me? You're just as insatiable." She wrapped her hands around his cocks, loving the feel of the hard shafts covered by silken skin. "Or why else would you already be hard before I even touch you?"

"You've got a point." He turned around to face her and put his arms around her to pull her to him, one hand sliding down over her ass until he reached her pussy. There, he rubbed his finger along her cleft. "Look who's talking. How come you're already wet, before I even touch you?"

"It's not something I can control," she murmured and lifted her face toward him, their lips only inches apart.

"Just as I can't control my cocks when I'm around you. No matter how exhausted we both are."

"Sleep's overrated."

"I agree," Ryder murmured before he slanted his mouth over hers and kissed her hungrily.

Scarlet barely noticed that he turned with her in his arms so the tiles of the shower were at her back now. Ryder ground his cocks against her stomach while he explored her with his tongue, kissing her as if they'd been separated for too long. She tasted his need in his kiss, her entire body prickling with excitement, her clit throbbing in anticipation of what was to come. His hands roamed her body, caressing her with such urgency that her own arousal spiraled higher with every second.

She ripped her lips from his. "I need you inside now."

Something flickered in his eyes, almost as if a flame of desire ignited there. "I've got you."

He lifted her off her feet, and kept her pressed against the wall, as if she was light as a feather. She spread her legs, and an instant later, Ryder thrust his lower cock into her, while his upper one slid against her clit. She gasped at the erotic sensation and held on to Ryder's shoulders, her legs crossed behind his back, while he pumped into her. He dipped his head to her neck and kissed her there. She felt her vein pulse against his lips as if calling out to him, while her clit throbbed in the same rhythm.

"Oh yes!" she cried out. She loved the way Ryder plowed into her, the way he took her without reservations, without holding back.

"You make me so fucking hot," he rasped into her ear, his breath hot, making her skin flush in response.

She felt his teeth brush against the sensitive skin below her ear, and shuddered at the touch.

"Fuck, baby!"

Ryder's cock spasmed, and her inner muscles contracted around him, her orgasm catching her by surprise. Warmth and wetness spread inside her pussy, and a corresponding stream of semen rained against her stomach, as his second cock exploded from the tip.

Ryder buried his face in the crook of her neck, shaking from the force of his orgasm, yet surprisingly still able to keep her suspended, pressed against the tiles.

"Oh God." She exhaled, her heart beating uncontrollably. "This keeps getting better with each time... I never knew I could feel this way..."

Ryder pressed open-mouthed kisses to her neck, his breath just as ragged as hers. "Scarlet?"

"Yes?"

"You have a devastating effect on me. I can't control myself when I'm with you. Your pussy must be raw by now."

"It's not. It feels better than ever." She rocked against him, making his cock sink deeper into her.

He moaned, his face still buried in the crook of her neck. "Baby, you do that again, and you'll find yourself facing the walls with my cocks inside you, fucking you again."

"If you need a break to recover your strength, I can wait," Scarlet said softly.

Ryder lifted his head and looked at her. His eyes shimmered golden under the bathroom lights. "You little vixen! You barely know me, and already you're pushing my buttons."

"What buttons would that be?"

"Implying that I might need a break to recover, when we both know that I can do this all night."

His words sent a thrill through her core. "Prove it."

30

Ryder stirred and felt Scarlet snuggling against him. They'd finally fallen asleep shortly after his parents had returned home. Vanessa had returned shortly after them, but he hadn't heard Ethan coming home.

Making love to Scarlet half the night had been the most satisfying thing he'd ever done in his life. To know that his future mate enjoyed sex with him, and couldn't get enough of it, was more than just thrilling. The way she'd tempted him to take her again and again, had nearly made him lose complete control. In the shower, his fangs had extended, and he'd been close to biting her, and drinking her blood. It had taken all his remaining willpower, not to give in to the urge.

But next time, he wouldn't be able to hold back. It made one thing crystal clear: he had to confess to her that he was a vampire. Before they had sex again—which meant it had to happen within the next twenty-four hours, most likely much sooner. Because one thing he couldn't allow to happen: him biting her without her permission. It would scare her off and destroy all the trust they'd started building between them.

Ryder pressed a kiss in Scarlet's hair. "How did you sleep?"

She sighed, exhaling deeply. "Like a log. What time is it?"

Ryder glanced to the clock on the nightstand on his side of the bed. "Just after five in the afternoon. Sun's still up."

"Damn!" She sat up.

"Something wrong?"

"Yes and no. I really need to do some work on the notes my professor gave me the other day. He's expecting an update."

"No problem. I can occupy myself while you study." It would help him keep his paws off Scarlet until he'd worked out an approach about how to tell her what he really was.

"But there's a problem. My computer is still in my room at home."

"That's not a problem. You can use mine, and just download your work from the cloud."

Scarlet frowned. "That's very sweet of you, but my stuff isn't in the cloud."

"You don't back up your computer?"

"I do, but I'm old-school. I back up on a physical drive." She shrugged. "I don't trust the cloud. With all the hacking, ransomware, and stuff, I'd rather have it where I can access it without having to go online."

"Well, then let's get your computer from home. I'll drive us."

Scarlet shook her head. "I don't wanna go home."

"You won't be staying. We'll just get your computer and a few clothes, and we'll be outta there."

"But what if Claudia is there?"

Ryder shrugged. "So?"

"I don't want to face her right now. She's probably annoyed that I told Dad what her nephew did."

"Okay then." He thought about it for a moment. "How about I go there on my own, get your computer and some clothes, and you'll just wait here?" As long as his parents and Vanessa were home, Scarlet would be safe here.

"But what if she sees you? I mean you punched Derek."

"I don't care. He's lucky he got away that easily. Besides, I can get in and out of your house without anybody noticing me. She won't even know that I'm there. Okay?"

Scarlet put her arms around him and kissed him. "Thank you. You're the best."

He freed himself from her embrace and grinned. "You can thank me later."

"How?"

"Oh, I leave that up to you." He winked, and jumped out of bed. "When I'm back, we can have dinner if you want."

"Do you mind if I cook something for us?"

"You don't have to, but if you insist, just check the fridge and the pantry. There should be plenty of options. Just promise not to leave the house. If there's any ingredient you can't find, text me, and I'll swing by the store before I come back."

"I will."

Fifteen minutes later, a list of things Scarlet needed from her home in his hand, Ryder left the house and walked to his car. He noticed that Vanessa's car was parked in the driveway, and Ethan's right behind her on the street, blocking her. Ethan was home after all.

It didn't take long to reach the King residence, but all parking spots on the block were taken, and Ryder had to park two blocks away. As he walked up to the residence, he couldn't tell if anybody was home. He listened before he put the key into the lock. Inside the house it was quiet. He opened the door and entered the foyer. His sneakers barely made a sound on the wood floor as he walked up the stairs and turned toward Scarlet's room that overlooked the street. He entered it.

The bed was unmade, and the rest of the room looked exactly like he'd left it the morning Scarlet's father had arrived unexpectedly. Ryder went to the walk-in closet, and stepped inside. On an upper shelf he found a leather travel bag, just like Scarlet had mentioned. He took it down and filled it with several items on Scarlet's list: panties and bras, socks, a pair of pants, several T-shirts, a cardigan, a casual dress, and two pairs of shoes. Satisfied, he stepped out of the closet and looked for Scarlet's laptop. He found it on the desk near the window and placed it in the bag on top of the clothes.

Then he looked around for the charger, but it wasn't on the desk. Where had she left it? He glanced around, wondering if she'd plugged the cable into an outlet somewhere else in the house. He walked into the ensuite bathroom, and looked around. When his eyes fell on an electric toothbrush, he took it together with a few other toiletries, even though they weren't on Scarlet's list. She'd probably forgotten them in her haste.

Back in the bedroom, his gaze fell on the bedside table. Between it and the bed, he saw the computer cable he'd been looking for. It was plugged into an outlet on the wall. Ryder crouched down and pulled it out, when he suddenly heard a loud sound. He froze. It sounded like somebody had hit the wall with a shoe or a fist.

Somebody was home after all. Ryder tossed the cable in the bag, and zipped it up. He took it, and went to the door. Quietly, he turned the doorknob and pulled the door open a couple of inches so he could peer down the hallway. He couldn't see anything, but more sounds were coming from somewhere in the back of the house now.

Ryder left Scarlet's room, intent on sneaking down the stairs as quickly as possible. When he reached the top of the stairs, a loud moan reached his ears. He stopped and looked over his shoulder. Something wasn't right. Was Claudia at home and had hurt herself? No matter his feelings about her nephew, he couldn't ignore his instinct, and had to check out if she was all right.

Ryder placed Scarlet's travel bag at the top of the stairs, and pivoted. Treading lightly, he walked to the end of the corridor, where the King's master bedroom was located. The door wasn't closed properly. As he reached it, there was another moan, this time accompanied by a second one, which definitely came from a second person.

Now more curious than worried, Ryder bent closer to peer through the gap between door and frame. His gaze fell on a mirror. In its reflection he saw the bed. On it, two people were having sex. He was about to retreat, wanting to give the couple their privacy, when he saw the faces of the couple. One was clearly Claudia, like he'd expected. But the man she was having rather wild and passionate sex with wasn't her husband. It was her nephew. Derek.

Ryder suppressed a stunned gasp and froze. He blinked, wondering if his eyes were playing a trick on him, but when he spied into the room again and saw the couple in the mirror, he couldn't deny it any longer. Claudia was fucking Derek.

"Fuck, I missed fucking you," he heard Derek grunt now as he flipped Claudia on her stomach and plowed into her from behind.

"I need this so bad, baby," she replied, "Brandon never fucks me like you do."

"I hate knowing that you still let him fuck you."

"Please, you know I have to. It won't be for much longer. You're the only one who fucks me like a real man. I only want you."

Ryder turned away. He'd seen enough. As quietly as he could, he hurried back to the stairs, grabbed Scarlet's bag and walked downstairs. Next to the bench that held several pairs of shoes, he spotted his own bag that he'd dropped there before he'd raced after Scarlet. He snatched it and made his way out the door, careful not to let it slam so as not to alert Claudia and Derek. Not that he believed that they would be able to hear the door close. Claudia was too busy cheating on her husband and committing incest with her nephew.

Back at his car, Ryder put the two bags on the back seat and got in. But he didn't speed away immediately. Instead, he let the entire scene play out in his mind once more. He wasn't a voyeur, no, that wasn't the reason. But something about Claudia and Derek having sex didn't sit right with him. Why would a woman sleep with her own nephew to cheat on her husband? A woman wanting a sexual affair behind her husband's back would choose someone who had no connection to her or her family. She wouldn't pick her nephew, because their interactions at family get-togethers could eventually betray them. She would pick a stranger, somebody she would never have to see again once it was over.

That's when the answer stared him right in the face. Derek wasn't Claudia's nephew. Ryder didn't know yet how to confirm it, but in his gut, he knew he was right. However, another thing made no sense, whether Derek was her nephew or not. Claudia had clearly tried to set Scarlet up with Derek, even facilitated it for Derek to make a pass at Scarlet—an unwelcome one—by leaving the house that night. Ryder had to assume that all this had happened at Claudia's direction. The question was, why? Why have her lover attempt to seduce Scarlet? What was the end game?

Something was afoot. And he was determined to get to the bottom of it. Another thing was clear too: he couldn't keep this information from Scarlet. She had to know about it. Perhaps she could fill in some of the blanks about Derek and Claudia.

He felt dread in his gut. This discovery wasn't something he could withhold from Brandon King. Ultimately, he was Scanguards' client, and an illicit affair represented a security issue, which made it Ryder's responsibility to alert him. However, he had to discuss it with Scarlet first. Together they would decide how to proceed.

31

Scarlet flipped on the broiler of the humongous gas stove in the Giles's kitchen, and turned back to the slices of bread on the kitchen island which she'd topped with garlic butter. Now she arranged slices of cheese on it, until the entire cookie sheet was covered. She checked the oven, but the broiler had still not turned on. She studied the controls again, and realized that she'd turned the dial to *Broil* but hadn't pressed *Start*. She corrected her error, then shoved the cookie sheet with the garlic bread onto the top rung of the oven and closed the door.

The Bolognese sauce she'd prepared was boiling happily on low heat. The water for the pasta was still not quite boiling. Scarlet looked at the large clock that hung on the wall next to the window that overlooked a narrow side yard with colorful flowers. The sun hung low on the horizon now and shone directly onto the island and the hallway beyond, though it seemed muted as if the window was tinted.

When she turned back to the stove, she noticed that the water was finally boiling. She pivoted to reach for the pasta. It wasn't where she'd thought she'd left it. She glanced around. What had she done with it?

"Come on," she murmured to herself.

But the pasta was nowhere to be found. She left the kitchen and turned to her left, where a door led into the small pantry. She flipped the light switch and saw the bag of pasta on the first shelf, right next to the canned tomatoes.

"Ah, there." She took the bag, then stopped for a second, before she reached for a second one. Maybe Ryder's parents and siblings wanted to have some food too, even if they didn't want to eat it right away. Leftovers were always good.

Scarlet returned to the stove, where the boiling water was already steaming up the kitchen. She hit the switch for the exhaust fan, then quickly emptied the two bags of pasta into the large pot of water.

The pasta sauce was bubbling up, and she realized that she'd forgotten to put the lid back on when she'd last stirred the sauce with a wooden spoon. She reared back so the hot sauce didn't splatter on the T-shirt she'd borrowed from Ryder, and promptly slipped on a wet spot on the marble floor. She managed to keep her balance by gripping the side of the sink for support, inadvertently knocking against the pile of dirty dishes she'd accumulated there during her prep work. The dishes shifted in the sink and made a noise so loud is sounded like a construction crew was doing demolition work.

It was lucky the dishes didn't break. She decided it was best to quickly wash and dry them before she could cause any more disasters. Maya Giles would probably not like it one bit if Scarlet made a mess out of her kitchen and damaged her good dishes. Scarlet knew that there was a dishwasher next to the sink, but she couldn't figure out how to open it. The door appeared to be stuck.

Careful not to break anything, Scarlet lifted the dirty dishes out of the sink, then looked for dishwashing liquid and a sponge. She found both underneath the sink, and began washing the utensils, bowls, and cutting boards she'd used earlier.

She was only halfway through washing the dishes, when something behind her hissed. She pivoted and realized that the pasta pot was boiling over and extinguishing the gas flame beneath it. She looked for a potholder, but couldn't find any. Smelling the gas escaping from the burner beneath the pot, Scarlet turned the dial to the off position.

"Fuck!" Maybe cooking hadn't been such a great idea after all.

She tried to calm herself, and opened the drawers next to the stove, and finally found a potholder. She moved the pot with the boiling pasta to a different burner, and was about to switch it on, when smoke rose to her nose. Her gaze drifted lower.

"Oh shit!"

Thick smoke was coming out of the oven. She turned the broiler off as quickly as she could, and opened the oven door. The smoke coming from the charred garlic bread knocked her backward, and she realized immediately that opening the oven door had been a mistake. The exhaust over the stove was already on its highest setting, and did nothing to clear the smoke from the kitchen.

The fire alarm suddenly went off, its high-pitched beeping sound nearly piercing her eardrums and sending her into a panic.

Scarlet charged to the kitchen window and opened it as wide as she could. She ran to the other side of the island into the living area, and opened the large window there too, hoping to get some cross-breeze going.

The sound of several pairs of feet running down the wooden staircase suddenly drifted to Scarlet's ears. Oh no! She'd woken the entire house! What a disaster! Ryder's parents would be so mad once they saw the mess she'd made of their beautiful kitchen. She wanted to sink into a hole in the ground to hide, but there was no escaping this. She was responsible for this.

"What's going on?" Vanessa called out from somewhere upstairs.

"Fire alarm. Wake your brothers!" Maya yelled from much closer.

"I'm sorry!" Scarlet cried out, just as Maya came running around the corner, dressed in nothing but a short red negligee.

"There's no fire. It's the oven," Scarlet said quickly, tears welling up in her eyes. "I burned the bread."

Maya was already in the middle of the kitchen and could see the mess for herself. Her lips parted to say something, when she suddenly yelled out in pain and shrank back. Scarlet's gaze shot to her. Had she touched the hot stove or bumped against the open oven door?

Scarlet caught a glimpse of steam or white smoke rising from Maya's forearm, before she turned her back to Scarlet as if to hide her arm from her. The smell of burned flesh filled her nostrils. From the hallway, Gabriel appeared, his long hair and entire body dripping wet. He was holding a towel around his lower half to cover his naked body.

"Gabriel, the window!" Maya yelled and ran toward him.

He froze right there, and stared at Maya. They looked at each other, but neither said anything else.

"I'm so sorry," Scarlet said, tears now streaming down her cheeks. "You're hurt because of me. Please let me—"

Gabriel lifted one hand to stop her. "It's all right, Scarlet."

"I don't know what happened," Scarlet said apologetically. "Mrs. Giles, I'm so sorry."

Maya looked over her shoulder, and to Scarlet's surprise Maya cast her a kind smile. "Please, it's Maya, and it's nothing. It'll heal in no time."

Ethan and Vanessa suddenly appeared behind their parents. Gabriel nodded toward Ethan, who walked into the kitchen and headed for the window.

"I think it's aired out enough now," he said, and closed it, while Vanessa was doing the same in the living room.

Finally, the fire alarm stopped beeping.

"Hmm, Bolognese sauce," Ethan said looking at the stove. "Yum! Though the pasta looks a little undercooked, and whatever this was"—he pointed to the remains of the garlic bread—"…is a little… well, fancy restaurants would call it charred, wouldn't they?"

"Don't make fun of her, Ethan," Vanessa scolded her brother. "You know yourself that the oven is temperamental at best. You've burned plenty of pizzas in there."

"How about you guys help Scarlet clean up here while we get ready for work?" Gabriel suggested, addressing his children.

As Maya and Gabriel turned to leave the kitchen, Scarlet looked back at the mess, and recalled the moment Maya had yelled out in pain. She hadn't been anywhere close to the stove or the open oven. So how had she burned her arm?

"What happened here?"

Scarlet spun around and saw Ryder walk past his parents and enter the kitchen.

"Nothing," Vanessa said. "Dinner will be ready in about twenty minutes, right, Scarlet?"

Scarlet smiled at Vanessa, grateful for her kindness.

32

Ryder had seen the burn mark on his mother's forearm, and knew it had come from the sun. While Vanessa helped Scarlet to finish preparing dinner, Ryder had briefly spoken to Ethan to find out that Scarlet had opened the windows and inadvertently let sunlight stream into the kitchen, exposing Maya to it. The incident cemented his decision to tell Scarlet the truth about himself, his family, and Scanguards tonight. Right after he'd informed Scarlet about Claudia's affair with Derek.

After a long leisurely dinner with Scarlet, Vanessa, and Ethan, Ryder took Scarlet's hand and ushered her to the sofa in the living room. Vanessa and Ethan had just finished cleaning up the kitchen, and were going upstairs. Maya and Gabriel had left for work over two hours earlier.

"Something happened when I was at your house earlier," Ryder started.

Scarlet gasped. "Did Claudia get mad at you because you beat up Derek? I shouldn't have let you go there—"

"No, she didn't see me," Ryder interrupted. "She had no idea I was in the house. But she wasn't alone."

"I thought Dad had business in Palo Alto."

"She wasn't with your father." Ryder sighed. There was no easy way to say this. "She was with Derek."

"She hasn't sent him packing? That's not fair! Dad promised that he would send him home! How could he lie like that?"

"It wasn't your father's fault. In fact, I believe he doesn't even know that Derek is still here. But that's not the worst thing."

"Not the worst?"

"No. Because I saw Claudia and Derek together. They were in the master bedroom…" He watched Scarlet's reaction closely. "They were having sex."

Scarlet's mouth dropped open, but no words came out.

"They're lovers, Scarlet. Your stepmother is cheating on your father with Derek."

"Oh my God." Scarlet put her hand over her mouth, tears suddenly welling up in her eyes. "No, no, that can't be. Dad loves her. She can't be cheating on him. She can't… And with her nephew? With Derek?" She shook her head. "Was he forcing himself on her? Because I rejected him?"

Ryder took her hands in his, trying to calm her. "Scarlet, it has nothing to do with you or what he tried to do to you. What I saw was consensual. And it wasn't the first time. The way they talked… they've been lovers for a while."

Agitated now, Scarlet protested, "But that's incest! She's his aunt!"

"I'm not so sure they're related. For one, I don't see a family resemblance, not that that's a definite indication," Ryder mused. "Also, they're very close in age… and… I just have that gut feeling that there's more to it than we know."

"Oh my God!" Scarlet's eyes suddenly widened as if she just realized something. "I never knew she had a nephew before this week. She never even mentioned that she had a sister. Why did she never mention her relatives before this week?"

Ryder nodded at the revelation. It made sense. "You're sure she never mentioned a sister or a nephew to you or your father?"

"Never. Dad would have told me if she did. The day you became my bodyguard, was the first day she ever mentioned her sister. And when I questioned her, she said that they didn't really talk, as if they'd had a big falling out, but that she had kept in touch with her nephew. Why would she lie about that? And why bring him here?"

"I don't know that yet," Ryder admitted.

"Ryder, are you absolutely sure about what you saw? Is there any way that you could have misinterpreted what you saw?" Scarlet asked, clearly grasping for straws.

"I'm sorry, Scarlet. But there was no room for misinterpretation. They fucked, and…" He hesitated.

"What is it? What are you not telling me?"

He cast her a regretful look. "During sex Claudia told Derek that her husband never fucked her like this, and that she needs a real man like Derek. I'm sorry."

A sob tore from Scarlet's chest. "What am I gonna do now? Dad needs to know about this." She locked eyes with Ryder, and he saw her pain. "How am I gonna tell him?"

"I'm not sure you can, at least not yet."

"Why not? If your mother cheated on your father, wouldn't you want to tell him immediately?"

Ryder knew such a thing would never happen. Vampires were devoted to their blood-bonded mates. Infidelity was virtually unheard of. But he understood what Scarlet meant with her words.

"Yes, of course. But the problem is, it's my word against Claudia's and Derek's. You weren't even there. Do you really think he'll believe me after you accused Derek of attempted rape, and I broke the asshole's nose? He'll claim that we're trying to get back at Derek, and at Claudia for making excuses for her supposed nephew."

"But Dad has to find out. He doesn't deserve this. He's a good man."

"I don't doubt that," Ryder said softly.

"I have to try. I owe him that much."

There was determination in Scarlet's voice, and Ryder knew he had to respect her decision. It was her father after all, and she knew him best.

"Okay, call him." Ryder took a deep inhale. "Let's hope he believes you. Perhaps leave out that the man Claudia is cheating on him with is Derek. He doesn't need to know that yet. It might be easier to swallow if he doesn't know that Derek is involved. Cross that bridge when you get to it. Besides, I want to look into Derek first, find out who he really is."

Scarlet nodded. "Okay." Then she took a deep inhale and pulled her phone from her jeans pocket. She sniffled and wiped the remaining tears from her eyes.

"Is there anything I can do?" Ryder asked, sensing Scarlet's apprehension.

"Just stay here with me."

He squeezed her hand and pressed a kiss on her forehead. "I'll be here for you."

Ryder noticed Scarlet's hand tremble as she dialed her father's number and let it ring. She put the call on speakerphone.

Brandon King answered on the second ring. "Scarlet, honey?"

"Hi, Dad."

"It's so good to hear your voice. I've been worried about you."

"I'm fine, Dad, but… but…"

Scarlet cast a glance at Ryder, looking worried. He took her hand in encouragement and squeezed it.

"But what? Are you okay?" Brandon King sounded alarmed. "Did something happen?"

She cleared her throat. "Dad, I'm fine but there's something I have to tell you."

"You're getting me worried," King replied. "Are you in some sort of trouble?"

"No." She took a quick breath. "Dad, it's about Claudia. She's having an affair with another man. She's cheating—"

A gasp came through the line, then a female voice shrieked.

"How dare you, Scarlet!" King thundered over the female voice that now became clearer.

"Why are you lying like that, Scarlet?" Claudia said, outrage coloring her voice.

Shit! Claudia was with her husband in Palo Alto?

"How can you hurt me like that?" Claudia asked. "I love you like my own…" Sobs swallowed her last words.

Ryder had to admit that Claudia sounded convincing. She was a good actress.

"You're cheating on him!" Scarlet cried out.

"Not another word out of your mouth! You apologize to Claudia right here and right now," King demanded, his voice laced with fury.

"Why don't you believe me, Dad? She's lying."

"After all Claudia has done for you, you hurt her like that? I won't have it. I don't want to lay eyes on you until you're ready to make amends."

There was a click in the line. Brandon King had disconnected the call.

Ryder put his arms around Scarlet and held her close to his chest.

"Why was she even with him?" Scarlet sobbed. "You said she was with Derek at the San Francisco house."

"She was, but that was almost three hours ago. She must have driven back to Palo Alto after…" He didn't have to finish his sentence.

Scarlet lifted her head. "How's he ever gonna believe me now?"

"We'll have to figure out a way for him to find out for himself. I'll think of something."

Scarlet sniffled.

"But right now, we need to go to Scanguards. They can help us look into Derek to see if there's anything that can help us expose him as Claudia's lover. If we can prove that he's not her nephew, your father will have to listen to you."

She hoped that Ryder was right. "Okay."

"Let's go."

33

Scarlet appeared to still be shaken from the revelations about Claudia as well as her father's rebuke. Ryder wished he'd insisted on Scarlet not mentioning anything to her father until they had verifiable proof of Claudia's infidelity.

"We'll figure out another way," Ryder said to her as they arrived at Scanguards. "We've got a few investigators here that can help us dig into Derek's background."

They rode up in the elevator, and exited on the top floor. The corridor was empty and quiet. Ryder was glad for it. Bringing a human to the top floor was strictly forbidden. There was only one exception to this rule: blood-bonded human mates. They were allowed on the executive floor where the offices of Scanguards' directors were located.

Ryder headed straight for Thomas and Eddie's office. Next to the door, a sign read *Thomas Brown-Martens & Eddie Brown-Martens, Directors of IT*. He knocked at the door.

Scarlet pointed to the sign. "Father and son, or brothers?"

"Spouses."

"Come in," Thomas's voice came from the inside.

Ryder took Scarlet's hand and opened the door, entering, then shutting the door behind them. Thomas was alone. He sat at his desk, several computer monitors next to each other. Eddie's station was empty.

"Ryder," Thomas greeted him, before his gaze swept to Scarlet. He lifted an eyebrow, then tossed Ryder an inquisitive look.

Ryder was aware that Thomas knew that Scarlet was human. Her scent and the lack of a preternatural aura only visible to vampires and other non-humans, identified her as such. But before Thomas could issue a reprimand, Ryder lifted his hand.

"I'm sorry to barge in, Thomas. I know Scarlet isn't supposed to be up here, but this is urgent."

Thomas nodded at Scarlet. "Nice to meet you, Scarlet."

"Nice to meet you too."

"So, what's so urgent?"

"We need your help," Ryder started. "I was assigned to Scarlet's protection detail. And something has happened."

"That goes without saying," Thomas replied and shook his head. "I hope I don't need to remind you that a relationship with your charge means you'll be removed as her bodyguard."

"It's not about that. Besides, don't tell me you never broke a rule in your life."

"Touché."

The door opened. "Hey, babe, I've got you—"

Ryder turned quickly to insert himself between Eddie and Scarlet. Eddie carried two bottles of blood.

"—tomato juice," Ryder interrupted quickly shooting Eddie a look to indicate he should go along.

"Yeah," Eddie said quickly. "For the Bloody Marys after work." He squeezed past Ryder and Scarlet, holding the bottles so Scarlet couldn't see the labels. "Better put those in the fridge." While he opened a small refrigerator and placed the bottles inside, he asked, "So who's your friend?"

"This is Scarlet King. Scarlet this is Eddie."

"Nice to meet you, Eddie," she said with a smile.

"Likewise. So what are you guys doing here?"

"Apparently they need our help with something urgent," Thomas said, while Eddie took sat down.

"Long story short," Ryder said, "we need help checking somebody's background."

Thomas and Eddie exchanged a look. Though neither was saying anything, Ryder knew they were communicating with each other through the special psychic bond all blood-bonded couples had.

"You've gotta make that short story a little longer," Thomas said.

Scarlet cleared her throat. "Well, it's about my stepmother and her nephew, with whom she's cheating on my dad."

Eddie rolled his office chair closer. "We definitely need to hear the full story."

Thomas nodded. "Most definitely."

In as few words as possible, Scarlet recounted what had passed between her and Derek, and Ryder filled the two IT geniuses in on what he'd seen happening between Claudia and Derek when he'd returned to the King residence to pick up Scarlet's computer.

"So we need something to prove to my dad that Claudia is cheating on him, and it would help if we could somehow prove that Derek isn't even her nephew," Scarlet said, casting a pleading look at Thomas and Eddie.

"Well," Thomas said slowly. "Something's definitely fishy."

"Worth a little digging," Eddie agreed.

"Do we have a last name for this Derek?" Thomas asked.

Ryder furrowed his forehead. "He only introduced himself as Derek to me."

"Claudia never mentioned his last name either," Scarlet said, but added, "but I got a glimpse of the name on his credit card when he paid at the restaurant." She closed her eyes for a moment. "Let me think. It started with an H. Something short. Reminded me of that hotel owner in New York, you know that one who was terrible to her employees. She died several years ago, and I saw a documentary."

"Leona Helmsley?" Eddie asked.

"Yes! That's it. Derek Helmsley. That's what it said on his credit card."

"Well, that's a start," Thomas agreed. "If there's something to find, we'll find it."

"Thank you," Scarlet said. "I don't know how else my father will believe what Ryder saw."

"Hmm," Eddie said, "have you thought of installing hidden cameras to record them?"

"And then give Dad the tapes?" Scarlet asked and shook her head. "He'll be furious with me for spying, no matter what's on the tapes."

"Not if you send them anonymously," Eddie added, "or you can make it look like somebody's blackmailing Claudia, and you can arrange it so your father sees the evidence by accident."

Ryder looked from Eddie to Scarlet. "Actually, that's not a bad idea. Particularly since we have no idea whether there's anything in Derek's past that'll help us convince your dad that Derek attacked you and is sleeping with Claudia."

Slowly, Scarlet nodded. "Okay. But how do we go about that?"

Thomas grinned at Eddie. "We've got all the equipment you'll need downstairs. And Ryder knows how to install it. I'll call the supply room and have them pack up what you'll need, and you just need to pick it up."

"Thanks, Thomas! Thanks, Eddie, you guys are the best," Ryder said.

34

In the hallway outside of Thomas and Eddie's office, Ryder gave Scarlet an encouraging look.

"Don't worry, we'll get proof that Claudia and Derek are having an affair. We'll go back to your house shortly, and set up the hidden cameras. Since Claudia is with your dad in Palo Alto, we should have no problem doing that."

"And what if Derek already left San Francisco and has returned to the East Coast?"

"I have the feeling that he never lived on the East Coast, nor in Paris," Ryder said.

"You might be right. His stories about Paris were so boring, they could be straight out of a travel guide. And if he lied about that, he probably also lied about flying in from the East Coast."

"Exactly."

They were already in the elevator, when Ryder's cell phone pinged. It was a text from his mother. "That's Mom. She wants us to meet her in the med center. Your blood test results are back."

He could sense Scarlet's heartrate accelerate a little showing that she was anxious. He realized that he too was curious about the results.

Scarlet's facial expression suddenly changed. "Damn it, I wanted to buy your mother flowers to apologize for making such a mess in her kitchen. She burned her arm because of me."

"I'm sure it's already healed," Ryder said while the elevator was going down. In fact he knew with certainty that it had. A little burn caused by the rays of the sun that had streamed into the house through the open window would heal within an hour or two if his mother drank sufficient blood—which he was sure she had.

"I doubt that very much. It looked really bad."

When they reached the medical floor and entered the hallway, it was busier than the previous night. Several people came in and out of various rooms along the corridor, before Scarlet and Ryder even reached the double doors. Outside of it, one of Luther's guards was posted. Ryder recognized him by his uniform, a full-body Kevlar suit complete with gloves and a helmet and face shield meant to shield the vampire inside the suit from dangerous UV-rays. At his waist, instead of a gun, he carried a UV-blaster, a weapon emitting UV-rays to subdue prisoners. The guard let them pass without questioning them.

Inside the medical suite, it was buzzing like a beehive. In the circular room with the nurse's station at its center, and various treatment bays and a waiting room surrounding it, at least a dozen people were present. The door to Maya's office as well as the two private patient rooms were closed. The curtains to several of the treatment bays were drawn, indicating that they were occupied by patients. Ryder was glad for the curtains, because there was always a chance that some of the patients were vampires who could at any point bare their fangs. To Ryder's surprise, Vanessa was at the nurse's station helping out a frazzled looking Jenny.

"Nessie, I didn't know you were coming in tonight. I could have given you a lift."

"I just got here, literally two minutes ago. I got a text to come in and help out. It's a circus here tonight. Did you know they admitted two V-CONs last night?"

"Luther mentioned it."

"V-CONs?" Scarlet asked.

Ryder exchanged a look with Vanessa. "Uhm, prison inmates."

"Oh," Scarlet said, looking stunned. "You treat prisoners here? Is that why there's a guard at the door?"

"Yep," Vanessa said. "So what are you guys doing here?"

"Mom wanted us to come down to talk about Scarlet's blood test. Where is she?"

Vanessa turned to the nurse. "Jenny?"

"She's in with Lizzy right now. Room two." Jenny jerked her thumb over her shoulder.

From one of the treatment bays, a man was yelling something unintelligible, moaning in pain.

"Your turn," Jenny said to Vanessa.

"What's he on?" Vanessa asked.

"A positive," Jenny replied while she took a clipboard and walked toward the waiting room.

Vanessa jumped up, and went to a large stainless-steel refrigerator. She opened it, revealing a large supply of blood, both in bottle form as well as in clear bags meant to be given intravenously. Vanessa grabbed one of the bags and hurried to bay three. She disappeared behind its curtain.

"Your sister is trained as a nurse? I didn't realize. No wonder she was so competent with Lizzy last night," Scarlet said, her gaze shifting from the refrigerator with the blood back to Ryder.

"Yeah, Nessie's pretty much a Jill-of-all-trades." What else could he say? Jenny wasn't a trained nurse either. She was a vampire whom Maya had recruited to help with running her growing practice.

"I hope Lizzy is doing better."

Ryder gave Scarlet a reassuring smile and looked past her and saw that the door to room two opened. "Let's ask her. Mom is just finishing with her."

Side by side, Ryder and Scarlet walked to the room, from which Maya was just emerging. When Maya saw them, she said, "Can you guys give me a couple of minutes? I quickly need to check on a patient."

"Take your time, Mom," Ryder said. "We'll say hi to Lizzy in the meantime."

"Good, she was asking about you." Maya turned back toward the door and opened it wider. "Lizzy, you've got visitors."

Maya walked away, and Ryder and Scarlet entered the room, where Lizzy was sitting up in a hospital bed, looking much better than the night before. She even smiled.

"Ryder, your mom told me that you saved my life when you—"

"Vanessa did much more than I did," Ryder interrupted before Lizzy could blurt that he'd given her his blood to help her heal. "She deserves the credit."

"I'm so grateful, to all of you," Lizzy said, then shifted her gaze to Scarlet, addressing her directly, "This guy's a keeper."

"Yes, he is." Scarlet beamed at him, making his heart swell with affection, before she looked back at Lizzy. "You look great today. I can't believe how fast you're healing."

Suddenly the sound of metal clanging against metal and heavy items crashing to the floor filled the medical suite amidst loud grunts and shouts. Ryder whirled around and saw the curtain of emergency bay three being ripped down from its rail on the ceiling, two people behind it fighting.

"Nessie!" Ryder screamed and charged out of Lizzy's room.

"The V-CON!", Vanessa yelped just as her attacker flung her across the room, knocking her against a hospital bed.

"Fuck!" Ryder cursed.

The V-CON she'd been treating emerged from the bay, one hand still in handcuffs. The handcuff was attached to a double rail, but he'd torn it loose from the gurney. His eyes were glaring red and orange, his fangs extended and dripping with blood. Shit!

"Guards!" Ryder screamed. "The V-CON is loose!" But he couldn't wait for the guards to help, because the V-CON was now coming toward him. His eyes focused on something behind Ryder, his chest heaving. His hands had turned into dangerous claws. He was in full attack mode.

Ryder had no choice but to lunge at the violent vampire, his intention clear, because behind Ryder was Lizzy's room with Scarlet in it.

"Scarlet, lock the—"

The rest of his words didn't make it over his lips, because he collided with the massive V-CON. The assailant kicked him with the metal rail attached to the handcuff on his wrist, but Ryder fought back, his body hardening, his vision tinting red. With the sharp barbs on his fingers, Ryder swiped the V-CON's arm, leaving deep cuts. Blood splattered, but his opponent didn't let his injury slow him down. Ryder punched him hard, then kicked him, flinging him against the nurse's station.

But the vampire growled, enraged even more now. He pushed off the counter and plowed into Ryder, this time knocking the wind out of him.

As Ryder went down, his back hitting a crash cart, he saw Vanessa get to her feet, her eyes red now, her fangs extended, ready to help him fight the V-CON. The bastard was heading toward Lizzy's room. Shit!

When Ryder scrambled to his feet to cut the V-CON off, he realized that the door to Lizzy's room was still open. Scarlet stood there as if paralyzed, her face a mask of horror. Behind her, Lizzy ripped her IV from her arm and jumped out of bed.

Fuck! The V-CON would attack Scarlet.

"The door!" Ryder yelled, before he lunged again and tackled the V-CON to the ground. "Nessie! Get Scarlet and Lizzy outta here!"

He didn't know if Vanessa had heard him, because several people screamed and the crazed vampire punched and kicked him, despite his position on the ground. He was strong, and a good fifty pounds heavier than Ryder—and by the crazed look in his eyes in a state of bloodlust. The V-CON managed to push Ryder off him, and scrambled to his feet. But Ryder was fast too, and motivated. He couldn't let the V-CON reach Scarlet and hurt her.

The assailant was only a few feet away from Scarlet now, when Ryder reached him. He grabbed the double rail attached to the V-CON's handcuffs and hooked his arm between the bars, then used all his weight and strength to twist it, and flung the assailant against the wall next to Lizzy's room.

Finally, he heard heavy boots hit the ground from the double doors.

"Fuck!" Ryder recognized Luther's curse.

Ryder kicked the V-CON in the back of his knees. But the bastard would still not go down. Ryder's arm still hooked in the double rail, he now gripped it with two hands and jerked it up under the V-CON's chin and pressed it back against his neck, trying to choke him.

"Noooo! No!" Lizzy screamed and pushed Scarlet out of the way to rush past her toward the V-CON. "Don't hurt him! Please don't hurt him!"

Finally, Luther grabbed hold of one side of the double rail, and together they flipped the V-CON, and he landed with his back on the floor.

"About fucking time! I warned you, Luther!" Ryder ground out.

"Please! Don't hurt him," Lizzy screamed again.

"Get back! He's in bloodlust," Luther ordered, but Lizzy just pushed in between him and Ryder to reach the vampire they were holding down.

"He won't hurt me," Lilly claimed. "We're blood-bonded."

Shock charged through Ryder.

"Lizzy…" the V-CON now murmured. "Lizzy…"

"I'm here, my love."

Ryder exchanged a look with Luther, who looked just as stunned.

"He needs my blood, or he'll die," Lizzy said. "Please let me feed him."

From behind Ryder, he heard a gasp. He looked over his shoulder to see Maya standing there, staring at them.

"That's why he was getting worse the more blood we gave him," Maya said, realization evident in her face. "How could we have missed that?"

Luther ran a hand through his hair. "Fuck!" Then he nodded to Lizzy. "Do what you have to do."

Lizzy kneeled down next to her mate, and leaned over him bringing her neck to his mouth. "Drink, my love."

Everybody fell silent.

"Lizzy," he murmured, before he sank his fangs into her neck and let his blood-bonded mate feed him.

Suddenly, a shocked gasp sounded from the door to Lizzy's room. Ryder lifted his gaze and saw Scarlet still standing there, watching in horror as the V-CON drank Lizzy's blood. She slowly turned her head and met Ryder's gaze.

This wasn't how he'd wanted Scarlet to find out what he was.

35

Scarlet was in shock. She couldn't believe what she'd seen, nor what was happening now. When the violent patient had flung Vanessa clear across the emergency room, and then attacked Ryder, she'd been scared for the two siblings' safety. That was before she'd seen the monster's fangs and claws, and the red eyes. At that point, she'd thought things couldn't get any worse than they already were.

She'd been wrong.

Ryder and his sister were suddenly showing the same signs as the inmate. Their canines had turned into fangs, sharp, dangerous fangs, and their hands were claws now with sharp barbs where their fingernails had been before. And then their eyes: glowing red. She realized now that Ryder had shown signs of his eyes glowing before tonight. When they'd had sex, she'd noticed his eyes shimmering golden, almost orange, and had dismissed it as light reflecting in his eyes. But she couldn't dismiss what she saw now. It was staring her in the face: the truth she'd not seen before.

"You're vampires."

When Ryder made a step toward her, she shrank back, fear clamping around her heart, panic choking off the air to breathe.

"I'm sorry, Scarlet." He made a movement with his hand toward the vampire on the floor. "This is not how I wanted you to find out."

"You should have told her last night," Vanessa said to her brother.

Ryder looked over his shoulder, where Maya was checking out Vanessa's injuries. "Not helping."

"Why don't you take Scarlet up to the lounge to talk to her," Maya suggested. "I'll be up once I've taken care of everybody's injuries."

Ryder looked back at Scarlet, his eyes looking normal again.

"I'm not going anywhere with you," Scarlet said, her chest heaving.

"I'm good, Mom," Vanessa said, despite the blood Scarlet saw gushing from her arm. "I just need a little blood."

"Okay, that's enough, Miller," Luther suddenly said. He was still crouched down next to the V-CON and Lizzy.

For some reason, Scarlet couldn't take her eyes from Lizzy and how the vampire beneath her finally took his fangs from her neck. Was he smiling at Lizzy? When he pulled her neck back down to her, Scarlet thought he'd plunge his sharp fangs back into her neck, but instead, he licked over the two bleeding holes his fangs had left. When he removed his lips from her neck, Scarlet noticed that the holes were gone.

"What the…" Scarlet couldn't finish her sentence, too stunned by what was happening right before her eyes.

Lizzy rose. She looked… happy. How was that possible? How could she have let this monster drink her blood? Wouldn't the bite turn her into a vampire too? Was that what had happened to Ryder and Vanessa? Had they been bitten and turned? And was that what would happen to her now?

Scarlet shuddered.

"Scarlet, baby, come with me. We'll talk."

While Luther helped the V-CON up, Ryder walked toward her, looking entirely human again. No red eyes, no fangs, no claws. As if she'd dreamed it. But she knew she hadn't. The claw marks on Ryder's chest and arms bore witness to the fact that he'd fought with the inmate.

Scarlet pressed her lips together, pushing back the tears that were welling up. She realized all of a sudden that she was in love with Ryder. But there would be no happy ending for her, because Ryder was a monster. A vampire out for blood.

"I'm sorry you had to see all this," he said, his voice gentle and soft. "But when he charged toward you, I had to stop him. I couldn't let him harm you." Ryder ran a shaking hand through his hair. "I had no idea he was trying to get to Lizzy. To his mate."

She shook her head. Nothing in her world made sense anymore. "Are you saying she's letting him bite her of her own free will? No! Why would she?"

"Because I love him," Lizzy said suddenly, pivoting. "He would do anything for me to keep me safe."

Scarlet looked past her, and noticed the loving look with which the convict looked at Lizzy. As if she could feel it, Lizzy turned her head and smiled back at him.

Then she addressed Luther, "I need to go with him, or he'll get worse again."

Luther nodded, though he seemed annoyed and growled at Miller, "You should have told me that you were blood-bonded. What the fuck were you thinking? You knew you'd get sick if you drank anybody's blood but Lizzy's."

Miller glared at Luther. "So you could punish her for falling in love with a prisoner? No, I'd rather die."

"Yeah, well, you nearly did," Luther hissed.

"What'll happen to him now?" Lizzy asked.

"He'll go back to prison."

"But, if he doesn't get my blood—"

"We'll arrange regular conjugal visits so he can feed. But he'll finish his sentence. There'll be no early release."

"Thank you, thank you so much," Lizzy said, beaming.

Luther looked at Maya. "I'm assuming the second V-CON has the exact same symptoms?"

Maya nodded. "We have to assume he's blood-bonded too."

"We'll have to find his mate, or he'll die," Luther said. "I'll talk to him."

Luther motioned to the guard that stood by the double doors. "Take him to lockup."

"Can I go with him?" Lizzy asked.

"For now."

As the three left the medical center, Maya looked at Scarlet. "Scarlet, I know all this is a shock for you, but give Ryder a chance to explain everything to you. Please."

Scarlet still stood rigid like a steel pipe, worried that if she moved and took a deep breath, she would burst out crying.

"And Ryder," Maya added, "Scarlet's DNA test was positive. She has the gene."

"What?" Scarlet's gaze bounced between Maya and Ryder. "What gene?"

"Let's go to the lounge, and I'll tell you everything," Ryder promised.

He locked eyes with her, and she couldn't tear her gaze from him. Something in them told her that he wasn't going to hurt her. Was it because he'd saved her before? Not just from the crazed vampire but also from Derek? And the days and nights she'd spent with him… not a single time had he tried to bite her or hurt her in any way, even though she'd been at his mercy, alone with him, without anyone who would have come to her aid. Yet he'd never laid a finger on her. He'd put her pleasure before his, and she'd felt safe in his arms.

"All right, I'll go to the lounge with you. And you'll tell me the truth, the entire truth."

Ryder slowly nodded. "No more secrets."

"And you'll let me go?"

"If after I tell you everything you decide you want nothing more to do with me, I'll let you go."

She took a few seconds, before she agreed, "All right, you have thirty minutes."

In the elevator they took up to the first floor, Ryder gave her space. She was glad for it, because she had no idea how she would react if he tried to touch her. Would she recoil from him?

On the first floor, Ryder swiped his access card at a door with the sign *V Lounge* on it. She could guess what the V stood for. Simultaneously she realized that *Waiting Room H*, where she'd been made to wait the night before, had to mean that it was a waiting room for humans, hence the H.

She didn't really know what she'd expected in a vampire lounge, certainly not the soft music, the warm lights, and the comfortable seating areas that reminded her of a VIP lounge in a fancy hotel or the First-Class lounge at an airport. There wasn't a coffin in sight, there were no heavy velvet curtains—there were no windows either—but rather tasteful prints and paintings decorating the walls. Fresh flower arrangements sat on coffee tables, and in one corner, there was even a fireplace.

Ryder ushered her toward the middle of the room, which had a bar at its center. An older man stood behind the pristine counter and polished glasses. When he saw them approach, he sat down his dish towel.

"Ryder, what may I get you?" He pointed to the taps behind the bar. "AB positive, fresh in."

Scarlet stared at the labels on the taps and felt her pulse quicken.

"Not today, Michael. Why don't you take a little break?"

Michael hesitated for a brief second, then nodded. "Thanks for reminding me. If you'll excuse me."

While he came out from behind the bar and disappeared through a door at the other end of the lounge, Scarlet realized that the taps weren't for beer or other drinks, but for blood. She'd seen the AB+ label before: on the bottles in Ryder's refrigerator.

"What I saw wasn't tomato juice, was it?"

"No, it wasn't." He pointed to a seating area. "Shall we sit?"

"You first."

Ryder raised an eyebrow, but didn't protest and sat down in an armchair opposite a sectional sofa. Scarlet sat down on the sofa, a large coffee table between them.

"There's so much I have to tell you," Ryder started, his voice calm and collected. "I don't really know where to start."

How often had he had to tell the girls he slept with what he really was? He probably had lots of practice in this.

She mustered all her courage to make him think she was strong so he wouldn't see her as prey. "Then let me ask you: how long have you been a vampire, because that's what you are, aren't you?"

"Technically, I'm a hybrid, because I was born a vampire. My parents were turned when they were both in their thirties."

"Are you telling me that vampires can have children? That's ridiculous." Just as ridiculous as this conversation was, because vampires shouldn't exist in the first place.

"A vampire male can impregnate his human mate, but—"

"So you lied to me!" Her breath hitched. "You're not sterile like you said. I could already be pregnant. Oh my God, and I let you fuck me with both your cocks! How stupid of me. How gullible."

"You're not gullible, and you're certainly not stupid. I told you the truth about my fertility. I was born sterile, all vampires are—"

"But—"

"—until they find their life mate and blood-bond. Only then can a vampire procreate. So you don't have to worry. You're not carrying my child."

There was a glint of something in his eyes. Annoyance? Disappointment? She couldn't be sure.

"So your mother was human, and then your father turned her after you and your siblings were born?"

"No. It's true, she was human, but she was turned against her will by another vampire. She almost didn't survive her turning, but my father saved her, and he won her love. My siblings and I were born because both my parents weren't entirely human—"

"Of course they're not. You said yourself they're vampires," she interrupted.

"They weren't entirely human *before* they were turned into vampires. They were both satyrs."

"What? Like minotaur? That's a total myth!"

"It's not. My siblings and I inherited the gene that makes us satyrs, the same that gives me my two cocks, and the same that causes Vanessa to go into heat every so often." He locked eyes with her. "The gene my mother found in your DNA. That's what causes the feverish episodes that you call PMS. In truth, what's happening to you is that you're in heat, like a feline, or like a dog. You're ready to mate. That's why your symptoms vanish when you have sex. Because you're giving your body what it desires."

Scarlet gasped and jumped up. "That's not possible. I'm human. I know I am. My father is human, my mother was human. I've seen my father in speedos when I was a kid, and trust me, he doesn't have two cocks like you."

"Then you inherited the satyr gene from your mother. She would have shown the same kind of fevers as you experience."

Scarlet shook her head, but even as she tried to deny Ryder's claims, it was possible that he was right. Her mother had suffered from terrible fevers and aches, and everybody had always assumed that she suffered from PMS. What if she'd actually been in heat? Was that why she'd committed suicide? Because she couldn't take it any longer?

"Scarlet," Ryder prompted her, and she looked at him. "Your mother had those symptoms, didn't she?"

Slowly, Scarlet nodded. "Is that why she killed herself?" Fear suddenly rose in her. "Is that what's gonna happen to me?"

"No!" Ryder jumped up. "I'll never let that happen."

"But how would you be able to prevent it? Dad couldn't stop Mom from going crazy and—"

"There's a reason satyr males have two cocks." He paused for a second. "To satisfy their mates when they go into heat. I know this is a lot to take in. But there's so much more I need to tell you. And you only gave me a half hour. Will you hear the rest of it?"

She nodded and sat back down on the sofa. She leaned back, the news hard to digest. "So you're both a satyr and a vampire? Have you killed people for their blood? Have you hurt—"

Ryder sat down in the armchair again. "Never. I've killed, yes, but only those who deserved it: evil vampires and demons. Never an innocent. Scanguards would never stand for it. We protect those who can't protect themselves."

"Like Lizzy?"

"Yes, like Lizzy, and many others. Samson founded this company to protect humans, and at the core, Scanguards' mission is still the same. Most of our employees are vampires and their hybrid children like Grayson and Benjamin and myself."

"Is Grayson a satyr too?"

Ryder suddenly laughed. "Thank God, no!"

"Why—"

"Could you imagine how full of himself he'd be if he had two cocks? He's arrogant enough with just one."

Involuntarily, Scarlet had to chuckle.

Ryder smiled at her. "I like it when you smile."

She evaded his gaze, not wanting to be distracted by his smile and what it did to her. She had to keep a cool head. Suddenly, she remembered something.

"If you and most of Scanguards are vampires, how come you can be out during daylight? I mean the lore says that the sun burns vampires."

"It does. That's why my mother's skin burned when you opened the window in the kitchen and she walked in. Our windows are covered with a special coating that filters out the sun's UV-rays so we don't have to draw the curtains during daylight hours."

"Yeah, that would explain your mother's injury, but I've seen you outside during daylight, and you didn't burn."

"Because I'm a hybrid. The other part of me, satyr in my case, and human in Grayson's and Benjamin's case, protects us from the rays of the sun. But we're still vulnerable."

"Let me guess? Stakes and garlic!" She'd watched plenty of vampire movies.

"Wooden stakes, yes. But garlic is just a myth. Silver will hurt vampires and hybrids alike. Otherwise we're pretty indestructible."

She knew what that meant. "You're immortal?"

"Yes."

She had to ask the next question. "How old are you really?"

"I'm thirty, though my body stopped aging at twenty-one."

Scarlet looked at his handsome face. He would always look like this. Young, handsome, irresistible. But a vampire, a creature who craved human blood. She recalled how she'd watched Lizzy offer herself to the crazed vampire she claimed she loved. Lizzy hadn't screamed, hadn't seemed to be in pain. It made her wonder what it would be like to be bitten.

"When you bite somebody… I mean… when you drink a human's blood… like, uhm, like that vampire who bit Lizzy…" She felt hot all of a sudden, unable to finish her sentence, not knowing how to ask what she wanted to know.

"Are you asking whether it hurts?" Ryder said softly, a kind smile on his face.

"Does it?"

"A vampire's bite is pleasurable. It's not just a feeding, it's a connection, a bond that—"

"Would you two just get a room?"

At the male voice behind her, Scarlet jumped up and whirled around. A man stood between the fireplace and two oversized wing chairs.

"Wesley, what the fuck!" Ryder cursed. "Were you listening this entire time?"

He walked toward them, a dark-haired man in his thirties with an easy smile that indicated that he was a charmer. "Sorry about that, but I was just relaxing by the fire. And by the time I realized your conversation was rather private, it was too late to leave. I mean, how would you have liked it if I'd piped up when your two cocks came up?"

Scarlet felt herself blush to the roots of her hair.

"Wesley, would you please get outta here?" Ryder said, letting out an exasperated breath.

"Actually, why don't you two find yourselves a private office and continue your chat there, while I relax in front of the fireplace, hmm? I hear that Blake is out for the rest of the night. Use his office."

"Thanks for the tip," Ryder said.

"And," Wesley said and winked, "you're right about Grayson. He'd be unbearable with two cocks." He chuckled to himself.

36

To Ryder's surprise, Scarlet didn't protest when he took her up to Blake's office on the executive floor to continue their talk. He also knew why Wesley had suggested it. Blake's office sported a Murphy bed and a full bathroom, because as chief of hybrid security Blake had often worked days and nights without going home to sleep, when the brood of a dozen young hybrids from infants to teenagers had demanded his full attention. Now that most of the hybrids were adults, his schedule had somewhat lightened up. But the Murphy bed and the bathroom were still there.

When Ryder ushered Scarlet into Blake's office, and closed the door, he looked at her. "Is it okay if I lock the door so we won't get disturbed by people like Wesley?"

"Okay. So, Wesley, he's a vampire too?"

"No, he's a witch."

"A wiccan?"

"No, a true witch, with amazing powers. You met his brother-in-law down in the medical center, Luther. Luther is blood-bonded to Wesley's sister, and he divides his time between Scanguards and the vampire prison in the Sierra Nevada."

Scarlet cast him a quizzical look. "So you really do punish vampires when they hurt people?"

"We do. We can't allow them to destroy the life Scanguards has built for all of us."

"Then you didn't lie when you said that Scanguards has a contract to look after the sex workers in San Francisco."

"It's only partially true," Ryder said. "I'm sorry, I could only tell you part of it. But the truth is that any crime involving a vampire, witch, hybrid, or any other preternatural creature is investigated by Scanguards, not the police department. That's the deal we have with the mayor's office."

"So the mayor knows." She shook her head in disbelief.

"And a few other people in the police department."

"You really don't hurt people… you protect them…"

There was a hopeful shimmer in Scarlet's eyes, and Ryder's heart skipped a beat. Was she coming around to accepting him?

"No, we don't hurt people." He stepped a little closer, very slowly, testing if Scarlet would let him approach. She didn't move, but stayed where she was, even when he took two more steps. "When Wesley interrupted us, I was trying to tell you about the bite."

Her lips parted, and a breath rushed from her mouth. "Yes, the bite."

"The bite is not just a way for a vampire to feed and get the nourishment he needs, it's also a way to intensify sexual pleasure. Blood-bonded couples engage in it almost daily, like my parents…"

"But they're both vampires."

"Even vampires drink each other's blood. It creates a high in both the vampire who bites, and the one who gets bitten."

He noticed how Scarlet's chest rose, and how her nipples were pressing through her T-shirt. He couldn't take his eyes off the erotic sight that made blood rush to his groin.

"Ryder," she murmured.

"Yes?"

"Is there anything else you haven't told me yet? Any other secrets you haven't shared with me?"

"There are two more things I haven't told you yet." He took a breath. "The night we met in the nightclub and had sex, I only had one cock."

She reared back. "What? That's not possible! That makes no sense. Two days later you had two. I can't believe—"

He put a finger to her lips. "Please, let me explain. A satyr is born with one fully functioning cock, and a mass of flesh and skin, a deformity of sorts, an inch or so above it. It's grotesque, and something I never wanted to show any woman. But there's no way around it. Only after a satyr has sex with his intended mate for the first time, the deformity grows into a second fully functioning cock within twenty-four hours. I had sex with you that night. Nobody else. And a day later, I had a second cock."

He paused to let the implications of his words sink in.

Her eyes widened. "Is that the second thing you haven't told me? That I'm supposed to be your intended mate?"

"You are, but there's something else I still need to tell you." In fact, it was the most important thing of all.

"What is it?"

He filled his lungs with air. "I love you, Scarlet, and if you will have me, I will do everything in my power to protect you and make you happy." He dropped his gaze, so he could continue what he had to say. "But if you don't feel the same for me, I will let you go so you can live the life you want for yourself. You are my intended mate, but you have free will. If you don't love me—"

Scarlet pulled in an audible breath. "Can you take me home now?"

Ryder's heart stopped. Scarlet didn't want him. She couldn't accept who he really was. But he'd made her a promise, and he was a man of his word. Even though this would break his heart.

He lifted his head and looked at her, his body tensing, steeling himself for the heartbreak ahead. "Yes, of course. I'll take you home. I would just ask you for one last favor. Please keep our secret. I'm sorry that I hurt you, and that I'm not who you hoped I would be." He turned on his heel and walked to the door, his hand on the lock, when he felt Scarlet's hand on his back.

"Ryder, look at me."

He turned slowly, unable to deny her even the smallest wish.

"When I said take me home, I meant your home."

His pulse started to race. "My home?"

Scarlet brushed her finger over his lips. "I want to make love to you. And I want to feel your bite." She pushed her hair away from her neck and tilted her head. "Is that where a vampire bites the woman he loves?"

His heart pounded in his chest as if it wanted to jump from his body to hers, while his fangs descended and pushed past his lips. His breathing suddenly turned ragged. "There, or your breasts, or the inside of your thigh, anywhere you want to."

"How about everywhere?" she whispered, her face close to his now.

"Are you trying to tell me that you have feelings for me?"

Scarlet brought her lips to within an inch of his. "Why don't I give you the answer to that question when you make love to me, and when I feel your fangs pierce my skin?"

"Deal!"

Ryder pressed Scarlet to him and took her lips, kissing her, careful not to hurt her with his fangs, but she instantly demanded more, her tongue licking against his lips. "Easy, baby, I don't want to hurt you."

"You won't," she murmured and licked her tongue against one fang.

A bolt of fire shot through his body, and a moan ripped from his throat. He let go of her lips instantly.

"Did that hurt?" Scarlet asked, a concerned look on her face.

"Christ, no! It felt as if you were licking my cocks."

"Oh!" A smile formed on her lips.

"A vampire's fangs are one of the most erogenous zones on his body."

"I'm gonna have to remember that." Scarlet's eyes sparkled with mischief. "I suppose that means if I lick them you'll get instant hard-ons?"

"Baby, just you being near me gives me instant hard-ons." He slid one hand down her ass and rubbed his groin against her stomach. "Feel that?"

She sucked in a breath. "What'll happen if I keep licking your fangs? Will you come?"

"Like a green teenager."

"I guess then I'd better stop that until we get home."

"I have a better idea." Ryder released her from his embrace and walked to the far wall in the office, where he pressed a button. The Murphy bed descended and turned into a king-size bed with crisp sheets.

"Oh my," Scarlet said on a gasp and bridged the distance between them with several steps. Then her eyes fell on his chest. "You need to get your wounds taken care of. The convict got you really bad."

Ryder looked down at his chest. The V-CON had slashed him with his claws, leaving several gashes that bled. On his arms too, he had superficial cuts from his opponent's claws.

"I've had worse." He lifted his eyes to Scarlet's face. "Your blood will heal me."

"Are you saying that human blood…"

"Yes, human blood will heal a vampire's wounds, just like vampire blood will heal a human's injuries."

Her eyes widened, and her pink tongue licked over her bottom lip. "You mean humans can drink vampire blood?"

He pulled her to him. "Yes."

"Won't that turn them into a vampire? I mean, the lore suggests…"

"Only if the human is on the verge of death. If the human's heartbeat is still strong, even if the injuries are grave, vampire blood will heal but not turn a human."

"There's so much I still don't know."

"Do you want me to tell you more now? I can, if you—"

"Later. Right now I want to feel you." She gave him a little push, and he landed with his back on the bed.

"I guess then I'll shut up."

"Good choice," she murmured and lowered herself over him, straddling him.

Ryder pulled her head to him and captured her lips for a kiss. His fangs were still out, but he wasn't concerned about scaring Scarlet off anymore. She'd already proven to him that she could handle him, and that she wanted to experience everything that made him a vampire. He explored her mouth, danced with her eager tongue, and let her take charge when she began to lick his fangs in earnest. The feeling of her tongue touching the razor-sharp instruments sent waves of pleasure into every cell of his body.

He started undressing her, freeing her of her T-shirt, her jeans and shoes, while Scarlet undressed him just as frantically. He'd never seen her so eager for sex, not even during the instances when she'd gone into heat. This wasn't Scarlet driven by her satyr side, this was Scarlet driven by something else entirely: her emotions. She wanted him, not because she was destined to be his mate, but because she cared about him. He could feel it with every fiber of his being, even though she'd not yet said the words he wanted to hear.

When they were finally naked, Ryder rolled over Scarlet, his weight braced on his elbows and knees, his lower cock poised at her pussy, his upper one sliding against her clit. "I'll take you with both my cocks later, but right now I need you to see me."

He parted his lips and let her see his fangs. With fascination in her eyes, Scarlet looked at him, her heartbeat racing now. It was pumping her blood through her veins faster, and he knew that once he pierced her skin, her blood would rush into his mouth.

"They're beautiful," she murmured.

"Oh, Scarlet, you have no idea what this means to me. You accepting what I am. You letting me drink from you, trusting me."

He thrust his cock into her, sinking into her wet warm cave. Scarlet's eyes closed for a brief moment, and she inhaled a deep breath.

"You feel so good," she whispered and looked up at him.

"Are you sure you want this? My fangs in your neck?"

"Taste me, Ryder. I want to know what it's like." She turned her head slightly to offer her neck.

He brought his lips to her smooth skin and licked over it with his tongue, preparing her for his bite. "I love you, Scarlet." He drove his fangs into her neck, and felt her blood on his tongue, the taste intoxicating. More blood rushed into his mouth, and he swallowed it.

He pumped his cock into her sweet pussy, pleasure spreading to every cell of his body, Scarlet's scent and taste engulfing him. He'd never felt anything better in his life.

Scarlet's hands were on his shoulders and his back, not trying to push him away, but to pull him closer, accepting him.

"I love you, Ryder."

At hearing Scarlet's declaration, Ryder's heart felt like exploding. Scarlet would be his.

37

Scarlet felt the erotic effect of Ryder's fangs in her neck instantly. Her entire body was floating as if on a cloud. She was feeling no pain; not even his sharp teeth piercing her skin had been painful. Instead, it had felt as if he was caressing her clitoris. And now, with Ryder drinking her blood, and his cock buried deep in her, his second cock sliding over her center of pleasure, every sane thought, every concern she'd ever had, left her brain to make space for pleasure to engulf her.

If she'd thought that sex with Ryder was pleasurable because of his two cocks and the way he used them to bring her to ecstasy, it was nothing compared to the sensations she experienced with his fangs in her while he plowed into her again and again. His skillful moves drove her arousal higher. She put one hand on his nape, and felt him shudder in response, before he gripped it and pulled it off him and pinned it to the mattress. He growled, the sound reverberating in her body like an echo that wouldn't stop.

She was panting now, her hips undulating to meet his thrusts and feel his second cock slide against her clit. With her free hand, she gripped his ass and forced him to thrust harder. He did, but then he pried her second hand off him, and pinned that one to the mattress as well. She was at his mercy now, imprisoned by his hands, impaled on his cock. To her surprise, she couldn't get enough of it. She wanted him to take her like this, wanted to feel his power, his strength. And she wanted even more.

"Take me with both your cocks inside me," she begged.

Another growl tore from his chest, and he ripped his lips from her, his head whipping back, his eyes glaring red, his fangs dripping with blood. To know that this powerful vampire loved her, sent ripples through her body, and she realized she was climaxing.

She pressed her head back onto the mattress and arched her back, the waves of her orgasm so strong that they robbed her of her breath. A moment later, Ryder flipped her and she found herself on her knees, facing the headboard, her hands braced against it. Still dazed from her orgasm, she felt Ryder kneeling behind her, his fingers dipping into her pussy, before he rimmed her anus with the plentiful juices. Then she felt his cocks again, one at the entrance to her pussy, the other at her anus.

"Oh, God, yes!" she cried out as Ryder thrust his cocks into her to the hilts.

There was no pain, no discomfort, only pleasure, when he impaled her on his twin erections. He brought his head back to her where he'd bitten her, and licked over the incisions.

"I want more," he said, his voice a deep growl. "Your blood tastes like pure paradise."

The sound of his voice sent a shudder through her body, and she knew she would never be able to deny him what he demanded. "Then bite me again."

"You like my bite?" he murmured at the other side of her neck that she was now turning toward him.

"Yes, I've never felt anything better."

He brushed his fangs along her skin, and the touch made her clit throb.

"You're making me come again by doing that," she said.

He withdrew his cocks but for the tips, before he plunged back into her. At the same time, he drove his fangs into her skin and sucked on her vein.

"Yes!"

Ryder's cocks suddenly spasmed inside her, and she felt warmth and wetness spread inside her as he came. His orgasm ignited her own, and waves of pleasure so powerful that she thought they could drown her, washed over her, until they both stilled, and Ryder removed his fangs from her and licked over the puncture wounds.

They collapsed on the bed together, and Scarlet instinctively touched the spot where he'd bitten her. But she didn't feel the holes his fangs had left. She checked the other side of her neck, but there too her skin was unmarred.

Her eyes flew open and she saw Ryder look at her, his eyes a rich brown again, and his fangs gone. "But you bit me. How—"

"A vampire's saliva seals small wounds like that instantly."

"So I wasn't hallucinating when I saw the V-CON lick over Lizzy's wounds… Wow… That's… amazing."

"You'll never have scars, no matter how often I bite you. I would never want to do anything to mar your beautiful skin." His eyes roamed over her body, and he caressed her heated skin with his hand, before he laid back and pulled her on top of him and sighed contentedly.

When her gaze fell on his chest and arms, where he'd gotten injured earlier, his skin was perfect again. No sign of an injury or any scars.

"You've healed."

"Because of your blood."

Scarlet snuggled against him, happy and sated like never before in her life.

"I'm sorry I was so rough with you. But tasting your blood, hmm… Do you regret it?" Ryder asked, caressing her back.

"Regret? No, not in a million years." She lifted her head and looked at him. His eyes suddenly shimmered golden. "Your eyes, they're shimmering again. I've seen them like that before. Back at the club, and every time when we had sex."

"The eyes reflect a vampire's emotions. When my eyes shimmer like this, it can mean a few different things, either arousal, desire, ecstasy, or satisfaction."

"What do they mean right now?"

"Pure and utter bliss."

She chuckled softly. "I was rather hoping for arousal," she joked.

Ryder rolled her beneath him in a split-second before she even realized what he was planning. "You insatiable little minx." He laughed and kissed her. "How am I ever gonna keep up with you?"

"I'm sure you won't have any problems in that department."

There was a loud bang at the door. "Are you guys done in there?"

Scarlet's heart beat into her throat. "Oh my God, did somebody hear us?" she whispered to Ryder.

A sheepish expression appeared on Ryder's face. "I might have forgotten to mention that vampires have rather sensitive hearing."

Scarlet felt heat rise into her cheeks.

Ryder turned his head toward the door. "What's your problem, Grayson?"

"We got a message from Brandon King. He claims you abducted Scarlet. And he'll have you arrested if you don't bring her back."

Scarlet almost choked on her next breath. "That's… that's…" She was speechless at her father's outrageous claim.

"Give us a few minutes," Ryder said and swung his legs out of bed. "We'll be right out."

Scarlet's head was spinning, fury and disbelief colliding inside her. "He can't do that! I'm an adult. He can't just…"

"We'll handle it. I promise."

Ryder pressed a kiss to her forehead and led her into the bathroom.

38

When Ryder and Scarlet left Blake's office a few minutes later, showered and dressed, Grayson was waiting impatiently in the hallway.

"Finally!" Grayson groused. He motioned them to follow him.

"What exactly did my father say?" Scarlet asked.

"I don't know. I didn't speak to him."

Realizing that Grayson was leading them toward Samson's office, Ryder asked, "He spoke to Samson?"

"My father is at the theater with Mom. King couldn't reach him, so the call went to Amaury instead." Grayson stopped in front of Amaury's office door, and knocked.

The door was ripped open, and Amaury, a huge, linebacker-sized vampire appeared in the door. "What the fuck took you so long?" Then his eyes fell on Scarlet. "I'm assuming you're Scarlet King."

"Yes, I'm…" Scarlet started, but her words died.

Amaury inhaled and shifted his gaze to Ryder. "You didn't need to shower on my account. I can still smell you on her. What the fuck is going on here?"

He ushered them inside with a quick hand movement, but when Grayson tried to follow, Amaury stopped him. "You, get out!"

It looked like Grayson wanted to say something—if Ryder had to guess something along the lines of the fact that Grayson was the boss's son—but he didn't and left, pulling the door shut behind him.

"Mr. Amaury, I don't know why my father is doing this…"

"It's just Amaury," he ground out. "And Ryder knows full well that we have rules here, and—"

Before Ryder could launch into an explanation, he heard a familiar female voice coming from the seating area.

"Baby, calm down," Nina, a beautiful blonde with a pixie haircut said as she rose from the couch, arranging her top, which looked a little crumpled. "You were reckless once too."

Ryder's gaze instinctively went to Nina's cleavage. Was there a drop of blood seeping through her top? It appeared that Amaury had just been feeding from his mate, and by the looks of it not from her neck, but her breasts.

"Guess King's call interrupted your dinner," Ryder said, not afraid of Amaury in the slightest. He was putty in Nina's hands. She would rein him in if need be.

"Watch what you say, Ryder," Amaury warned.

"Scarlet knows," Ryder said.

"Knows what?"

"Who we are, what we are." He put his arm around Scarlet's waist and pulled her closer to his side. "That's Amaury, he's Damian's and Benjamin's father, and this is Nina, his mate, and the twin's mother."

Amaury let out a breath, while Nina smiled at Scarlet.

"It's nice to meet you…" Scarlet said hesitantly. "I've met your sons. They're nice."

"They're hellions. No need to sugar-coat it," Nina said. She looked at Amaury. "Are you gonna be civil now?"

"I'm always civil," Amaury claimed. He looked at Ryder and Scarlet. "So by the looks of it, you didn't abduct your charge, you seduced her, and alienated her father so—"

"Actually," Scarlet interrupted. "Ryder didn't seduce me. I seduced him. So, it's all my fault."

"It's not," Ryder protested, astonished that Scarlet wanted to shoulder the blame. "I knew what I was doing, and I did it anyway."

Amaury shook his head and chuckled all of a sudden. "Ryder, you never had a chance resisting her. When a woman makes up her mind, we're powerless." His gaze swept to Nina, and Ryder couldn't help but notice the lusting looks he raked over her. The twin's claim that their parents couldn't keep their hands off each other, was definitely true. He knew with certainty that the moment Ryder and Scarlet left Amaury's office, Amaury would make love to Nina, and bite her again, not for the nourishment her blood provided, but because the bite would heighten their arousal and make their climax even more satisfying.

"Anyway," Amaury said, his demeanor calmer now as he addressed Scarlet directly. "The point is that your father called me and threatened to have Ryder arrested for kidnapping you. Listen, I've never spoken to him before, but believe me when I tell you he was absolutely serious. He'll make good on his threat."

"We can deal with the police. They won't arrest me," Ryder said. "The mayor won't let it happen."

"The police aren't our problem. The press is," Amaury said. "Once this leaks we've gotta do damage control. I'd rather not put ourselves through that if we can avoid it. We don't need the press snooping around in our business."

"Fine," Ryder said, "then I'll talk to King and explain the situation."

"But Dad's in the wrong! He knows you didn't abduct me. You spoke to him. I was right there when he told you to take care of me. I don't understand why he suddenly changed his mind."

Ryder looked into Scarlet's eyes. "I do. Claudia got to him after you told him that I saw her cheating on him with Derek. She's turned him against you and me."

"What's that about?" Amaury asked. "Who are these people?"

"Claudia is my stepmother," Scarlet explained. "And Derek is supposedly her nephew. Only, she's never before mentioned a nephew, or a sibling for that matter."

"I saw them having sex," Ryder added. "Scarlet told her father over the phone, not knowing that Claudia was with him. And of course she denied it. I think Claudia is turning King against Scarlet, and the way to punish her is to take me out of the picture."

"And that can't happen," Scarlet said, and pressed herself close to Ryder.

Amaury nodded. "Have you tried to figure out who this Derek guy is? I have the feeling Brandon King needs hard evidence before he believes that his wife is cheating on him."

"I've already spoken to Thomas and Eddie. They're working on it."

"Good," Amaury said, "but in the meantime, you've got no choice but to take Scarlet back to him and hope you can explain to him that Scarlet is with you out of her own free will. I mean, you're over eighteen, right?" He looked at Scarlet.

"I'll be twenty-five in three months."

"Well, legally he can't do anything to keep you from seeing Ryder. But," Amaury said, "he needs to see you so he can't claim that Ryder is keeping you locked up somewhere."

"He'll try to blackmail me into staying," Scarlet said.

"Blackmail? How?" Ryder asked.

"I'll get access to my trust when I turn twenty-five. There are stipulations… he can try to convince the trustees that I'm mentally unstable, and legally, they'd have to prevent me from accessing my trust…"

"You're not mentally unstable," Ryder protested, grinding his teeth. "It doesn't matter. Let him keep the money if that means you're free to live your life the way you want to." Free to love him, to be his mate, his forever.

Scarlet lifted her eyes to him. "I don't care about the money. I just don't want his cheating wife to get it. Because if the trust goes back to my father, it might as well be hers. She already spends his money with both hands, I'm sure she'll do the same with my trust, once it reverts back to my father."

"One thing at a time," Ryder said. "Let's first see your father and show him that you're well, and that I'm not keeping you against your will. Then we'll deal with the rest. Once we have some dirt on Derek, your father will see reason."

Slowly, Scarlet nodded. "I hope you're right."

39

Ryder drove through the late-night traffic from the Mission to Pacific Heights. Scarlet sat on the passenger seat of his SUV, lost in her thoughts. It was almost midnight. So much had happened in the last six hours. It felt like a lifetime had passed, because the life ahead of her was so very different from everything she'd ever known. The man she loved was a vampire and a satyr, a creature she should fear, yet no such fear spread in her heart, because it was full of love, the love she felt for Ryder, and the love Ryder felt for her. There was no space for fear or doubt or regret.

Scarlet looked at Ryder's profile while he navigated through the city streets that turned more deserted the closer they were to her home.

Ryder glanced at her, and put one hand on hers, squeezing it gently. "Everything will be all right. We'll convince your father that he can't trust Claudia, maybe not tonight, or tomorrow, but soon. And once he sees that you only had his best interest in mind when you told him about Claudia's infidelity, you and he will make up. He was your father first, before he met Claudia. He loves you."

Scarlet let out a sigh. "Despite the fact that he wants to have you arrested, you have nothing bad to say about him. You're much kinder than I am. I'm so angry with him."

"I'm not. Without him, you wouldn't exist, and that would mean I would've never experienced true love."

His last words sank deep into her, filling her with hope that all the obstacles ahead of them would soon come crumbling down.

"You have such a big heart. How is it possible that a vampire, a creature the lore paints as violent and heartless can be so caring?"

Ryder smiled and brought her hand to his lips. He pressed a kiss on her knuckles. "Because a vampire's heart beats the same way any other creature's does, be that human or animal. Our emotions run as deep as those of a human, maybe even deeper. And while we may be almost indestructible physically, our hearts can break as easily as a human's."

"I love you, Ryder."

"And I love you."

"There are so many more questions I have about your life, about all the other vampires, about… everything."

"I'll tell you whatever you want to know."

She hesitated. "There is something I'm curious about."

"Yes?"

"It's about the women. You said Nina is Amaury's mate and Damian's and Benjamin's mother, and like your mother, she looks so young, so I'm assuming she's a vampire. But what happens to the human women who are… uhm… in relationships with vampires? If the vampire stops aging like you did, then what happens when the women age…"

"You believe Nina is a vampire?"

"Yes, of course, otherwise how would she look so young yet have two grown sons?"

"Nina is human. She and Amaury have been together for thirty-two or thirty-three years, since before Samson's first child was born."

Stunned, Scarlet stared at Ryder. "But then, how does she stay so young?"

"It's the blood-bond she shares with Amaury. She drinks his blood. Because of it, she remains as young as on the day she bonded with him."

"Ohh." Would Ryder want her to drink his blood? And would she want that? Would she find it as erotic as when he'd drunk her blood?

"We're here," Ryder announced and parked the car in the first empty parking spot he found.

Scarlet got out of the car, and with Ryder holding her hand, she crossed the street and looked up at the stately Victorian that had been in her family for three generations. There was light in the foyer as well as in the living room. Her room, which overlooked the street, was dark, but behind the window next to it, which was part of the second-floor corridor, she saw a dim light.

In front of the entrance door, she stopped, her hand shaking too much for her to put the key in the lock. Ryder steadied her hand.

"He's not gonna bite you," Ryder said. Then he seemed to realize what he'd said, and added, "Sorry, stupid idiom. You know what I mean."

Scarlet took a deep inhale and unlocked the door. She entered, Ryder behind her, shutting the door.

"Dad? I'm back." She waited for his reply, but it was quiet in the house.

She cast a look at Ryder. He shrugged. "Maybe he fell asleep waiting for you?" Though by the look on his face, he didn't believe it either.

Scarlet walked into the living room, Ryder on her heels. She glanced around. There was a glass on the coffee table, a tumbler which by the looks of it still had a little bit of whiskey in it. Next to it was a whiskey bottle.

"That's Dad's favorite drink."

But he was definitely not in the living room.

"I saw a light upstairs," Ryder said.

They walked back into the foyer, and Scarlet glanced to the back of the house where the kitchen, a laundry room, and her father's study was located. But it was dark back there.

"Let's check upstairs then," Scarlet agreed.

As they walked up the stairs, Scarlet called out again, "Dad? Where are you? I'm home."

"What's that sound?" Ryder asked.

"What sound?" She hadn't heard anything.

"A clicking sound, but now it's gone."

"I didn't hear anything." At the second-floor landing, Scarlet didn't bother turning left to go to her room. She knew he wouldn't be there. Besides, the room was dark. She pointed to the master bedroom at the end of the hallway. The door was ajar, and from it, light streamed into the corridor.

Her boots made a click-clack sound on the old hardwood floors.

"Dad?"

At the door, Scarlet knocked, despite it being open a sliver. She didn't want to walk in on her dad if he was getting undressed.

When he still didn't answer, she exchanged a look with Ryder. He nodded and pushed the door open, entering ahead of her. As she opened the door wider, she saw the unmade bed. The bedside lamps and the recessed ceiling lights illuminated the room.

"Dad?" she called out toward the bathroom. The door to it was closed, but from underneath the door, she could see the light. "Dad?"

Still no answer.

"What if he fell again?" Scarlet asked.

"What do you mean?"

"Last week he slipped in the bathroom in Palo Alto and sprained his ankle."

"Yeah, I saw him limping the other day," Ryder confirmed.

"Yeah, he told me that he slipped on some spilled lotion or shampoo. He didn't know what. Claudia has so many different bottles. What if it happened again?"

"Mr. King," Ryder called out at the bathroom door. "I'm coming in." He turned the knob and pushed, but the door didn't budge. "It's locked."

Now Scarlet felt a pit in her stomach. "Oh my God, we have to get inside. If he's hit his head or had a stroke… please, Ryder. We have to get in there."

"I'll break the door down. Step back."

Scarlet took a few steps back and watched as Ryder kicked his foot against the door just above the doorknob. With a loud crash, the wood splintered, and the door separated from the frame and swung inside.

Ryder hurried inside. Scarlet rushed after him, fear clamping her throat shut, preventing her from breathing. But the moment she stood in the bathroom with the extra-large shower, the soaking tub, the double vanity and the separate toilet, she realized that the bathroom was empty.

"But it was locked from inside," Scarlet said.

"Easy to do," Ryder said. "Turn the knob lock, leave the bathroom, and pull the door shut, and it appears as if somebody has locked himself in."

"But why? Why would he do that?" Scarlet said.

"He wouldn't," Ryder said. "Because your father was never here."

"But his drink in the living room…"

"It's all staged." Ryder ran a hand through his hair. "Fuck! It's a trap! We've gotta go! Now!" He grabbed Scarlet's hand.

Scarlet didn't have a chance to ask any more questions, because Ryder was already pulling her away from the bathroom and toward the door to the hallway.

"Shit!" he cursed before they even reached it. "I smell smoke."

"What? I don't smell anything."

Ryder ripped the door open. Finally, Scarlet could smell it too: smoke. It was coming from the first floor.

"Oh my God!" Scarlet cried out.

By the time they reached the landing, flames were already shooting up from the stairs. The old house was burning like tinder. She looked down the flight of stairs, but the smoke was getting thicker, and the flames had already devoured the middle of the staircase, making a descent impossible.

Panic shot through her. "We can't get out."

Ryder snatched her hand. "Back to the master bedroom. We'll have to get out through the back."

As they ran back into the master bedroom, Ryder pulled his cell phone from his pocket and punched a number. Almost immediately a voice answered, "Scanguards, emergency line."

They rushed into the master bedroom, and Scarlet slammed the door shut.

"Ryder Giles. Emergency protocol foxtrot, send fire and ambulance to 2447 Pacific Avenue, Brandon King's residence. I'm with a human. Exit route is compromised. I repeat: I'm with a human."

Ryder was already looking out the windows that overlooked the garden.

"Understood. Emergency protocol foxtrot invoked. Keep your line open," the woman on the end of the line said.

He placed the phone in his jacket pocket. "Is there a fire escape out of here?"

"No."

"Okay, get me all the bedsheets you can find in here. I'll have to lower you down to the ground."

"And what about you? Who's gonna lower you down?"

"Don't worry about me. Immortal, remember?" He squeezed her arm. "Sheets?"

"Okay." As quickly as she could, she opened the drawers of the antique linen closet and rifled through the stacks of sheet, taking out the largest and thickest ones. "Here." She turned to Ryder who was trying to pry the window open.

"It's nailed shut," he cursed.

"Who would—"

"If I had to take a wild guess, the same person who set the fire. Probably Derek. " Then he grabbed a pillow from an armchair and held it against the window. "Watch out for the glass. And start knotting the sheets together. Double knots."

Ryder used his fist to smash in the window, then continued to knock out the jagged edges so there was a large enough opening for a person to get through without cutting themselves.

"How're you doing on the sheets?" Ryder asked and came to help her.

Together, they knotted half a dozen sheets together. Ryder tested all the knots, pulling hard to make sure they wouldn't loosen.

"Okay," he said with a nod at Scarlet. "Lift your arms over your head."

She did as he asked, and he tied one end of the sheets around her belly, then tested the strength of the knots he'd tied. They held. Scarlet's gaze was drawn to the door. From the gap between the floor and door, smoke was now coming into the room. Ryder saw it too.

"You have to go, now," he said and kissed her hard. "I'll be right behind you. Promise me once you're in the garden, climb over the fence to the neighbor's house. You'll be able to get out with their help. I'll meet you at the car, okay?"

"Promise. How are you gonna get out?"

"Go, now." He lifted her up and sat her on the window sill, with her legs dangling. The long end of the sheet-chain was already draped around his back, and he was holding on to it with both hands. Scarlet felt dizzy when she looked down, and leaned back.

"I've got you, baby, trust me."

"I love you, Ryder."

Slowly, he started dropping her. With every foot that she got closer to the ground, she felt more confident that they would get out of this alive. When her feet finally hit the ground, she sighed with relief and turned around to look up at the window.

"I made it!" she cried out to Ryder, but she wasn't sure he could hear her. The fire in the house now sounded like a freight train. "Ryder!"

"Run!"

40

Ryder watched as Scarlet climbed over the neighbor's fence.

"Ryder?"

He pulled out his cell phone from his pocket. "Thomas?"

"Are you injured?" Thomas asked through the open emergency line.

"No. I'm fine. I lowered Scarlet down into the garden, she's getting out via the neighbor's yard," he replied.

"The fire brigade is thirty seconds away," the emergency operator cut in. "I'll have them check on her."

"Thanks," Ryder replied.

"Ryder," Thomas continued now, "We found stuff on Derek Helmsley. It's not good."

"Yeah, I figured."

"He's definitely not Claudia's nephew. He and Claudia are a con couple. They run long cons, and are wanted in Canada and in Texas. They're after rich men and women, and fleece them for all they've got."

"And apparently they don't shy away from using violence," Ryder guessed. "This fire is arson. It was a trap to kill Scarlet." What Scarlet had said about her trust fund suddenly came to mind. Something else became clear at the same moment. "You have to warn Brandon King."

"Eddie's already on that."

Ryder saw the first flames shoot underneath the bedroom door. "I've gotta get out of here. The fire is getting too close."

"Brandon King isn't answering his cell phone," Eddie said through the line.

"Fuck!" Ryder cursed. He feared the worst—that Claudia and Derek had already killed him. "Triangulate his cell phone!"

"On it!" Eddie confirmed.

Ryder slipped his cell phone back into his jacket pocket. He hopped onto the windowsill and swung his legs through the opening, ready to jump.

"Fuck!" Eddie cursed. "King is in the 2400-block on Pacific Avenue!"

"Shit!"

"He must be in the house, Ryder!" Thomas added.

"Those fucking bastards!" Ryder cursed and got off the windowsill, hopping back into the room. "I've gotta find him."

"The fire truck is there now," the emergency operator reported.

Ryder cast a look at the bedroom door. He could feel the heat coming from it. Quickly, he ran into the bathroom, grabbed a large bath towel and soaked it in water. Then he put it over his head and shoulders, his head bending downward.

When he reached the door, he grabbed the knob and turned it, ignoring that the hot metal was burning his hand, and pain was shooting up his arm. He dipped his head and ripped the door open. Flames hit him, but the wet towel helped. He raced out into the corridor. Everything combustible was in flames. He headed for the first door to his right, one of the guest rooms, and ripped it open. The flames hadn't reached the room yet, but were now slowly licking into it.

The guestroom was empty, the ensuite bathroom as well.

Ryder quickly left the room, heading back into the flames. When he reached the second guestroom, the door to it was already standing in flames, and the room behind it was burning hotter than hell. The floor was giving way, and several floorboards had already burned through. The subfloor was gone, and soon the joists would give way too.

In a split-second Ryder assessed the situation. He couldn't reach the second guestroom nor Scarlet's room, and could only hope that Brandon King wasn't up here.

"Have the firemen concentrate their hoses on the foyer and the stairs," Ryder called out, hoping the cell phone in his pocket could pick up his voice. "I'm coming down the stairs."

The stairs were gone. It was clear that the fire had started somewhere underneath them to cut off his and Scarlet's escape route. The clicking sound he'd heard when he and Scarlet had gone upstairs could have been some sort of trigger that started the fire.

Ryder heard a garbled voice come through his phone, but the fire created such a noise that he couldn't make out the words. "I'm jumping now!"

Ryder took the ten-foot jump, landing on his feet, then rolled to his side. Beneath him were hot embers, remains of floorboards and joists. But he also felt sludge. The water from the hoses had extinguished some of the flames in the foyer.

"I'm in the foyer," he yelled. "Heading for the kitchen and study."

The living room had been empty when he'd arrived with Scarlet, which only left the back of the house. The flames were raging there too. The half-bath along the corridor was burning. Opposite of it was the study. The door was already damaged by the fire, holding on by only one hinge. Ryder kicked it in, and felt a rush of air, then the flames in the hallway shot past him into the room with such force that he lost his balance and fell forward into the study.

Despite the burns he'd already sustained, Ryder got back on his feet. The smoke and flames made it hard to see anything in the room, but his honed vampire senses told him that Brandon King was here.

"He's in the study," Ryder called out toward his cell phone, "the room behind the living room. Hit it with the hoses! Now!"

Ryder reached the heavy mahogany desk and made his way around it. Behind it, a man lay on the ground. Brandon King. He wasn't moving.

A heavy burning joist came crashing down from the upper floor, the desk breaking its fall, missing Ryder and King by only a few inches. Ryder bent down to King and put his fingers on his neck, checking for a pulse. It was there, but just barely.

He also saw now why King hadn't replied to Scarlet calling out for him. He was gagged and bound. Ryder pulled the gag from his mouth and hooked his arms underneath King's armpits, when the window shattered. Ryder turned his back to it instantly, shielding King from the flying glass shards, which now embedded themselves in Ryder's jacket.

Water suddenly streamed into the room, and a figure in a heavy Kevlar suit jumped through the window, and though Ryder couldn't immediately see the man's face, he recognized him anyway.

"Dad! Help me get him out!"

"I've got him," Gabriel said, grabbing King. "Get out, the house is about to collapse. I'll lift him through the window."

Ryder headed toward the window and jumped through it. Outside, he pivoted and reached his arms through the opening, ready to help his father lift King through, when he heard joists crashing and window panes exploding. The framing of the old Victorian was breaking like matchsticks, collapsing under the weight of the second floor.

"Dad!" Ryder screamed.

41

Scarlet stood on the opposite side of the street in front of her home. Flames were shooting out of all the windows. A fire truck was aiming several hoses at the house, dousing it in water, but the flames showed no sign of abating. Frantically, she searched for Ryder to come out through the side of the neighbor's yard, the same way she'd made it out. But there was no sign of him.

Tears shot to her eyes, and fear choked her as she ran toward the house. "Ryder! Ryder! Please!" she screamed over the din of the fire and the loud shouts of the firefighters as they tried to bring the fire under control.

"Scarlet!"

At the sound of her name, she whirled around and saw Maya jump out of the back of an ambulance, running toward her.

"Maya!" Scarlet cried out and pointed to the house. "He's still in there. Ryder is still in there!"

Maya pulled her into her arms. "I know, honey."

"He should be out by now. Why isn't he out? We have to help him. Please!" Through tear-stained eyes she looked at Maya.

"Listen, Scarlet, he's still in there because he's trying to get your father out."

"My father?" She freed herself from the embrace, and spun around, staring at the house. "Oh God, no!" She would lose them both. "No! I have to do something!"

She tried to run toward the flames, but Maya pulled her back. "Gabriel went after him. Please, you have to stay here. Ryder will never forgive me should anything happen to you."

Her last words were swallowed by the loud sound of the building collapsing.

"Nooooooo! Noooooo!" Scarlet screamed. The pain of her heart breaking buckled her knees, and the sobs tearing from her chest blurred her vision. Maya's arms held her upright, or she would have collapsed.

Maya caressed her back and pressed kisses in her hair. "They're alive, I know it. They'll make it. Please trust me."

The last few days flashed before her eyes, making the pain even more intense. Everybody she'd ever loved was gone, her mother, her half-brother, and now her father, and Ryder. There was no reason for her to go on living. It was over. She lifted her head from Maya's chest, and Maya loosened her grip. Scarlet turned back to look at the smoldering flames.

"I love you, Ryder," she murmured to herself and ran toward the house, past a firefighter. The heat became more intense the closer she got.

"Scarlet!"

She whirled her head toward the sound of Ryder's voice. Was she hallucinating? She blinked and wiped her eyes, trying to clear her vision, when she saw him with a man in a full-body Kevlar suit—like the vampire prison guard had worn—carrying out a third man. They were hurrying past the left side of the building where a narrow path separated it from the house next to it.

"Ryder!"

Maya pulled her farther back now, leading her back to the ambulance. For the first time Scarlet read the writing on it. *Scanguards Emergency Response*, it said. This wasn't an ordinary ambulance. Ryder and Gabriel lifted her father onto the waiting gurney.

"I told you they'd make it," Maya said, before she embraced her husband.

Scarlet threw herself into Ryder's arms. "I thought you were dead."

He kissed her hard for a second, before he freed himself from her arms and turned to the gurney.

Scarlet leaned over her father. "Dad, please, you're safe now." But her father didn't move, didn't open his eyes.

Ryder put his fingers to his neck. "The pulse is weak." He looked to Maya, who with Gabriel's help was already lifting the gurney into the ambulance.

Maya jumped in with the gurney and listened for a pulse.

"You have to save him, please!" Scarlet cried. "Ryder, please, you said vampire blood can heal a human."

Ryder took her hand, then exchanged a look with his mother.

"Get in," Maya ordered, and they both jumped in.

Gabriel closed the ambulance door behind them. A moment later, he jumped into the passenger side of the ambulance, and Benjamin—or Damian, she couldn't tell them apart—started driving.

Scarlet was painfully aware of the fact that Ryder hadn't replied to her request to heal her father with vampire blood.

"I'm sorry, Scarlet," Maya said, "it's too late to heal him. His injuries are too extensive."

"No! I can't lose him. You don't understand. The last time we spoke, I said terrible things. I can't... he can't die."

Ryder held her hands. "Scarlet, there's something that we can do. But it's for you to decide."

She noticed how he shared another silent look with his mother, who nodded.

"What?"

"When he takes his last breath, we can turn him into a vampire," Ryder said.

Scarlet stared at him, her heart pounding.

"But it's not a decision taken lightly. He may not want to live as a vampire. He won't be like me. He'll be like my parents, having to avoid sunlight. There'll be many adjustments, and he'll need to get his hunger for blood under control. It's not an easy thing to do..."

Ryder looked at her with kindness in his eyes, and only now Scarlet noticed the burns that covered his body. But he didn't even seem to notice them. She tore her gaze from him and looked at her father. The burns on his body were extensive, but he had other injuries too. Blood oozed from deep gashes on his torso, probably caused by falling debris. One leg was shattered in two places. His chest barely rose with each breath, and his face was grey beneath the soot that covered his skin.

"Will he still be the same person?"

Ryder nodded. "His personality will still be the same, though he'll feel different at first. But we'll all help him adjust to his new life. He won't be alone in this. Scanguards will be his family. If that's what you truly want for him."

"There isn't much time, Scarlet," Maya said, her fingers on Brandon King's neck to feel his pulse. "We only have a couple of minutes left. We can't wait much longer. Once his heart stops, he'll be gone for good. And nothing will bring him back."

"Nobody will judge you, no matter what you decide," Ryder said softly.

Scarlet wiped the remaining tears from her eyes and looked at Ryder and his mother. They had a life, a good one, a loving family, friends. And they had jobs, they had Scanguards and its mission, a calling to help others. And while Scarlet had only found out about vampires a few hours earlier, she knew that a vampire could be happy. Her father would get another chance at love. And maybe this time it would be forever. She wanted that for him, because she had found it for herself, with Ryder. She wanted the same for her father.

Her decision was made. "Turn him."

"Okay," Ryder said and lifted his own wrist to his lips, his fangs already extending.

"Son, I'll do it," Gabriel said from the front seat and squeezed through the opening between the driver's and passenger's seat into the back of the ambulance. "Your relationship with Scarlet's father is gonna be complicated enough. If it turns out that he doesn't want this, let him be mad at me, not at you. I'll be his sire."

"Thank you," Scarlet said and watched Gabriel take off his Kevlar gloves and jacket, so he could access his wrist.

Gabriel's fangs lengthened, and for a moment, Scarlet noticed how frightening Gabriel could look when he showed his vampire side, but she wasn't scared of him.

"Pulse?" Gabriel asked with a look at his wife.

"Thirty and falling fast. Get ready."

Gabriel brought his wrist to his mouth and plunged his fangs into it. Blood dripped from them when he removed his fangs.

"It's time," Maya said.

Gabriel moved his arm, so his bleeding wrist was right above Brandon King's mouth. The blood dripped onto his lips, and Maya used two hands to open his mouth gently. Gabriel's blood dripped into the open mouth in a steady stream.

"Drink!" Gabriel urged. "Damn it, drink!"

Scarlet felt the tension in the ambulance as the three members of the Giles family watched the blood fill Brandon King's mouth. Nobody breathed. Nobody spoke. Everybody waited. Scarlet's heart clenched. What if it didn't work? What if it was too late? Had she waited too long to make a decision?

All of a sudden, there was the tiniest of movements of her father's throat, the Adam's apple moving slightly as he swallowed. His eyes remained closed, but he took the blood, swallowed it.

Ryder let out a sigh of relief, and gave her an encouraging look. He squeezed her hand and pulled her closer to his side, while he continued to watch. Scarlet couldn't take her eyes off Gabriel's wrist and the blood he fed her father. There was something fascinating about seeing a vampire like Gabriel engage in the selfless act of giving his blood to a human to save him. Ryder had offered the same without hesitation, simply because she'd asked him to do it. She looked at Ryder now, and he met her gaze.

"I love you," she murmured.

He pressed his forehead to hers. "And I love you."

She perceived a movement, and looked back at Gabriel. He removed his wrist from her father's mouth and was about to bring it to his lips, when Maya took it and dipped her mouth to it.

"Let me." She licked over Gabriel's puncture wounds with her tongue, lapping up the remaining blood and sealing them, stopping the blood flow.

Fascinated, Scarlet stared at Maya, and noticed that her eyes were shimmering golden the same way she'd seen Ryder's eyes shimmer.

The ambulance suddenly stopped. The driver—and she still couldn't figure out which one of the twins he was—looked over his shoulder. "We're here."

Scarlet looked outside and realized that they were in Scanguards' underground garage.

Jenny, the nurse Scarlet had met before, was waiting for them and opened the ambulance doors, helping Ryder's parents to transport the gurney with Scarlet's father to the elevator.

Ryder lifted Scarlet out of the back of the ambulance. Scarlet hurried toward the elevator, ready to join them.

But Maya lifted her hand. "No, you can't be near him now."

"What?" Panic rose in her. "Why not?"

"Ryder, take care of Scarlet," Gabriel said before the doors closed.

Scarlet turned to Ryder. "What's going on? Why can't I be with him?"

"It's too dangerous."

Behind them, the ambulance moved into a parking spot farther down the garage.

"Your father can't be around any humans when he wakes up. He might get overwhelmed by the smell of human blood and attack somebody."

"Dad would never hurt me!" Scarlet protested, tears rising into her eyes again.

Ryder pulled her into his arms. "Shhh, easy, baby. You'll get to see him soon. It'll just be for a few days. He needs time to adjust to his new body."

"But he needs me."

"My parents will take care of him. My father is responsible for him now. He won't let anything happen to him. I give you my word. And once your father can be trusted around humans, I'll bring you to him."

"He'll have questions."

"My mother will talk to him. She went through this herself. She never chose to become a vampire. She was turned against her will. She knows what he'll be going through. If anybody can help him, it's my mother." Ryder's eyes shimmered golden. "Your father is in the best possible hands."

Slowly, she calmed and nodded. "Okay."

Ryder looked over his shoulder. "Benjamin, you coming?"

The elevator pinged and the doors opened. Benjamin entered the elevator with them.

"Thomas just called me," Benjamin said. "He couldn't get through to you. He needs to see you."

Ryder touched his jacket pocket. "My cell must have fallen out somewhere in the house. It's probably toast right now." He punched the button for the top floor.

"Pretty charred toast, I'd say," Benjamin commented. Then he smiled at Scarlet. "Glad you're all right."

"Thanks to Ryder. If he hadn't lowered me out of the second floor risking his own life..."

She looked at Ryder, and he suddenly swayed. "Ryder?"

Ryder would have tumbled to the floor had Benjamin not caught him instantly.

"What's wrong with him?" Scarlet asked, panicked.

Benjamin lifted one hand, which suddenly was drenched in blood and slid Ryder's jacket to the side. There was a gaping wound in his side bleeding profusely. "Oh, fuck! He's injured. He's losing a shitload of blood."

"Why didn't he say anything? Oh my God! What can I do?"

"He needs blood. Bottled is fine, but coming directly from a human's vein would be better."

"I'll do it!" There was no hesitation. She didn't merely owe him her life, and her father's, but she loved him.

Benjamin lowered Ryder down on the floor. "I'll keep pressure on his wound. Give me your wrist. I'll have to pierce it."

Scarlet kneeled down on the floor and Benjamin shifted Ryder, so his head was in her lap. Then he took Scarlet's wrist.

"Sorry about that," Benjamin said, before he bit into her wrist.

It took a second or two before he removed his fangs, and she couldn't help but notice him swallowing some of her blood, his eyes shimmering golden.

"Now let him drink."

She put her bleeding wrist to Ryder's mouth and felt him latch onto it, sucking hard. A shaky breath rolled over her lips.

Benjamin let out a breath, and Scarlet raised her gaze to look at him.

"What a lucky bastard," Benjamin said as he licked a last drop of Scarlet's blood from his lower lip, his fangs still extended.

42

Ryder felt his senses sharpen, and became aware of his surroundings. He lay on a cold surface, his head cradled in a warm lap, drinking from a human's wrist, the delicious liquid familiar.

Scarlet...

His eyes flew open, and he jerked up, the bleeding wrist dropping in his lap.

"Fuck, Scarlet! Did I attack you? I'm sorry—"

"No," she said, "you collapsed from the blood loss."

Only now he realized that they weren't alone. Benjamin was pressing his hand into Ryder's side, and Ryder realized that he was putting pressure on the wound he'd sustained when a metal rod had pierced him when the house had come crashing down.

"Scarlet offered to feed you her blood so you could heal," Benjamin said and removed his hand from Ryder's wound. "Looks like it's healing already."

"You should have stopped her!"

Scarlet gasped and pulled back. "You don't want my blood?"

He took her arm and pulled her to him. "Of course I do, but I already took so much from you earlier...when we..."

"But you needed it..." Scarlet said.

He brought her wrist to his lips and licked over the incisions to close them. "Thank you, Scarlet."

Benjamin helped him and Scarlet up.

"Thanks," Ryder said, "and Benjamin?"

"Yeah?"

"If you ever bite Scarlet again, I will beat you senseless."

Benjamin shrugged. "Sounds fair." He pressed the button to open the elevator door. "Thomas wants to see you urgently."

Ryder took Scarlet's hand into his, and together they exited the elevator and walked to Thomas's office.

"Why were you threatening Benjamin?" Scarlet asked. "He was only trying to help."

Ryder cast her a sideways look. "He wouldn't have needed to bite your wrist. He could have just used his claws to make a little cut. But he wanted to get a taste of your blood, and he knows full well that I wouldn't approve."

Scarlet shook her head. "Are all vampires so possessive?"

"I'll show you possessive later," he said, raking a hungry look over her. Having fed on Scarlet's blood was not simply healing him, it was arousing him. "But right now we've got something important to do."

Thomas and Eddie were both waiting for them, when Ryder and Scarlet entered the office.

"Have you found anything else about Derek and Claudia?" Ryder asked immediately.

Scarlet put her hand on his forearm, making him look at her. "So it was Derek? He did all this?"

"Not just Derek," Thomas said and turned his monitor so that Ryder and Scarlet could see it too. On the screen were two photos. Derek sported a goatee, and his hair was blond. Claudia was almost unrecognizable. She had long, straight, red hair in the photo instead of blond curls, and her eyes were brown not gray.

"Meet Claudia and Derek Ditmore. They're married," Thomas continued.

Scarlet gasped.

"There's more. They're wanted in Canada as well as in Texas for fraud. They're running long cons. Once they identify a mark, they get to work. If it's a rich woman, Derek will romance her, and get her to marry him, then skim as much money from the victim as possible, before disappearing. And in the case of older rich men, Claudia will use her charms to seduce the guy, then fleece him. Their con in Canada went so far as to set up an accident so Claudia would inherit her victim's money, but the guy she was conning was a lucky bastard. He survived the attempt on his life, and contacted the police. But by then, Claudia and Derek had already fled the country with false passports."

"Shit!" Scarlet cursed. "Dad's fall in the bathroom! It wasn't an accident. She was really trying to get rid of him."

Thomas nodded. "And you. We found paperwork Claudia tried to file on your behalf to sign over your trust, but because of a technicality that she got wrong, the document was rejected."

Scarlet's chin dropped. "She told me a few days ago that I needed to sign some papers for the trust, so there wouldn't be any delay in me accessing it when I turn twenty-five in three months. But I didn't get around to it."

"It's likely that she realized that the paperwork would never fly, that's why she and Derek came up with the arson plot," Eddie mused, exchanging a look with Thomas.

"I think they had a different plan before that," Ryder interjected. When Scarlet looked at him, he continued, "Setting you up with Derek, so they could work it both ends. And when Derek messed up Claudia's plan by almost raping you, they had to come up with a quick solution."

"So that they could get the five million dollars in my trust?" Scarlet asked.

"Five million?" Eddie asked and pulled something up on his screen.

"Yeah, that's what I'll get in three months."

Eddie shook his head. "Not according to this statement. That's your trust, isn't it?"

Scarlet leaned closer so she could see the name on the statement Eddie was showing her. "Yes. That's my trust. How were you able to get access to this?"

Eddie smirked. "Let's just say that Thomas and I can hack into pretty much anything we please." He pointed to the screen again. "Anyway, there's no five million dollars in there. Not anymore. Over the past year, huge withdrawals were made. My guess? Claudia managed to withdraw money and was slowly moving it off-shore."

Ryder looked at the statement, and then at Scarlet, realizing what this meant. "That's why they had to act quickly. In three months you would have seen that most of the money in your trust was gone. They couldn't allow that."

Scarlet stared at him, her eyes widening. "Oh my God. Ryder, my half-brother had the same kind of trust. But he died before he was able to access it. Do you think…"

Tears welled up in her eyes. Ryder pulled her into his arms.

"Thomas? Eddie?" Ryder asked. "His name was Joshua King."

"We'll look into it," Thomas said. "I hate to say it, but it's possible. They tried to kill Brandon King and you, Scarlet. But right now, we need to find Claudia and Derek. The good thing is that the banks are closed tomorrow and Sunday. They won't be able to execute any wires. That gives us a fighting chance before they disappear."

"Have you traced Claudia's phone?" Ryder asked.

"Tried that," Eddie said, "but it's switched off. Her last location before she switched it off was Palo Alto."

"She was with Dad earlier," Scarlet said. "But they would have had to knock Dad out to bring him to San Francisco—" She looked at Ryder. "Where in the house did you find Dad?"

"He was tied up and gagged in his study."

"Derek and Claudia could still be in San Francisco," Scarlet mused. "Somebody had to start the fire just after we went inside. They had to be close."

Ryder nodded. "One of them, yes, though there is always the possibility of triggering a fire remotely, but I have no idea if either of them has those skills." He thought about it for an instant. "Problem is, with both you and your father dying in the fire, Claudia would be an instant suspect, which means she needed an alibi. She would have been nowhere close to San Francisco when the fire broke out."

"I agree," Thomas said. "She would have established an alibi in Palo Alto, somewhere where she could be seen." He addressed Eddie, "Check her credit cards, and see where she used them in the last six hours."

"Already on it," Eddie said and typed something on his keyboard. Moments later, he shared his findings. "She ordered pizza from Massimo's in Palo Alto, and then later there's a DoorDash order from Sinful Desserts."

"They're both not far from our house," Scarlet confirmed. "Massimo's only delivers within a two-mile radius."

"We're heading to Palo Alto," Ryder decided. "I need a few guys. By now, Derek is probably back with Claudia."

"Sun's coming up in less than two hours," Thomas warned. "You can take every available hybrid, but no vampires; too risky. Let me check who's not on a pressing assignment." Thomas sat down behind his desk and pulled up a schedule. "Take Grayson, Ethan, Isabelle, and Benjamin. I'm sending them messages right now."

"And what if Derek saw that Dad and I made it out alive? Wouldn't they be on the run by now?"

Ryder shook his head. "Derek would have only stayed long enough to see the house burning. It would have been too risky for him to wait around. Somebody could have seen him, neighbors, firefighters..."

"I hope you're right," Scarlet said.

"So am I," Ryder replied. "I'll drop you off with Vanessa. She'll look after you until I'm back."

"No! Claudia tried to kill Dad and me; she betrayed us. I need to be there when you confront her. I want to spit in her face, and kick the living crap—"

"Okay," Ryder said, realizing that there was no use in saying no to Scarlet. She needed to see this through to the end. And so did he. Besides, five hybrids against two humans was no contest. "You can come with us, but no heroics, okay?"

"Okay."

43

Fifteen minutes later, they were in two SUVs heading down the freeway toward Palo Alto—Ryder, Scarlet, and Ethan in one, with Ethan driving, and Grayson driving the other with Isabelle and Benjamin as his passengers. When they reached Brandon King's mansion, it was still dark, but Ryder could sense the sun wanting to breach the horizon.

The King residence was a sprawling single-story estate surrounded by high walls, lush vegetation, and mature trees, with a pool and pool house in the back. According to Scarlet, there was an intruder alarm, but Scarlet had the code for it as well as the house key. The key worked for the front door and gate as well as the side door leading into the kitchen.

"Getting in shouldn't be a problem," Ryder said over his speaker phone as both SUVs had stopped a few yards outside the property's high walls, hidden from view. "Let's do this quietly and quickly. We don't want Claudia and Derek to get a chance to hear us coming."

As they got out of the SUV, Ryder turned back to Scarlet. "Are you sure you wouldn't rather stay in the car, and wait until—"

Her determined facial expression told him her answer.

Ryder sighed. "Then stay behind me, please."

She nodded.

Ryder unlocked the gate and pushed it open. Scarlet had told him that the gate wasn't connected to the alarm system to allow for delivery people to be buzzed into the front courtyard. All six of them walked toward the front door, keeping their eyes and ears open. Everything was quiet.

At the front door, Ryder inserted the key into the lock and turned it, then tested the knob. It turned. He pulled the key out, then handed it to Grayson. "Kitchen door."

Grayson knew what he had to do and disappeared around the corner, Benjamin following him.

"Isabelle and Ethan, you'll cover the sliding doors that lead out to the pool, in case they're trying to escape out the back," Ryder said below his breath. "There's a gate behind the pool house that leads to a maintenance path behind the walls. They might use that route to escape."

"Don't worry, they won't get past us," Isabelle reassured them.

"That's hardly any fun," Ethan complained in a whisper.

Ryder glared at him. "It's not supposed to be fun."

Without another word, Ethan and Isabelle turned and walked around the other side of the house to get to the pool area. Ryder let another few seconds pass, giving everybody sufficient time to get to their positions, and Grayson time to unlock, but not open the side door to the kitchen yet.

Ryder nodded at Scarlet, then pushed the door open and turned to the alarm panel. There was no beeping to alert the person entering to disarm the system. Scarlet had told him that it was by design. Ryder punched in the code Scarlet had given him. But the light on the panel stayed red. He tossed Scarlet a look. She stared at him in surprise, then punched the code in herself. The alarm was still armed.

"She must have changed the code," Scarlet whispered.

"Shit!" Ryder cursed.

They only had seconds now, until a loud alarm would alert Claudia and Derek to their presence. They had to act quickly.

"How long till the police show up here once the alarm sounds?"

"At least five minutes, but the alarm company will call the house phone first to check if it was a false alarm. If Claudia hasn't changed the verbal password too, then I can call off the police."

Right then, an ear-shattering noise nearly pierced Ryder's eardrum.

"Do it!"

As he ran toward the left wing of the house, where the master bedroom was located, Ryder heard the phone ringing twice, before it stopped. No time to look over his shoulder he trusted that Scarlet had picked up the receiver and was talking to the alarm company to stop the police from coming. Had they been in San Francisco, the police wouldn't be a problem. But Scanguards had no special deal with the local police department in Palo Alto. Here, they couldn't risk being dragged into a police investigation.

Amidst the blaring sound of the alarm, Ryder heard other sounds, footsteps, thudding, and shouting. So far nobody had switched on the lights in the house, though Ryder didn't care. He could see just fine, better than any human anyway.

The door to the master bedroom was open, and there, the bedside lamps illuminated the vast room. Benjamin was holding a kicking and screaming Derek, only dressed in tighty-whities, pinned against the wall.

The bed was slept-in, clothes—his and hers—strewn on the floor, evidence that the couple had undressed in a frenzy, probably celebrating the presumed death of Brandon King and his daughter with a marathon sex session. An empty champagne bottle lay on its side on the floor, and two glasses stood on the bedside table.

But Claudia wasn't here.

Ryder charged at Derek, and Benjamin pried him off the wall and turned him so Ryder could land a hard punch in his gut. "Where is she? Where is Claudia?"

Derek screamed in pain.

"Grayson?" Ryder asked with a quick look at Benjamin.

"Searching the house for her."

"You can't do this," Derek cried out. "I'll have you arrested! The police will come, and—"

Ryder punched him again. Just then, the blaring sound stopped. "Guess the police have been called off. False alarm. Happens all the time."

"Let him go!"

At the sound of Claudia's voice, Ryder whirled around on his heel and froze in terror. Claudia, dressed in only a negligee, had one arm around Scarlet's neck, holding her as a shield in front of her, while she pointed a small handgun at Scarlet's temple with the other.

Fuck! He should have never allowed Scarlet to enter the house. He should have insisted on her staying in the SUV, or even better, in San Francisco.

"Or I'll blow this little bitch's brains out." Hatred spilled from Claudia's voice. "The two of you should've died in the fire like her father!"

Ryder lifted his arms. "Let her go, and we'll release Derek." He exchanged a look with Benjamin, who nodded. They had to stall her, until Grayson was back from wherever he was searching for Claudia.

Claudia narrowed her eyes. "You think I'm stupid? Let him go now."

"No!" Scarlet cried out. "You can't let him go! He's a murderer and an arsonist, and so is she!"

"Shut up!" Claudia ground out. "I'm sick of your constant bitching and whining. Poor little rich girl!"

"Fine, you can have Derek." Ryder made a motion to Benjamin, who slowly released Derek, pushing him in Claudia's direction.

"Derek," she said, and moved her head to indicate that he should step aside.

Derek turned his head to look back at Ryder and Benjamin, glaring at them. "You'll pay for this, you fucking bastards!"

Claudia moved her gun hand and swung the gun away from Scarlet's temple, directing it toward Benjamin and Ryder.

"Now!" Ryder yelled and sprinted toward Claudia.

Scarlet suddenly lifted her foot and stabbed her heel down onto the top of Claudia's bare foot, while using her elbow to jab Claudia in the stomach, taking her by surprise. Claudia screamed in pain and swayed, when the gun all of a sudden went off.

Ryder was only a foot away from reaching Scarlet, wrenching her out of Claudia's hold. Behind her, Grayson now appeared, charging at Claudia.

Ryder lunged sideways, Scarlet in his arms. He spun around, protecting Scarlet with his body. From the corner of his eye, he saw Grayson colliding with Claudia, the hand in which she held the gun jerking upward toward her own face, when a shot went off.

Blood splattered, and Claudia fell to the floor, her face hitting the plush carpet, revealing the damage the bullet had done. The impact of the bullet had shattered her skull and sent brain matter flying. Grayson had gotten the brunt of it.

"Fuck!" he ground out, disgusted. "That jacket is ruined."

Normally, Ryder would have barked at Grayson's insensitive comment, but he couldn't bring himself to feel any sympathy for Claudia either, and he'd seen that Grayson had merely tried to disarm Claudia, when she'd accidentally shot herself.

Ryder turned with the trembling Scarlet in his arms. When her eyes fell on Claudia's body, she didn't scream, didn't cry, just nodded.

Ryder's gaze went to Benjamin and Derek. Benjamin was unhurt, but Derek lay on the ground, blood spilling from his chest, and gurgling out of his mouth. He was drowning in his own blood. Nobody in the room moved.

"Claudia…" Derek murmured barely audible. A moment later, his heart stopped beating. He was dead. Accidentally shot by his partner in crime.

"Looks like a murder suicide to me," Benjamin said.

"Yeah, lover's quarrel. Claudia shoots Derek, sees what she's done, and kills herself. Works for me," Grayson agreed.

Ryder nodded. "Let's get outta here. I'm sure they'll be found soon enough."

On the way back to San Francisco, Ryder cradled Scarlet in his arms, both sitting in the back seat, while Ethan was driving.

"It's over, baby," he murmured and kissed her on the forehead.

"I'm glad they're dead. It will be easier for Dad to never have to lay eyes on her again."

"You were very brave. I would have reached you in time, even if you hadn't kicked Claudia. Vampires are faster than humans."

"I didn't know that. I just hoped that if she managed to shoot me, my heart would beat long enough for you to turn me. I want you to know that should anything like this ever happen to me, I don't want to die. You have my permission to—"

He put a finger to her lips. "I will never let you go, Scarlet. Because without your love, I have nothing."

He kissed her and felt her respond to him, her love and trust filling his heart.

"Get a room, you two. You're worse than Mom and Dad," Ethan said and chuckled from the driver's seat.

44

Two weeks later

The V lounge Scarlet had visited the night she'd first found out about vampires was packed. Scanguards had organized a party to welcome the newest member of their community: Brandon King.

She'd seen her father almost every day since the fateful night when their beautiful Victorian home had gone up in flames. He'd spent the past two weeks in a comfortable suite attached to the medical center at Scanguards' headquarters in the Mission. While Scarlet had been allowed to talk to her father as often as she wanted, she'd only been allowed into his suite under protection from another vampire.

The worry that Brandon King would try to bite her and drink her blood was the reason she'd not been allowed to hug him. At first, she'd thought the precaution had been overblown, but when she'd noticed her father's nostrils flare when she'd entered his room for the first time, accompanied by both Gabriel and Maya, she'd realized that he was driven by his vampire instincts.

But he'd made great progress in the past two weeks, accepting his new circumstances, and coming to terms with the fact that Claudia had betrayed him and paid for it with her life. Scarlet hadn't told him about the gene she'd inherited from her mother. Knowing her father, he would blame himself for her mother's suicide once he knew the whole truth about what had truly driven her to take her life: being born a satyr who'd never found her intended mate and had instead fallen into depression from which there was no way out. Ryder and she had decided to tell him the truth about Scarlet's mother when the time was right.

But tonight wasn't the right time.

Tonight, the extended Scanguards family, many of whom Scarlet had been introduced to in the preceding days, had come to celebrate.

Scarlet wore a short red dress she'd purchased during the past week, together with a whole stack of other clothes, since everything she possessed had been destroyed in the fire. Vanessa and Isabelle had accompanied her and helped her choose a new wardrobe. They treated her like the sisters she'd never had.

Scarlet caught Samson's eye, and he waved his hand to approach him. The founder and owner of Scanguards looked dashing in his dark suit and white shirt. He was tall and slim, with almost black hair, and hazel eyes. Next to him his wife, Delilah, looked petite. She wore a royal-blue dress, and looked stunning, and far too young to have three adult children. Would she ever get used to the fact that the vampires and their blood-bonded mates didn't age?

"You look gorgeous tonight," Delilah said and took Scarlet's hands into hers.

"And you look stunning, Delilah." Scarlet smiled and turned her gaze to Samson. "I don't know how to thank you for what all of you are doing for my father."

"Your father is a good man," Samson said. "And he's adjusting better than expected."

"It looks like he's found a new zest for life, after all that happened," Scarlet replied. "I still can't fathom how Claudia managed to lie to him for so long."

"It's a tragedy," Delilah said. "But at least she's gone, and so is Derek."

"And the police?" Scarlet asked, looking back at Samson. "Did they buy the murder/suicide story?"

Samson nodded. "Yes. It helped tremendously that both shots were fired from the same gun, and that Claudia was the only one with gunshot residue on her hand. They're not looking at other suspects. And the fire that destroyed your home was ruled arson, committed by Derek. Our liaison at the San Francisco Police Department took your father's statement that Claudia drugged him and then transported him to San Francisco where she left him bound and gagged so he would die in the fire. SFPD submitted the statement to the authorities in Palo Alto."

"What if the police in Palo Alto want to interview my father? I mean, he can't just go to the station if they ask him…"

"We've made sure it won't happen," Samson said confidently. "The police in Palo Alto have been informed that your father suffered such severe burns all over his body, including his face, that he has to remain under medical care for months, if not years, and undergo reconstructive surgery."

Scarlet took a deep breath. "Thank you for doing all this. I don't know how I can ever repay you and everybody at Scanguards the kindness you're showing us."

From the corner of her eye, she saw her father approach. "I think I've figured out a way to repay Scanguards," Brandon King said.

"Hey, Dad." He looked good, better than he had for a long time. His body had healed completely. There wasn't a single scratch on him, nor any burns or fractures. He looked virile, and his face had a healthy color. Which was another thing that surprised her: none of the vampires she'd met so far had pale skin like she'd expected from creatures who had to avoid the sun.

"Are you gonna finally hug me?" he asked with a smile.

She beamed at him. "Is it gonna be okay?"

He nodded. "I'm well fed, and I actually like the bottled blood. So you're quite safe from me."

Scarlet put her arms around him, and hugged him for the first time in a long time. "Oh Dad, I'm so happy."

Her father chuckled. "So am I, honey." He released her from his embrace, then looked at Samson. "As for repaying your kindness, Samson—"

"There's no need," Samson interrupted.

"There is," Brandon King insisted, "I have a proposal for you. I can help you expand Scanguards."

"How so?" Samson asked.

"By investing in your company. I realize that I can't continue my existing business, not when I'm unable to travel as freely as I could before all this happened. But I still want to do something useful. I'd like to talk about that with you. But I don't just want to be a silent investor. I want an active part in it."

"But Dad, don't you think you're taking on too much so soon?" Scarlet interrupted. "You'll be busy with rebuilding our home. It will take a year, at least, to bring it back to its original glory."

"Scarlet, I don't own the house anymore."

Shock jolted her. "You sold the property? But you loved the house." And so did she.

He smiled at her. "I did. But it's time for a new family to make it their own. It's in good hands."

Scarlet sniffled.

"So, you see, I can devote all my energy to a new project," he added.

"Well, Brandon, then we should talk," Samson said. "Tomorrow night. Tonight is about family."

Brandon King reached for Samson's hand, and they shook hands.

"Mind if I steal Scarlet?" Vanessa asked from behind her.

"Sure," Samson and Brandon said at the same time.

"Great!" Vanessa said and pulled her away.

"What's going on?" Scarlet asked as Vanessa dragged her across the room toward the fireplace, still shocked at the news that her father had sold their San Francisco home.

"You asked me the other day how Lizzy is doing, and I know Luther has some news to report," Vanessa explained.

"Is Lizzy all right?" Scarlet asked, just as she spotted Luther standing next to Wesley, his brother-in-law, in front of the fireplace.

"She is," Luther answered, having picked up her voice despite the music and the many conversations going on in the room.

That was another thing she'd have to get used to: the fact that vampires had much more sensitive hearing than humans.

"Hi, Luther," Scarlet greeted him, then cast a quick glance at his brother. "Uhm, Wesley."

When Wesley greeted her with a smile, she felt her cheeks heat with embarrassment, remembering that he'd been the one who'd overheard her conversation with Ryder, in which two cocks had featured prominently.

"Hi, Scarlet," Luther said, "I thought you might want to know that Lizzy is doing fine, and she's now got daily visiting rights at the prison, until Phil Miller will be released."

"I'm so happy to hear that. Did you ever find out who attacked her?"

"We caught him last week. A recently released V-CON, Richard Gleason, who had a beef with Miller and wanted to exact his revenge on him by hurting Lizzy. He's back in prison now."

"Won't that be a problem with Miller, and Lizzy, when she visits?" Scarlet asked, concerned about the woman's safety.

"We'll keep them apart. Gleason will be kept in the wing for repeat offenders, and won't have any contact with Miller."

"A lot of things have changed there, since Luther did time there," Wesley added. "Lots of improvements—"

Scarlet had to do a double-take. "Luther was in prison?" She shot Luther a look. "I mean, you were locked up?"

"Thanks, Wes, way to drop a bomb," Luther said with a sideways glance at his brother-in-law.

"It's not like it's a secret," Wes said, shrugging.

"I think you and I should talk about which stories can be shared in mixed company and which can't."

"Where's the fun in that?" Wesley asked. "I think everything should be game."

"Oh, you do?" Luther asked, then turned back to Scarlet. "Scarlet, have you ever heard the story about how Wesley turned two Labrador puppies into piglets, because he screwed up with his potions?"

"Ah, that's not fair," Wesley complained. "I was still learning my craft. Besides, I managed to turn them back."

Scarlet laughed.

"Yeah, but their nicknames stuck," Vanessa said. "Bacon and sausage, can you believe it, Scarlet?" Then she waved at somebody in the crowd. "Gotta go."

Scarlet followed her with her eyes, when she finally saw Ryder. They'd arrived at the V lounge a little while earlier, but shortly afterward, Gabriel had pulled him away on urgent business, and she hadn't seen him since. She noticed that he was shaking Brandon King's hand, and her father patted him on the shoulder. Scarlet was happy to see that the two men she loved most in her life were settling into an amicable relationship.

"Handsome," Maya said next to her.

Scarlet turned her head to look at Maya, who'd joined her. "As handsome as his mother."

Maya chuckled. "Thank you, Scarlet, but I was talking about your father."

"Oh."

"One day when he's gotten over Claudia's betrayal, he'll find a woman who really loves him," Maya said and put her arm around Scarlet's waist.

"I hope so. He deserves love."

"When he's ready, there'll be plenty of women standing in line in the hope he takes notice of one of them," Maya predicted.

"I hope he's all right," Scarlet said. "I'm just worried that he's making rash decisions."

"What do you mean?"

"He doesn't want to rebuild our home. He just told me that he sold it. He loved that house. It's where we all lived when my mother was still alive. I can't believe he turned his back on it…"

"Too many memories. Sometimes they can be crushing for the soul. Your father needs a new start. A clean slate. You have to respect that."

"I know. I'm just worried about him…"

Scarlet noticed Ryder making his way through the crowd walking toward her.

"Don't worry about him. He has all of Scanguards to watch out for him. It's time for you to live your own life." Maya leaned closer and whispered, "I hope Ryder is everything you want in a man."

"Everything and more," Scarlet said.

"That makes Gabriel and me very happy." Maya pressed a kiss on Scarlet's cheek before she walked away.

Ryder stopped in front of Scarlet, his eyes shimmering golden. "Have you had enough time to mingle?"

"Yes. Did you finish whatever your father wanted you to do?"

There was a flicker that suddenly flared up in Ryder's eyes. "I have no more obligations for tonight. Would you be very upset if we left this party early?" His gaze dropped to her cleavage, and she noticed his fangs peek past his lips.

"Ryder, your fangs," she whispered below her breath. "What will everybody think?"

He pulled her against his body, and dipped his mouth to her ear. "They will think that I'm a lucky bastard because I get to feast on the blood of the most beautiful woman I've ever seen, while I have my cocks buried inside her, pleasuring her until she can't take any more."

Scarlet gasped for air as heat shot through her, scorching her from the inside. "I think we should leave."

"I think so too." He released her from his embrace, then took her hand. "Come, I have a surprise for you."

"Does your surprise include lovemaking?"

Ryder chuckled, and the sound reverberated deep inside her body. "I think you haven't quite grasped the concept of a surprise."

45

Ryder had received a key from Samson. It unlocked a tiny cottage in Sausalito surrounded by a lush garden and mature trees. Its location on a hill afforded a stunning view over the bay and the skyline of San Francisco. Beyond the water, the lights of the city sparkled. Inside the cottage, lights of a different kind illuminated the cozy interior: dozens of candles gave the place a magical atmosphere.

In the fireplace where once wood fires had been burning, candles were arranged in the form of a heart. On the coffee table, the pattern was repeated. In another corner stood a king-size four poster bed with crisp white sheets and a canopy made of white lace.

"Ryder," Scarlet murmured as she let her eyes roam. She turned to him, and he saw tears of joy brimming in her eyes. "When you said you had a surprise, I never expected this. It's so romantic. Whose place is this?"

"It belongs to Scanguards. They let their employees use it for special occasions. Like tonight."

Scarlet looked at him, her breath hitching. "What special occasion?"

With a pounding heart, Ryder stepped closer to her, never once taking his eyes off her. The short, red cocktail dress accentuated her beautiful curves perfectly. He'd noticed several of the unbonded vampires and hybrids in the V lounge casting second and third glances at Scarlet, and while he'd felt a fierce possessiveness grip him at the thought of other men looking at her, he pushed that feeling away. Everybody knew that Scarlet was his; every vampire in the room could smell that he'd made love to her only hours before the party, cementing his claim.

"I spoke to your father earlier," Ryder said, his throat parched all of a sudden.

Scarlet nodded. "I saw you two shaking hands. He likes you, and not just because you and your father saved his life."

"I'm happy we got him out in time, otherwise I wouldn't have been able to get his permission to ask you this…"—Ryder dropped to one knee and pulled out a small jewelry box from the pocket of his blazer— "…Scarlet, will you blood-bond with me, and become my wife and my mate for eternity?"

"Ryder…" Scarlet choked up, pressing her hand to her lips, her chest rising, and filling with air.

With wide eyes she looked at the ring he'd selected for her, a sapphire that matched the blue color of her eyes, before locking eyes with him.

She dropped down to her knees opposite him and reached in the tiny handbag she held in her hand. When she opened her hand again, it revealed a simple platinum band.

"I wanted to ask you the same thing," she said softly. "I've been carrying this ring with me for almost a week, trying to find the courage to ask you to make me yours in every sense of the word."

Ryder's heart felt so full with love, he thought it would burst. "You wanted to ask me?" He smiled and choked back a tear of joy. "I forced myself to wait a couple of weeks, because of everything you've been through, the fire, your father's turning… I didn't want to add any more stress to—"

"Stress?" she asked softly and put her palm on his cheek, cupping it. "Oh, Ryder, I've wanted to be yours since the moment you first touched me…"

Ryder chuckled and took her hand. "I take that as a yes to my question." He slipped the sapphire on her finger.

She looked at it, then took the platinum band and slid it on Ryder's ring finger. It fit perfectly.

"I want to bond with you," she murmured, "with all that you are, the satyr and the vampire."

He rose and pulled her up with him, then lifted her into his arms and carried her the few steps to the bed, where he laid her on the duvet.

Scarlet's halter-neck dress was the color of fresh blood. It contrasted against the white sheets, and her long black hair fanned out like a halo. The dress was made of silk, and hugged her body without being too tight or too loose. He reached behind her neck and undid the knot with which the halter top was fastened. Once open, he simply pulled the dress down her torso and laid her breasts bare.

His mouth went dry at the sight of her suddenly stiffening nipples.

Behind his black pants, he felt his cocks hardening in anticipation. While Scarlet dropped her gaze to his groin and licked her plump lower lip, Ryder pulled the dress over her hips and legs, and freed her from it. She wore a tiny thong in the same color, and the scent of her arousal already drifted to him. He pulled the miniscule garment down her legs and tossed it behind him.

"Spread your legs for me, baby," he demanded, and she did.

Scarlet still wore her high-heeled red sandals, but he wanted her to keep them on, because she looked even sexier wearing them than entirely naked. She brought her knees up, spread wide so he could feast his eyes on her pussy.

"Now you," she murmured, while she slipped one hand to her sex and ran it along her cleft, collecting the juices that were already seeping from her.

Ryder took off his jacket and shirt, then his shoes and socks, before he put his hand on his pants and unbuttoned them. He slid the zipper down and looked at Scarlet's face. Then, he dropped his pants and stepped out of them.

Scarlet gasped. "You went commando."

Ryder grinned. "My cocks needed some extra space."

"I can see that," she murmured and licked her lips, while she circled her center of pleasure with her fingertip and moaned softly. "They keep getting bigger."

"Because you're making me so horny," he replied and stepped closer. "Look at you. You're already wet and ready for me, aren't you?"

"I don't like waiting."

Ryder reached to the bedside table and took the tube of lubricant from there. Very deliberately he lathered his lower cock with it, because tonight when he bonded with her, he would take her with both cocks while facing her.

"Oh," she sighed, "I was wondering if you would ever take my ass with your bigger cock." She licked her lips, and her hand on her sex was suddenly moving in a faster tempo.

Seeing that the thought of his larger cock in her anus turned her on, he said, "If that's what you wanted, you should have just asked…" He tugged on his lower cock, adding more lubrication. "You know I can't deny you anything."

Ryder put the tube of lubricant aside and joined Scarlet on the bed, gripping her thighs and pressing them back toward her torso, revealing both her channels. He nudged closer, both cocks now touching her body.

Scarlet shuddered visibly. "Ryder, please, don't make me wait."

Her last word hadn't left her lips yet, when he thrust into her to the hilts. Scarlet arched her back and let out a moan. Fuck, she was tight! There was a reason why his upper cock was slightly smaller than his lower one, because the satyr's preferred mating position was taking his woman from behind, thus his larger cock would take her pussy. But like this, with Ryder facing Scarlet, his bigger cock now stretched Scarlet's anus to capacity. He knew he should give her time to get used to him, but he couldn't.

He withdrew and plunged back into her, loving the way her muscles clamped down on him and squeezed him tightly.

"Yes!" Scarlet suddenly cried out, and spasmed, climaxing without warning.

"Fuck!"

Ryder rode her hard and fast, unable to stop himself now, holding on to her thighs to keep her legs spread wide.

"So good," she murmured, her lids closed halfway, her body covered in a sheen of perspiration. "Ryder… bite me, please…"

He would do more than that. Because tonight, he wouldn't be the only one drinking blood.

He let go of one of her thighs, and willed his hands to turn into claws, then sliced into his skin where his shoulder met his neck, so blood was dripping from it.

Scarlet stared at it, her eyes full of desire and need. He lowered himself to her, his fangs already extending to their full length, when Scarlet's lips touched the open cut and her mouth latched around it. When he felt her sucking on his vein, Ryder shuddered and drove his fangs into her neck to drink from her carotid artery.

Rich, warm blood filled his mouth, and he gulped it down like never before. The beasts inside him, the satyr and the vampire, now took over his body. His twin erections impaled her over and over again, and his fangs remained lodged in her neck, drinking the sweet blood she so willingly gave him. All the while, Scarlet was drinking his blood, the blood that joined them together for eternity, the blood that would keep her young for as long as Ryder lived.

They were one. She was his, and he was hers.

Ryder felt Scarlet climax again, and this time, he joined her, his twin orgasms sending shudders through his body, until he collapsed on the bed. Somehow he managed to roll off Scarlet, and a moment later, he found himself on his back, with Scarlet on top of him, both of them breathing raggedly.

When Scarlet lifted her head, he realized that he hadn't closed her puncture wounds yet, so he brought his lips to her neck and licked over the spot.

"Christ, Scarlet, I've never felt anything so amazing in my entire life."

She lifted her head and looked at him. "After you bit me for the first time in Blake's office, I didn't think it could get any better." She let out a breath. "I was wrong."

He laughed, truly happy. "I hope you'll always feel this way."

"I love you more every day."

"You can't possibly love me more than I love you," Ryder said, and rolled them so she was underneath him.

She smirked. "Oh, ready again so soon?"

"Yes, but before I forget it, there's something your father wanted me to tell you."

She raised her eyebrows. "Something wrong?"

"No. On the contrary. He asked me to tell you about his wedding gift to you, to us. The property on Pacific Avenue belongs to you now together with the funds to rebuild it and bring it back to all its former glory."

Tears shot to Scarlet's eyes. "But he told me he sold it."

Ryder shook his head, smiling. "He told you that it's time for a new family to make it their own. Our family."

Scarlet sniffled, smiling. "Our family... I don't know what to say."

"I told him that you'll be overjoyed... but he made me promise him something."

"What is it?"

"He wants grandchildren, lots of them." Ryder smirked. "I told him I'd get right on it—as long as that's what you want too."

"A horde of boys with two cocks? What could possibly go wrong?"

Scarlet laughed, and Ryder chuckled and captured her lips in a searing kiss.

~ ~ ~

ABOUT THE AUTHOR

Tina Folsom was born in Germany and has been living in English speaking countries for over 25 years, since 2001 in California, where she married an American.

Tina has always been a bit of a globe trotter. She lived in Munich (Germany), Lausanne (Switzerland), London (England), New York City, Los Angeles, San Francisco, and Sacramento. She has now made a beach town in Southern California her permanent home with her husband and her dog.

She's written 46 romance novels in English most of which are translated into German, French, and Spanish. Under her pen name T.R. Folsom, she also writes thrillers.

For more about Tina Folsom:
http://www.tinawritesromance.com
http://trfolsom.com
http://www.instagram.com/authortinafolsom
http://www.facebook.com/TinaFolsomFans
https://www.youtube.com/c/TinaFolsomAuthor
tina@tinawritesromance.com

Printed in Great Britain
by Amazon

23560622R00148